T0278639

THE LAST BOOKSTORE ON EARTH

LILY BRAUN-ARNOLD

DELACORTE PRESS

This is a work of fiction. Names, characters, places, and incidents either are the product of the author's imagination or are used fictitiously. Any resemblance to actual persons, living or dead, events, or locales is entirely coincidental.

Jacket art by Travis Commeau based on art by Wacoma,
used under license from Shutterstock.com

 Published in the United States by Delacorte Press, an imprint of Random House Children's Books, a division of Penguin Random House LLC, New York.

Delacorte Press is a registered trademark and the colophon is a trademark of Penguin Random House LLC.

Visit us on the Web! GetUnderlined.com

Educators and librarians, for a variety of teaching tools,
visit us at RHTeachersLibrarians.com

Library of Congress Cataloging-in-Publication Data is available upon request.
ISBN 978-0-593-89948-9 (trade) — ISBN 979-8-217-02775-0 (int'l ed.) —
ISBN 978-0-593-89950-2 (ebook)

The text of this book is set in 11.75-point Adobe Garamond Pro.

Editor: Hannah Hill
Cover designer: Ray Shappell
Interior designer: Michelle Canoni
Production editor: Colleen Fellingham
Managing editor: Tamar Schwartz
Production manager: Shameiza Ally

Printed in the United States of America
10 9 8 7 6 5 4 3 2 1
First Edition

To Bea—

Sorry for killing you off in everything I write.

CHAPTER ONE

I've given this whole thing enough thought that I can confidently say overtime sucks. Especially 9,667 hours of it.

Girlboss! you might say. *You earn that dough!*

In response, I roll my eyes.

In response I say: I will die in this godforsaken bookstore, and there will be no one to remove my rotting body from the floor. I will die surrounded by Poe, Nietzsche, and Shusterman, wedged halfway between Young Adult and Classics, and one day some alien archaeologist will find my body and study it like Pompeii. He will not say, *Girlboss! You earn that dough!* He will say ⊑⏃⊑⏃ ⌇⎍☊☍⟒⍀, which roughly translates to *Sucker!*

I will die here alone, bored out of my mind.

I will die here, staring at the lock-and-key journals, the ribbon twirlers, and the overly dramatic book covers that litter the Business section. *How to Win Yourself a Wife* and *Make a Million Dollars in Ten Easy Steps!* the titles read, as a man with a fake tan and a receding hairline poses below them. On the rack to my right, the birthday cards with their corny slogans about needing to drink more wine and hating your children have faded almost completely to white. They taunt me, as if to say, *Why did you even bother staying? Nothing else here did!*

I wasn't always so alone at the last bookstore on Earth. (At least I think it is. Most cell-phone towers are down, and global communication is on the fritz, so who knows if it's *actually* the last bookstore on Earth. It is to me.) I used to have Eva, who was three years older than me and twenty years too old to be dealing with my BS. Eva didn't mince words. Eva wasn't afraid of going into the basement at night, even though god knows what was hiding down there. Eva couldn't sing, but she sure as hell tried. She left nine months and seventeen days ago.

She said that she wanted to "explore." She wanted to "see what was left of the world." She said it in the same way parents say, "I'm not mad, I'm disappointed," and "I really did enjoy your band concert and didn't at all notice when you messed up in measure thirteen of *Contrapunctus Nine.*" She wouldn't look me in the eye.

I told myself it was okay and that I was fine with it. I told myself that I liked the quiet that hung in the air because how much did I really like people in the first place? How much did I really need someone to talk too loudly and chew with their mouth open? I told myself that there was a difference between being alone and being lonely. They weren't a package deal.

I told myself she would be back soon, like she said she would be, and I counted the days on the wall, adding tally marks in permanent marker until I lost count and energy. After the *almost*-end-of-the-world, when I realized I had no home to go back to, I had chosen to come back here. So had Eva, until she didn't.

I unhook the CLOSED sign in the front window, the metal

uncomfortably warm between my sweaty fingers. I try not to think about Eva and the tally marks and how unbearably hot it is. Tendrils of hair slick themselves to the back of my neck, having managed to weasel their way out of a sloppy ponytail. I try not to think about anything as I look at the miles of nothingness outside.

The middle of suburban New Jersey, of course, is no more interesting after the almost-end-of-the-world than it was before. Even though there are no more terrible drivers or men with scary accents who say things like "pork roll," "Bruce Springsteen," and "down the shore," there are also no more Coke slushies or Wawas. It's a net-zero equation.

I flip the CLOSED sign on the door so that it says OPEN, even though what I really want to do is hurl it at the wall. But I don't, because I did that yesterday and it absolutely didn't help. Instead, I stare through the glass at the voids left behind. The shadows where people used to be, sitting under the husk of an oak tree that looms in the square. Crawling through the debris, the smashed windowpanes, and splintered wood. Sliding out of the cars that lurk, discarded, on the side of the road.

Wouldn't it be funny if it were all a dream? Like a bad story written in the fifth grade that ends with *And then, she woke up.* A slapdash ending to a half-assed tale. Some cursed, messed-up nightmare of a dream. I'd wake up in bed, a thousand light-years away, a sheen of sweat on my forehead, and stare out at the moon from between the slits in my curtains. I'd say to my parents the next morning at breakfast, *You won't believe the cursed, messed-up nightmare of a dream I had,* and the statement would hang in the air until I remembered that *it's over.* It didn't matter anymore.

Through the fogged-up window, I can see a man in a faded navy peacoat stumble down the road. He fumbles with his coat buttons and looks around the desolate open space. He does not see me watching him yet. He does not know that he is the first person I have seen in days. He does not look happy to be here.

I didn't think I'd be seeing him again so soon.

When he sees my shadow in the window, he pauses and looks around the deserted town square before grimacing and striding toward the door.

CHAPTER TWO

When I first met the man in the faded navy peacoat, or Peacoat Man, as I've taken to calling him, Eva had been gone for two days. I'd devolved into a vampiric existence, not sleeping, not eating. And sure, it's not like we were ever anything more than friends—although my crush had grown to a size that I had never before encountered—but it hurt like something more. I spent my time picking at my fingernails and watching them bleed. I didn't know what to do except stare at the ceiling and wallow in my own uselessness.

I thought I had gone mad when I first looked out the window and saw a figure approaching. For an instant, I was transported back to normal times, when I'd pass the hours watching people walk by from inside the comfort of the air-conditioned store. And sure, maybe I shouldn't have, but out of reflex, I smiled at him.

I don't know if that's what started it all. My gleaming smile could have been the catalyst that led me to this particular point in time. Or maybe the man was going to come into the bookstore whether I let him in or not. Maybe he would have gone all zombie movie on me and busted down the door with a rusted chain saw. Still, as he reached for the door handle, he smiled back, and I let him in.

He had come to buy a book about birds, or at least that's what he said, and he even tried to hand me a crumpled twenty-dollar bill in payment.

He said, "I have nothing else to give you."

I laughed at its uselessness, but I took it anyway. At that time, I couldn't understand what value a book had in this new world. I mean, I understood what it meant to me, but to the rest of the world? It soon became clear that I severely underestimated the power of distraction. Peacoat Man chuckled when I asked him if he wanted a paper bag, or birthday wrapping.

He said, "No thank you. My birthday isn't until March. But thank you for making my day a little less dull."

I said, "Thank you for stopping by. Please do come again."

• • •

The bell above the door chimes as Peacoat Man walks in, and I smile. He pauses for a moment before he plasters on a smile in return, and I watch the corners of his eyes crinkle slightly as he combs his fingers through his sweat-slicked hair. I watch something flicker across his face, as if he's wondering whether to hide his emotions for my sake. I make the choice for him, sticking to our normal pleasantries as I put down my copy of *The Island of Dr. Moreau.*

"It's a little hot to be wearing a coat." I can feel the back of my tank top adhering to my skin in the sticky July heat. I say it as if he hasn't been wearing the same coat every single time

I've seen him, even as the months slipped into summer and the temperature climbed. I say it as if I haven't said it a million times before in the seventeen times I've seen him these past nine months.

The man laughs. "I'd lose it if I wasn't wearing it. I'd lose my head if it wasn't screwed on." His fingers shake slightly as he pulls at the collar of his shirt.

"Ah. I know the feeling."

I don't know the man's name. He's never told me, and I've never asked. I don't want to know until he's ready to tell me. It might be rude and go against some apocalyptic rule of etiquette. It's not in any of the volumes of etiquette books that I have here in the bookstore, and I've read them all out of sheer boredom. I've read most of the store at this point and have become rather fond of the more tragic endings. Anything that finishes with more desolation than it started with, but beggars can't be choosers.

Everyone who comes through these doors learns my name. *Elizabeth. Liz. Eliza. Lizbeth. E. Don't wear it out.* I'm not afraid of them knowing.

When the last person who knew you forgets your name, it's like you never really existed in the first place. It's like you were never really there. *Poof,* gone. I figure that I'll spread my name far and wide, considering how few people are left. I'll offer it to anyone who walks through that door, if they're willing to listen. If they're willing to remember me.

"What are you looking for today?" I ask, sliding into customer-service mode. That chipper lilt creeps into my voice again, like it always does. Old habits die hard. I rub my hands against the wooden counter, tracing gentle curves into the dust. I'll try to clean that later, even if dust accumulates faster than I can remove it.

Peacoat Man wrinkles his nose and wipes his hands on his pants. "A mystery, I think. One that I can figure out, though. Nothing too dark, if you know what I mean."

"I know what you mean." I smile again. This time a real one, not one formed by years of muscle memory. "I'll let you look for yourself. I know how peeved you get when I try to give you a recommendation."

"That's because your taste in books couldn't be any worse. *A Canticle for Leibowitz*? In this climate?"

I'm going to be perfectly honest and say that I've never read *A Canticle for Leibowitz,* some postapocalyptic epic about a Catholic monastery that worships Saint Leibowitz throughout centuries of desolation and destruction. It was one of the options on my freshman-year summer reading list. I almost chose it until my dad told me he'd read it once and hated it so much that at the age of thirteen, he was scarred for life. I have never read *A Canticle for Leibowitz,* because I am a chicken who doesn't want her life ruined. So, of course, I now try to get absolutely anyone and everyone to read the ridiculous book and report back to me. So far, no one has taken my bait.

"You're pretty fresh this morning, old man." I don't know how old he is, but I assume he'd qualify for a senior-citizen discount on NJ Transit.

Peacoat Man just grins, allowing a strand of hair to fall over his hard eyes. "Watch your mouth, young lady." We stand in silence for a second, slowly melting in the late summer heat.

His face softens as he reaches into his breast pocket and

takes out a piece of wrinkled yellow paper, which he holds out to me. "It's for my sister." He pauses. "Could you keep it for me, in case she comes through?"

"Of course," I manage. I lift the message gingerly from his hands, tacking it on the corkboard behind the register.

Peacoat Man also gives me a photograph printed on shiny paper from CVS. A woman beams up at me from the four-by-six rectangle, bundled up in an argyle sweater and a gray beanie. She seems like the type of person who would hike the Appalachian Trail for fun or run a marathon barefoot. Something like that.

It wasn't my idea to start functioning as a post office. It started eight months ago when an older woman came in with an envelope and offered me a six-pack of chicken-flavored ramen in exchange for making sure that her letter ended up in the right hands. She had been traveling to a western compound with a new group but knew that a friend of hers might pass through the area. Or at least she hoped so. It was an offer that I couldn't refuse. The letter's intended recipient arrived three months later, and I gave him his mail. As he held the flimsy piece of paper in his shaking hands, the man cried.

So far, I've had thirteen successful deliveries, making my makeshift postal service one of the best bets for people around here. Still, there's a pile of undelivered letters sitting behind the counter. There are a few dozen people in the area, based on the number of people who have visited in the past year, with others passing through town occasionally. I'm hopeful that at least some of the letters will find their recipients, but I can't help but feel like I've failed. I can't help but feel like I'm letting everyone down.

"Thanks," Peacoat Man says. "I'm planning on getting out of here before The Storm passes through. Hunker down somewhere far away, where the damage won't be as bad." The man continues, "She should be passing through soon, and I wanted to make sure she has directions to my campsite." He says it so nonchalantly, like he doesn't notice the blood draining from my cheeks. Like he doesn't realize that our casual conversation has morphed into something more sinister.

"What do you mean?" I ask. "About The Storm?"

That grimace tugs at his mouth again. "There's another one coming," he says gravely.

"What are you talking about?"

"I've heard things. People are starting to talk. They say the clouds have already started to gather over the Atlantic."

His words slice through me, creating a pit in the bottom of my stomach. *The Storm.* I had almost pushed The Storm out of my mind entirely. After what happened last year, I told myself that it wouldn't come again, that it was a one-time thing. It had to be. Because I'm not sure that I can survive another one. I'm not sure if I want to.

"Do you know that it's coming again?" I ask, my voice dry and harsh. "Or are you guessing?"

The man shakes his head slowly, as if to say *How can you possibly be so naive?* I hate the look in his eyes, so I straighten my spine and purse my lips.

"Remember last time, how all the birds left?"

I don't remember how all the birds left, because I honestly couldn't care less about birds. I didn't care then, and I don't now. But then I think back to this time last year, before *it* happened, and how quiet it was, like the entire world had been shrouded in stillness. At the time, I had simply liked the way that quiet made me feel. Like everything else had gone away. I never dreamed that it was a signal of something so much bigger. So I nod at Peacoat Man, and he nods back.

"It was like they could sense it was coming. I've heard that animals can do that sometimes. They know before us when bad things are headed our way. Tsunamis and stuff like that. You see it on television sometimes." He pauses, staring at some faraway object. "But this time, it's not only the birds. It's the deer and the rabbits and who knows what else. I'm not the only one who's realized it. I'm sure you've noticed how few people are in the area."

I don't know when Peacoat Man became an expert on predicting weather patterns, but I bite my tongue.

"So it's coming," I murmur, allowing myself to play into his macabre fantasy. *He doesn't know anything for certain,* I tell myself. *He could be totally wrong, and it might not come at all. He knows nothing more than you do.* "When?"

"I'm not sure. It could be a couple of weeks. Less, if we're unlucky. And it's going to be so much worse. I can tell. Bad enough for the deer and the rabbits that didn't run last time to pick up on it." He breathes softly. "I'm going to head out before it's too late. Try to find a place that won't be hit quite as hard. I suggest you batten down the hatches, okay?"

He sounds like my dad. I pretend not to notice as his eyes reflexively flick toward the ceiling, acknowledging the gaping hole in the roof two stories above us, blown apart during The Storm. But this place is all I've got, even if it's falling apart.

"Okay." My mind is swimming, drowning, struggling to stay afloat. I've known him for almost a year. He knows me, right? He wouldn't lie to me.

I glance down toward the small, puckered scars on my left arm. I remember how the rain burned, and I'm sure he does too. The area around his right eye is waxy, the iris faded into a milky white. We all bear our own scars, even if some of them are more than skin deep.

Peacoat Man clears his throat and plasters on a small grimace. "Enough of this doom-and-gloom talk," he says. "We'll be fine. We've made it out of worse."

"Sure," I reply. I'm not sure he knows what he's talking about, but I don't press the matter further. It doesn't matter what he believes; The Storm might not ever come at all.

"And don't forget about the letter. My sister should be coming through any day now; I only wish I had the time to stay here and wait for her."

"Got it," I say, trying to muster up some energy to fuel my smile. "Happy to help."

"You're a lifesaver."

And I almost laugh at that because I've never saved anyone's life. Ever. I've never even gotten close. If passing letters from one person to the next saves lives, every postman and third-grade girl deserves a Presidential Medal of Freedom. I do what I can to stay relevant.

I let him retreat to the back of the room to get lost in Agatha Christie and Stieg Larsson. Alone at the cash register, I take stock of the store. Rusted hinges on the front door. Those need to be replaced. Broken windows. Rotten floorboards. Dust everywhere. And don't forget the massive, gaping hole in the roof. This place is one wind gust away from blowing over completely.

The world as it exists now is not the "end of days" aesthetic that I imagined from my years of binge-watching *The 100* and devouring the Hunger Games trilogy. This isn't the visually pleasing techno-cyberpunk dystopia that used to feature in my daydreams, especially since the electricity went out months ago. I used to devour apocalyptic books when things were normal-ish. I used to validate my fear of the future with the cynical belief that the end times could come any day. In a weird way, I hoped for them. With civilization collapsed, I wouldn't have to figure out what I wanted to major in at college. Instead, I could live out my Pinterest-inspired, hot-girl zombie-busting dreams, chain saw in my uncharacteristically muscular hands.

I can't help but wish that I still had a future to be afraid of. A fear that was so far off that I'd never have to confront it. But that's not an option. The constant braid of time that seems to expand in front of me endlessly has run out. All I have is the past. The past and today.

I shift my gaze over to a set of leather-bound books, lying haphazardly on the shelf behind the dust-encrusted Dell computer. The computer was already inoperable before all of this. At this point? It's a relic. A fossil for our future alien overlords to discover. ᑎᑊᐠɯᑎꝊ⊕!, they'll say, which roughly translates to *Idiots! Why do their browsers still default to Microsoft Bing?!*

According to Eva, it came from a virus someone accidentally downloaded in 2008 when trying to access a bootleg copy of *Breaking Dawn.* I'd been trying to get rid of it for months when the computer finally kicked the bucket. Bing is stubborn as hell. It will inevitably outlast all of us.

The journal behind the computer is filled with my slightly illegible writing. My fifth-grade English teacher called my penmanship "the script of a psychopathic killer." I call it sexy and mysterious. It's not my fault that I had the flu when we were supposed to be learning cursive in the third grade.

I've gotten into the habit of taking down the stories of my favorite regulars at the bookstore. (I haven't yet decided if this habit is good or incredibly tedious.) When they stop by to get a book or leave me with a letter, I ask them to share a little about themselves. What they were like before The Storm, where they were when it hit, who they are now. I take down the stories because they keep me sane. If I can put words on a page, then it means I was here. No matter what happens, I was undeniably here, and absolutely and utterly real. And it means they were real too.

Peacoat Man yanks me back to reality from my heat-induced stupor as he *thwack*s the hardcover of a book with the palm of his hands. He's never given me his story. Something about the misty-eyed look he got when I asked made me think that it was too painful for him to tell.

"Well, I'm ready to head out," he grumbles.

I shake off my daze. "That's all?" I ask as I lean a little closer, even though I don't quite know what else he could want. But the phrase is programmed into my brain, so I say it anyway. I look at the cover of his book. *The Alienist.* I bury my ever-present need to give my opinion.

"That's all." His free hand fiddles with the button on his pocket before he pulls out a fistful of something that I can't quite discern.

He reaches his arm out toward me, and purely on instinct, I offer him my hand. Three objects drop into my palm, one by one. They clink and roll around, warm in my hand.

When I pull back, I see batteries. Double-A batteries.

Double-A batteries that he could have probably traded for a week's worth of food instead of a musty old book.

"Thank you, but I—I—" I stammer, my eyes betraying my thoughts, but the man shakes his head. It's always worth a try. Some part of me, passed down by my father, who inherited it from his father, and his father's father, genetically requires me to refuse any sort of gift. In my family, it was always a race to see who could procure a credit card the fastest when we went out to dinner, like some messed-up high-noon duel. But that's not how it works anymore, right? Chivalry is dead. Nothing comes for free.

"Don't even." He clutches his book and walks out, the floorboards creaking as his boots trod across the dusty wood. He pauses, looking back at me as he adjusts the buttons on his dirty coat. Then he adds, "Please stay safe. Things are so much worse than you think."

All I can think about is the hole in the roof, and the rotting floorboards, and the front door that won't lock. All the things that are broken. All the things that are waiting for the perfect time to fall apart. Now seems as good as ever.

"I'm not going anywhere."

Chris Nickelson

33 Years Old

Portland, Maine

It wasn't at all like it is in the movies. Screaming and fire and destruction and all that stuff that comes with it. Sure, there was screaming at first. It makes sense to scream if your skin is being burned off. But it lasted maybe only twenty minutes before there was no one left outside to scream. It took the unlucky ones out quickly. No mercy. The rest of it, though? It was silent. The rain pounded, and the winds roared outside, but in my solitude, everything was absolutely silent. No voices echoing through the hallways of my apartment building. No slamming doors or music playing a few doors over. Just completely quiet.

CHAPTER THREE

I still haven't figured out what to do with the batteries, so I've been carrying them around with me for two days. That way, I can't lose them. That way, they can't magically disappear the moment that I look away like most things normally do. Right now, they're lined up in a row on the checkout counter like some sort of weird domino set.

That's a bad habit of mine, leaving things for later. My dad used to say it was one of my worst habits. It drove him nuts. He used to find my half-eaten packages of peanut butter crackers littered on the kitchen table and toss them. Then I'd come back from work looking for those same peanut butter crackers, and they'd be gone, and I'd be sad and hungry, and Dad would be upset about the crumbs on his kitchen table. Naturally, I'd get myself another package of peanut butter crackers, eat a couple, start my statistics homework, and once again forget about my crackers, causing Dad to throw out the abandoned package. It was a vicious cycle.

Still, I leave the batteries on the counter and peer out the front window one last time, just to make sure that no one is walking down the road toward me. I know no one is. Visits are somewhat randomly spaced, but it's rare to have more than one every couple of days, and someone came through just this morning. My dwindling customer base is loyal, if nothing else. It was a familiar face, as they often are—a kid I knew from high school, Isaac, who has grown even taller in the past year, a feat that I didn't think was possible for a towering twenty-year-old. He's been living in the basement of a RadioShack, two miles away, the building above his sun-less room almost entirely collapsed. His skin was a deep gray, almost fully devoid of color from the lack of sunlight, but he swore it was better than trying to move into one of the still-standing homes that dot suburbia. Homes mean people. People mean death, and rot, and memories we try too hard to keep out.

When he left he took my prized copy of *The Girl with the Dragon Tattoo,* pages dog-eared from overreading and highlighted in all my favorite places, but he left an unopened bag of jerky in return and enough conversation to tide me over until the next person came through. That seemed well worth it to me. He swore up and down that he'd return it, and he even offered to pinkie swear on it, but I know that it'll probably never come back. They rarely do. People tend to hold close the things that they have nowadays.

The bookstore is on the bottom floor of a two-story building, with an apartment unit on top, connected to the shop by a narrow hallway and a set of stairs. On the other side of that narrow hallway are the stairs to the basement, but the basement is creepy and prone to flooding, so I tend to avoid it entirely. The hallway is dark, with off-white walls tarnished slightly from all the times I've bumped into them carrying pointy things that leave dents. The staircase is no less sad, with small, sagging steps that creak each time I walk up them.

I didn't know the guy who lived in the apartment above the bookstore before The Storm, because I never saw him. Sure, I heard his speakers sometimes as we were closing up shop, blasting songs with obnoxious bass levels that shook the ceiling. And sure, we had to deal with his misdelivered Amazon packages, but I never saw him. Not in person, anyway. I liked to imagine him when it was slow at the shop, always picturing him as young and in love. Someone who rode a motorcycle and shaved part of his head and said cool things like *enigmatic* and *inconsequential.*

When I went up to the apartment for the first time after The Storm and knocked on the door, no one answered. Whoever lived there was gone before I got to say hello. There wasn't a body, so I still have hope that he survived. But it's a bit of a pipe dream. I know there are plenty of places to die. We don't all die in our homes, surrounded by the things we love.

What I do know, now, is that his name was Greyson. He really liked the *Matrix* movies and had posters on his wall of each one. He had a girlfriend with bright pink hair and an awesome smile. At least, I assume it was his girlfriend. I found her picture propped up on his desk, right in the middle, right where he could see it every single day. I've decided that meant they were in love.

I didn't keep his photos. I didn't think I could. When I left my home for the last time, after *it* happened, I brought only one picture with me. I don't like the idea of anyone finding the photos *I* left behind, so I couldn't very well keep his. The picture I took is of my family: me and my twin sister and my parents. I was nine. In the photo, my parents sit on yellow chairs, holding hands. My sister and I sit on their laps, looking up at their bright faces. At the time the picture was taken, it was the only way life could be. Happy and mundane and normal.

So I put my photo in the middle of the desk, sliding it into the frame over Greyson's girlfriend, right where I can see it every day. When I look at us, happy and together, it's like everything is okay. It's like I didn't screw everything up. I can pretend we still exist, together, in that moment. Forever. When I look at it, I can forget the guilt that constantly simmers in the far-off reaches of my brain. For a moment, it's gone.

The apartment itself is small, though the kitchen is big enough to hold one of those oversize refrigerators with two doors and a built-in freezer, but too tiny to fit a real table. The bedroom is a bit of a mess, the solitary desk shoved into a corner with a now-useless lamp hovering above it. My mattress is stacked in the other corner, deep red covers rumpled, balled up and tossed out of the way. My pillow looks a little worse for wear and a little thinner than I might like it to, but it's home. It's what I have and it's all I need, although I don't think I'd be super upset if someone came in and decided to trade me another pillow for a book.

I grab a spare notepad from the desk, flipping frantically past horrible doodles and half-written poems, and begin writing a list. One that I have to complete so that I won't die sad and alone when the next Storm comes. If it even comes at all.

to-Do List (of utmost importance) :)

1. the roof

The roof is a disaster. Most of it was blown away by the original Storm, and in my infinite laziness I've managed to only half fix it by nailing a tarp to what remained of the outer walls. It's kind of like camping, but shittier. Every time there's even the slightest bit of breeze, the makeshift roof flutters back and forth, sounding like an overworked banshee. When the sun shines hard enough, the entire room is enveloped in an eerie shade of blue, like some low-budget science-fiction movie. It wouldn't do in a regular storm, not to mention the type with rain that could burn through your skin.

I swing open the kitchen cupboard with a bang. The shelves are dangerously empty, but I don't stop to think about it, because there's absolutely nothing I can do that will make more cans appear. The nearest food store was ransacked a long time ago. It sucks. Right now, my dad would tell me to have *agency.* Then I'd narrow my eyes and clench my jaw and tell him that *he didn't know what the hell he was talking about.* I eye a can of baked beans, disgusting yet available, which I'll likely have for dinner. Just like the night before. And the night before that.

I twist open the faucet, partly to test the water pressure and partly so I can have something semicool to splash onto my face and lower my body temperature even slightly. I wait there, arm outstretched, seconds slowly passing, before I realize that absolutely nothing is coming out.

I stare at the faucet as it starts to make a low, guttural hissing noise, which grows louder and louder until the entire sink shudders and heaves and a quick shot of gunk bursts forth from the spout, landing with a splash in the basin. Then the sink is silent again. Thick, brown water swirls to the drain. So much for drinking water. Unlike with the beans, I cannot sweet-talk myself into drinking water that would probably give me some horrible disease that comes only from gross faucets in New Jersey. I'm not that brainless.

I'm lucky it even lasted this long, I think as something acrid twists through my insides. But I've seen too many survival movies to not realize what this means. Fresh water is life, right? There's a reason why people hallucinate water in the desert and not something more exciting, like a meatball sub or a car to ferry them to safety. Without water, none of that matters. Without water, I'm screwed. Sure, I might have enough squirreled away in bottles around the bookstore to last me for a day or two, but that's not something to rely on. My tongue adheres itself to the roof of my mouth, feeling like sawdust and clay. I add it to the list.

2. Water

I decided to underline that one, just in case. I leave the rest of my bedroom behind, trotting through the open doorway and into the kitchen. I look at the crack in the top right windowpane. And the one that's missing completely below it, the gaping hole covered by duct tape and the dust jacket from a copy of *Wonder.* Not going to cut it.

3. Kitchen windows

I continue downstairs, into the actual bookstore, still devoid of people and full of dust. I stacked some old milk crates against the wall in the back of the store, carefully placed to hide the damage Eva and I caused when we accidentally knocked over a bookcase filled with hardcovers. The falling shelf made a gaping hole in the plaster, and I can see the pink, pillow-like insulation seeping out from the wall.

4. Insulation
5. Water stain on ceiling?
6. Door doesn't lock
7. Broken windows *again* (downstairs)

When I look at my ever-growing list, my pulse quickens, especially considering that I haven't yet looked at the building from the outside. That'll add at least another three entries. My stomach lurches. I don't know how to fix insulation, or replace windowpanes, or repair giant holes in the roof. I didn't think I would have to. My expertise probably ends at noisy hinges. I always assumed that Eva would be here to help once things got bad.

When I make it outside, I look at the half-gone roof and the clogged gutters and the cracked windowpanes. I notice the way the small oak tree is leaning toward the building, as if one gust of wind could send it toppling. I would add that to the list, but I don't know what I could do about that. I hate that I don't know what to do.

When I was younger, really young, I used to have every single thing planned out. Like, as a fifth grader, I wanted to go to Dartmouth and become a surgeon. I wanted to go to Dartmouth because my best friend's dad went there and told me that during the winter they drank beer and ice-skated and jumped over barrels. To me that seemed "fun" and like "what cool people would do." I wanted to be a surgeon because I had memorized the names of fifty bones and thought that was all I needed to know. I would go around offering people the most incorrect medical advice in the world. I decided to not become a surgeon when I realized that I would have to go to medical school for four years, plus a residency, which would cause me to miss my prime Broadway-performing years. I wanted to do it all.

High school forced me to face reality. My school guidance counselor put an end to the color-coded spreadsheets that dictated every aspect of my future. She introduced me to things like "acceptance rates" and "common applications." After that, everything was out the window. I was no longer good enough to do everything at once.

Well-meaning adults would ask, "Now, where do you want to go to college?" or "What are you planning to major in?" and I'd just smile and say, "I have a couple of top choices" or "I'm deciding between English, music, and biochemistry." They'd nod and reply with "That's nice," and I'd die inside a little bit. I hated not knowing what I wanted and knowing that I'd have to figure it out sooner rather than later. I had a future, but I didn't want one. Now I miss the future I never had. Joni Mitchell would have a field day with my predicament.

I look back toward the leaning tree and stare at its dead limbs. Not a single green leaf clings onto its branches. It's been dead and gone for a long time, and I didn't even notice—though I suppose it's easy to miss when the streets are covered in bits of buildings and the shops you used to visit on Fridays after school are half reduced to ruins. My world has crumbled around me, and I'm still trying to hold together the pieces that are left.

CHAPTER FOUR

JANUARY 14: BEFORE THE FIRST STORM

The Christmas decorations are still up, even though January is halfway over. School is in full swing. There are no more bogus preholiday class periods wasted away with study times or barely relevant documentaries.

My mom hates taking the Christmas decorations down. I've pointed out to her that she doesn't have to spend so much time putting them up and staring at them and adding little cardinals and jingle bells to the roping. The fake greenery from the ACME uptown does the same job, *and* I don't have to vacuum up a forest's worth of pine needles when I should be working on my English essay. Still, Mom refuses to change her ways. We have to drive into New York every year to tie a particular tree to the top of our car and buy roping from the hole-in-the-wall florist shop on the bottom floor of a building that should have been condemned years ago. Mom doesn't appreciate my commentary.

So I don't say anything about the Christmas decorations or the pine needles stuck in my wool socks as I make my way to the dinner table. Dad has warned me that I have a bad habit of ruining dinner conversation before the meal has even begun, as I tend to be the one to bring up the most uncomfortable topics. Sometimes I don't even notice I'm doing it, the words slipping out of my mouth like it's my god-given duty to remind my family of the state of the world. But I'm trying to keep my streak of unruined dinners going. I'm up to six.

My sister, Thea, is sitting in my seat, but I don't say anything. I am not going to ruin dinner.

The newspaper is sitting on the kitchen counter, its headline barely visible. I'm sure that it says something about snow, and melting ice caps, and god knows what else. But I don't comment on it, because I am not going to ruin dinner.

In fact, I am so focused on not ruining dinner that I do nothing except stare at my limp asparagus and meat loaf. I shove my macaroni around on my plate with the tip of my fork and wait for someone else to speak first.

Mom takes the bait, using a thin finger to push her blond hair behind her ear.

"Elizabeth," she chides. "I worked hard on this meal."

It takes me a second to realize that she's talking about the macaroni and not the fact that I've come down to dinner in slightly stained sweatpants.

"It's not meant to be offensive, I swear."

"You know how she has that weird thing about different foods touching," Thea adds, her just-as-blond hair pulled back into a slick ponytail.

Dad clears his throat, looking up from his plate to smile at me. I got my looks from him. His hard eyes and square jaw. "She likes to compartmentalize, honey." A pause. "Right, Liz?"

"Sure."

Dad chuckles, letting his fork rest on the side of his plate.

Mom has always cared too much about how she sets the table. The napkins match the tablecloth. The cutlery is always adorned with overly intricate metalwork. It's all picked up from yard sales, and it's all vintage. Her philosophy is that you can forget about all the shitty little things that happened today if your dinner table looks like it was stolen from an episode of *I Love Lucy.* Dad encourages her, and so I've never experienced a night when the Flannery family hasn't dined by candlelight. Even if we're eating takeout.

"When you were little, you used to tell us that you had different compartments in your body, for different foods," Dad says.

"I know."

And I do know, because I hear this story about once a week, whenever I dare to refuse seconds of Mom's spaghetti.

Thea shakes her head, turning to meet my glance. "What? Is your macaroni compartment full? Poor thing."

"Woe is me. God always gives his toughest soldiers his toughest battles."

"Yeah, macaroni and college essays," Thea fires back.

At those two golden words, Mom perks up, pulled out of her macaroni-induced trance and back to the present.

"Any college news, girls?" she asks, her dangling earrings swinging back and forth as she pivots her head between the two of us. We've entered interrogation mode.

"It's January," I answer.

"What about early action?" Dad adds, picking up his fork once again.

Thea huffs. "I've heard from all of those already. Nothing new."

"Me too," I add.

But Mom ignores me, instead focusing on my sister. "Really, Thea?" She leans back in her chair, crossing her arms. "There's nothing that you'd care to share?"

It's as if my mom doesn't even realize how much her questions irk my sister. But her recent string of rejections has caused Thea to be more than prickly, whether my mom has noticed or not.

"No," Thea replies, sighing. "It doesn't matter anyway, right?"

I can't help but smile. I'm sure she's just trying to goad Mom, but I appreciate the effort. I'm used to being the resident cynic in the family, and so I scooch my foot toward Thea under the table and nudge her slightly. A love tap, as Dad would call it. She gets the message, and she blushes slightly.

"Don't say that," my mother says as she hunches over her macaroni, turning beet red.

"Let her speak, Ivy. We raise independent thinkers in this household."

But Mom shakes her head. "Not if she's going to say things like that."

I can see the discarded newspaper out of the corner of my eye. Thea sees it too.

"It's true!" Thea protests, pushing her plate away from her. "You can't be that oblivious."

"I'm not oblivious."

And the staring contest begins. Like mother, like daughter. My dad looks at me, as if to say, *Please do something. I can't watch World War III break out right now.*

"It said in the *Times* that we have until next January before things get to the point of no return," I offer. "That's long enough to start college."

"Not helping, Liz," Dad mutters, his eyes suddenly like daggers. Apparently that wasn't what he was looking for.

"She's not wrong," Thea fires back.

Mom isn't one to surrender, though. "There's no such thing as the point of no return. They keep saying that, but it never happens. They were saying that before you two were even born."

Thea doesn't bat an eye. "It hasn't happened *yet,* you mean."

Dad takes a long, deep breath. I watch his chest rise and fall as his eyes scan the three of us. I know what he believes. He doesn't have to say it. I know that if Mom weren't here, he would say, *You're right.* But he's a peace broker. So he swallows and puts on a brave face.

"Your mother worked hard on this dinner. Let's not ruin it."

"Thank you, *David.*"

I say nothing, watching as pine needles fall from the roping by the stairs.

CHAPTER FIVE

I was dreaming about my family when I was awoken by the sound of the downstairs door creaking open. The dream wasn't a new one. My mind has been a rather unimaginative place in recent months.

My eyes slowly adjust to the darkness. My to-do list sits on the table next to my mattress, collecting both metaphorical and literal dust. People used to say that it was bad to keep your cell phone next to your bed because you'd always know it was there, subconsciously, and that knowledge of your phone would keep you from getting a good night's sleep. My to-do list has the same effect. I tell myself that it's the reason for my recurring nightmare, even if I know that it's not.

I pause, staring up at the blue tarp fluttering above my head, wondering if I imagined the sound of the door opening. It's possible, for sure. With the tarp fluttering and the wind blowing outside, it's easy to hear things that don't exist. But then again, I know what the tarp sounds like. It's one of those things you get used to, like our old neighbor's hound dog that always howled at exactly six in the morning. I got used to that, eventually.

I close my eyes, willing myself to go back to sleep. I'm nearly there when the sound of hinges screeching downstairs jolts me awake.

And then I hear a crash.

I'm not making it up this time. The first time I could play it off as a hallucination, but I don't think my mind is advanced enough to play the same prank twice.

I sit up in bed and get on my feet. I walk across the kitchen, carefully, before pausing by the door, listening. I don't hear the door hinges, but I do hear something else. It sounds like rustling, footsteps shuffling. I think I hear voices. Or maybe just one voice. Maybe it's some wacko muttering to themselves about how much they like murdering teenage girls. I'm not sure. I start down the stairs, using the banister to propel myself in the dark.

My insides toss and turn, doing somersaults. A part of me wants to say that I'm being ridiculous. There could be a million things happening in the bookstore, and only one of them is that someone is walking around in there. But a bigger part of me, the part of me that loves reading ghost stories even though they give me nightmares, knows better. I've seen enough horror films to know that a creaking floorboard in the night is usually cause for concern.

I exhale, open the door, and step into the bookstore.

The world is silent except for my footsteps. The whole thing is slightly unsettling, making me realize that I've never been down here in the dark before. By the time the sun sets, there are no customers to be watching for, and so I'm already upstairs, crawling into bed and dreaming about things I try hard to forget when I'm awake. Before everything ended, the bookstore kept lights on overnight—little LEDs, left over from the holidays, twinkling brightly above the shelves. It was never dark. It was never like this.

The room is completely empty, a fact that is both unsettling and relieving. Maybe I made the whole thing up. Maybe I didn't hear anything at all. Maybe I'm going insane. Either that or tonight's intruder is still somewhere inside, watching me creak through the room with no shoes on.

But then I look outside.

Resting by the front entrance, there's a cart waiting in the open doorway, sitting out on the sidewalk in front of the store.

It could probably be more accurately described as a wagon, almost like a Radio Flyer with the sides replaced by wire mesh. The sort of mesh that makes up picnic tables at a playground, or the sides of a beaten-up lumber truck. It's rusted; the holes in the mesh are warped and out of shape. The handle has been discarded on the ground, making its mark on the dusty sidewalk. The cart is full—filled with trinkets and bags and pots and pans and cans and cloth. The cans remind me of how hungry I am. The cans remind me of the lack of water and the lack of food in the kitchen cupboard. This isn't the sort of thing someone would leave on the side of the road. This belongs to someone who wouldn't just run off and leave it behind. This is valuable.

And so, the intruder must still be in the store.

I don't see them yet, so I slowly make my way toward the Classics section to nab a hardcover copy of *Anna Karenina* for self-defense purposes. It's the biggest book I see, and so I assume it will hurt the most if used to smack someone in the face. Not that I've tried that before. I grip it tightly, my knuckles turning white with strain, and tread lightly, letting one foot cross over the other like I saw in an episode of *Criminal Minds,* holding my hardcover edition firmly by my head so that I can swing it in front of me when necessary.

I begin my sweep of the bookstore. I tell myself that if someone *were* going to jump out at me, they've had plenty of opportunities to do so and have probably missed their window at this point. I keep moving forward until I reach the entrance to the Children's section. The Children's "room" is the only part of the store that isn't a rectangle. Instead, it juts off to the left like a wonky *Tetris* piece. Maybe it was meant to give kids privacy as they read, far from the watchful eyes of their parents. Maybe it's because the back of the building always gets the nicest lighting. Either way, I can't see into the room until I enter it, making it the perfect hiding place for our intruder.

I rack my brain for the right warning to give before I enter. But the intruder beats me to it, a clear voice echoing through the empty bookstore. A girl's voice.

"Leave now and I won't hurt you," she growls, her voice hoarse and worn.

That wasn't what I was expecting. I was expecting an apology or a cry for help or something more like, *Oh my goodness! You caught me! I'm so sorry! Please don't hurt me with that clothbound deluxe copy of* Anna Karenina *that you have gripped in your hands!*

"What?" is all I can say in response as I press myself against a bookshelf, making sure that my uninvited guest can't see me.

"I don't want to hurt you. Just go back upstairs and pretend

I wasn't here." Although that sentence holds no real malice—in fact, it hints at desperation—it still sounds more like a threat than anything else.

While a small part of me feels scared, like the girl with the hoarse voice could tear me to shreds, the other part of me feels insulted. Who does she think she is, breaking into my home and giving *me* orders? Why should *I* be afraid? So I take a deep breath and decide to, for once in my life, grow a spine.

I move into the room, holding *Anna Karenina* a bit tighter in my sweaty fingers. "I'm sorry, I don't think that you're in the position to—"

Suddenly, I'm face to face with the intruder, slamming straight into her chest, her sternum colliding with mine. I quickly back away, tumbling backward toward a shelf of picture books, heat rising to my face. She follows me down toward the ground, her elbow against my chest, pinning me to the carpeted floor. She stares at me, nose mere inches from mine.

She's shorter than I imagined, maybe five and a half feet tall. She's young, too, probably a year younger than me, although that might just be her height. Her hair is a mess, shaved on one side, the other half a cascading tangle of dark brown waves. There are a few scrapes on her face, scabbed over but still red and puffy. And above her hard green eyes are two thin eyebrows, knitted into a scowl.

As I lie on the ground next to a display of Dr. Seuss books, I find myself almost wanting to apologize. But then, I shake the feeling and remind myself that I do, in fact, have a spine.

"Who the *hell* are you?" I ask, trying to mimic the gravelly quality of her voice.

The intruder eases her grip slightly, positioning her free

hand on the floor next to my head. There's a small tattoo on her forearm. It's simple, just black lines etching an open eye into her skin, a full moon where the iris should be. For a second I think she might let me go, but then she places her knee on my torso, throwing all her weight onto me. I hold my breath.

"I said that I don't want to hurt you."

But the look on her face, and the way she's reaching toward her back pocket, make me think that she *does* want to hurt me. These days, people will do almost anything to survive.

"I could say the same," I reply, glancing at my now-discarded copy of *Anna Karenina,* which lies open on the ground a few feet away. I hope I don't sound as pathetic as I feel.

"I doubt that you could."

I want to strangle her, and the fact that I can't is actively killing my brain cells. It's one thing to break in; it's another thing to insult my competence. I realize that I need to protect the one thing I have from this outsider. I use the only strength I have to push upward, forcing her knee off my torso. To my surprise, she eases her grip and removes her leg, moving backward a few inches. It's not quite a victory for me, but it'll do. I prop myself up on my elbows hesitantly, waiting for her reaction. When she doesn't force me back down, I take it as permission to slowly stand.

"What do you want from me?" I ask, my energy store now depleted.

"I need you to leave me alone. Go upstairs. Pretend you didn't see me. I'll be gone in the morning."

"I'm sorry," I sputter. "That's not how this works. I *caught* you. You're supposed to give up now."

The girl clears her throat, rolling her eyes. "I don't think you understand. I'm not going anywhere until I get what I need."

"You're out of luck," I reply, even though I realize that I don't have any power at all in this situation. I'm scrawny, I have no upper body strength, and the most violent thing I've ever done is throw a book across the room when I'm upset with the ending. But she doesn't know that. "There's nothing here for you to take."

The girl seems to shrink slightly, and she stands up straight, no longer looking like a wannabe superhero. Instead, she looks like a teenager. A teenager who has been through hell, sure, but who hasn't?

"What?"

"Unless you're looking for a book, of course," I add.

But the girl grits her teeth in a way that says she hasn't read a book that wasn't assigned for school in a long time.

"I'm not in the mood," she says. "Don't quite have time for reading right now. Never did."

"Then I don't have anything to give you, even if you hadn't pinned me to the ground. I have no food for you to take. No water either. There is absolutely nothing that you could take from me that hasn't been taken already." I'm on a roll. There's nothing stopping me now. I watch as her face softens, the malice it holds slowly turning into something else. "I bet you came in here thinking that I must have it so much better than you—"

"I didn't know that there was anyone here—" the girl starts, but I wave my hand, silencing her.

"But I have nothing. This place is falling apart. I'm tired. I'm hungry. You don't see me going around and stealing from others." I pause before adding, "You really are a lowlife, aren't you? Aren't you ashamed of yourself?" I cringe, realizing how much I sound like my mother.

But the girl isn't paying attention to my rant anymore. Her face is once again hard, her eyebrows pressed together. She's deep in thought.

"I'm not looking to steal from you," she says.

"Huh?"

"Well, I *was.* Take some supplies, maybe spend the night, and hit the road. But since you're here now, what I really need is a place to crash."

"Why?"

"My tent broke," the girl says matter-of-factly. "Word is there's another Storm coming, maybe a month if we're lucky, and I'd rather not be outside when it does."

I raise my eyebrows. "How do you know that's true?" Am I the only person to have been left out of the meteorological loop?

The girl bites her lip, squinting slightly before she responds. Eventually she says, "I have my sources."

What a wonderful and informative answer!

"You don't know that it's coming for sure," I mutter before pausing. I bite the inside of my cheek. "And what's in it for me?"

"You just said you need food. Water. Supplies," she responds. "I can help you get them."

"By stealing things?" I scoff. "I'm sorry, but unlike you I actually have a moral compass."

I watch as a vein in the girl's forehead throbs, watch as her jaw tenses. She stares at me with steely eyes. "I'm good at repairs," she says, gesturing toward the cracked windowpanes and the insulation seeping out of the wall. "My dad was a super. I basically grew up with a screwdriver in my hand."

I look at the girl. I stare at the cuts on her face, and her mess of hair.

"You could have killed me."

"But I didn't."

My to-do list tells me that I am royally screwed. There's not much keeping this place together besides a hope and a prayer. And now a second person tells me that another Storm is rolling through.

I don't have to like her. We don't have to be friends. I can keep her at arm's length and keep myself safe. I need food. I need water. Although I hate to admit it, I need someone. This might be something that I can't do alone.

"Fine" is all I say.

• • •

We sit in the kids' room together in the dark. Even though I'm tired and I'd rather be upstairs sleeping, I stay awake the whole night, just in case. Just in case this was all a part of her plan and she wants to steal everything I have as soon as I close my eyes and let my guard down. But we don't say a word to one another. We sit and glare.

My back is digging into a box set of *Elephant & Piggie.* She sits on the other side of the room, over by the graphic novels, a half-opened copy of *Amulet* in her hands.

Finally, the silence gets the better of me. "What's your name?"

"Maeve," she replies, raising her eyebrows nonchalantly.

"Oh."

Maeve pauses, as if wondering whether she's morally obligated to ask the question in return, before finally caving.

"Yours?"

"Elizabeth," I reply. "Liz."

"Like Elizabeth Swann. From *Pirates of the Caribbean*?"

I regret asking her anything at all.

"I guess."

I've never seen *Pirates of the Caribbean*. I'm not sure if saying I'm like Elizabeth Swann is a compliment or a half-hearted attempt at a joke. I decide not to think of it as either.

"I'm from New York," Maeve offers as she shuts her book and slides it back onto the shelf. I want to tell her that she's putting it in the wrong place and that I worked hard to get everything in alphabetical order, but I bite my tongue.

"Cool" is what I say instead.

"What about you?"

"I'm from here," I reply.

"Ah."

We don't say anything else for the rest of the night. Eventually, Maeve falls asleep, her head lolling backward until it's wedged inside the Middle Readers' shelf. I don't sleep. I watch.

I watch the way she grimaces in her sleep. I watch the way she clenches her hands every once in a while. I can't help but wonder if I've made a huge mistake.

CHAPTER SIX

We stand outside the front door the next morning, staring down into Maeve's wagon, piled high with so many objects that I can't even discern what all of them are. She begins riffling through them, picking up a can in one hand and a blanket in the other as if there's some sort of method to her madness. I can tell that there absolutely isn't, but I allow her to pretend. Whatever floats her boat. It makes so much noise, the clashing and clanging of each object.

"So you'll leave after you fix the tent?" I ask, struggling to make my voice heard over all of the ruckus. Maeve doesn't seem to hear me, or if she does, she ignores my question completely. I decide to try again.

"Can I help?" I gesture wildly at the cart. I'm not sure why I should help, but it seems like the right thing to do.

Maeve whips her head up, tendrils of brown hair extending in every single direction. She purses her lips, her brow furrowed in concentration. "We need to bring it all in."

"Inside? All of it?"

Maeve nods.

I'm not sure what I've gotten myself into as I look from Maeve to her cart back to Maeve. I've spent the past year expertly cultivating a rhythm to my life. After Eva left, I got so used to doing things alone. On my own schedule. Maeve could mess everything up. I want her out of here as soon as possible, and I'll do absolutely anything to get her tent fixed in a timely manner. After, of course, she's helped me check off a bit of my to-do list. Expedited the process.

I look at her cart and shake my head. The ridiculous cart that for some reason can't fit through a perfectly reasonably sized doorway. The ridiculous cart that is going to force me to bring all the junk inside by hand, piece by piece.

"Here," I say, reaching out toward a crate filled with blankets and candles and rope and scissors. "Let me take that one, and then you can follow me upstairs."

"Why would we bring it upstairs?"

"Because that's where we sleep?"

"You mean, that's where *you* sleep."

"What do you mean?"

"Can't I just sleep down here?" Maeve asks, her voice dripping with judgment. "It was kind of weird, waking up to you watching me sleep."

"Absolutely not."

"I'm not going to *cuddle* with you, Liz, if that's what you're looking for."

I scoff before realizing that Maeve is perfectly serious. "I don't trust you. *That's* why we sleep in the same room."

"That's not fair," Maeve says matter-of-factly. "Our deal was that you let me stay here, and I make sure that you don't die. There was nothing in our agreement about a shared living space."

"I want to be able to keep an eye on you. Make sure you're not trying to take advantage of me."

"That's actually really creepy," Maeve mutters. "Plus, I wouldn't do that."

I laugh, for real this time. "*You* are the one who tried to rob me last night. *I'm* the one who doesn't do that."

"I don't trust you either."

I look from the cart, at the piles of food and supplies, to Maeve, with her arms crossed over her chest. If she's as desperate for shelter as she says she is, she'll cave. I know she will.

"Fine," Maeve says finally.

Ha. I was right.

"Okay. Glad we got that settled."

Maeve scoops a pair of pants and a six-pack of instant ramen into her arms. "Lead the way, Elizabeth Swann."

"Liz is fine."

I nudge the front door open with the tip of my sandal, sliding my way inside. I can hear a slight shuffle behind me as Maeve follows, banging her hip against the doorknob on her way through. Even the bookstore doesn't want her here.

I lead her around the counter and through the dark hallway, up the creaky stairs, careful not to trip on the sagging parts in the middle. Once at the top, I fumble with the knob, twisting it two or three times before the door finally gives up and lets me in.

I plop her crate down on the kitchen counter and slide it over a bit to make room for her pants and ramen, which she tosses onto the surface haphazardly.

"Do you want to make your own corner for your stuff?"

Maeve shrugs her shoulders. "Whatever you think is best."

I don't know what's best, and so I head back downstairs to

take another load up from the cart. I'm rummaging through her crap, wondering how she accumulated so much, when I see it.

Sitting, only half-visible, on an old red T-shirt with *Jackson Hole, Wyoming* on it, is a knife. It's sheathed in a triangle of worn leather, golden studs holding it together. A dark wooden handle juts out from the top. I have no choice but to stare at it. It commands my attention.

It's not like I haven't seen a knife before. Maybe because it's a *knife* knife, and not just one of the run-of-the mill-kitchen ones, that it holds my gaze. I pick it up, gingerly, as if it might explode in my hands. Slowly I pull it out of the leather, careful not to nick myself. Judging from how easily I stapled my fingers together when I was seven and making paper chains in art class, it isn't too far-fetched for me to chop a finger off, right here, right now, which is exactly what I need.

It's one of those knives I used to see on Instagram, probably made by some man in the back of his camper van with giant chunks of reclaimed wood. It's the type of knife that, in the old days, would set you back a couple hundred dollars and would be called "artisanal." The blade isn't clean; something's caked on. Something deep and just slightly red.

It scares me.

I know nothing about Maeve. That fact hits me now as I'm standing, totally vulnerable, alone. I know absolutely nothing about this person whom I've allowed into my home. She could have killed me last night. Is this what she'd been reaching for in her pocket? Her knife? But then why didn't she use it? It would have been much more convenient to end me and take the building for herself. And why is she taking so long? Why is she still up there, taking her sweet time?

I hear the back door creak from inside, and I turn to face Maeve, who is standing in the doorway. When her eyes meet mine, she freezes.

"Why do you have a knife?"

She takes a couple of tentative steps toward me, craning her neck to see what exactly it is that I have in my hands.

"What?" Even though she asks the question, she doesn't seem confused at all. Her face remains perfectly composed.

I repeat myself, even though her grimace makes me uncomfortable. "Why do you have a knife?"

"Don't you have a knife?"

"Sure I do. I have a *kitchen knife* that probably hasn't been sharpened in years. It couldn't even make a clean cut through Styrofoam." And it has never once been caked in a mysterious red substance.

"Okay," Maeve says, continuing to walk toward me. "And how do you eat?"

"With a *spoon*."

She smirks. I can feel heat rising into my cheeks. I can't tell if it's from embarrassment or anger. Maybe a horrible mixture of both.

Maeve is practically a foot away from me now. She reaches her hand out for the knife that I'm holding. I grip it tighter.

"Don't you ever have to hunt?" she asks.

"No."

Her eyebrows shoot up when I say this, and I can't understand why. I hate that I don't understand why. "So you've been eating what, exactly?"

I swallow hard before answering. "Things that I don't have to *kill*."

Eva had already begun a stockpile when I arrived, driving from supermarket to supermarket in her Subaru, grabbing what she could. I added what I could from my own kitchen and from my dad's vain attempts at doomsday prepping. We ate sparingly, filling in whatever gaps appeared with the trades we got from others. And when two became one, I suddenly didn't have to worry about food for a while. But stores are low, and fall is fast approaching. Luck runs out, as it always does.

"And how do you defend yourself? All alone here?"

I look down at my feet, unsure if there's a correct answer to this question. "I've never had to," I say, before adding, "at least not until last night."

Maeve laughs at this, the sound less grating than I expected. "Have you even left this building in the last six months?"

I repeat my response. "I've never had to."

"Let me tell you something, *Elizabeth Swann,*" she says. "The world isn't the same as how you last left it. It's worse."

"That doesn't mean that you need a bloody knife."

"Look, Liz," Maeve spits as she plucks the knife from my hands. For some reason, I don't even try to hold on to it. "Don't judge me for what I've done to survive. I've had to get my hands a little dirty, because unlike you, I live in the real world. Some of us don't have fancy bookstores to hide out in. Some of us have to look out for ourselves." I watch as she brushes past me, gathering more of her belongings from the cart. I open my mouth to speak, but Maeve's glare quiets me. I freeze as she points the tip of her knife toward me, my heart leaping up into my throat. "And don't look through my stuff."

Lynn Porter
56 years old
Northampton, Massachusetts

Dogs are smart. Smarter than we are, I can tell you that much. Because we were floundering about whether anything was going to happen. "Oh, are we sure that this will even affect us in the first place?" "Can we really be certain about that sort of thing?" But my dogs? They knew immediately, no doubt about it. I woke up that morning to them scratching at the bedroom door—both of them, even though Quint is basically blind and senile. And they're well-behaved dogs, both of them. Once the sun set, they were barking. Basically taking turns like some sort of coordinated alarm system, so I sat on the floor with them trying to calm them down instead of going on our nightly walk. I swear to god that those dogs saved my life. Saved their own too.

CHAPTER SEVEN

That night, we sit in the kitchen together, silently fuming. I don't think I could speak even if I wanted to.

Part of me burns from the hypocrisy of it all. Looking through her stuff? While she was sneaking around the bookstore for god knows how long looking through *my* belongings? She came to me because she needed shelter and then told me that *I* don't understand what it's like to be hungry. That I don't understand what it's like to be alone. But I do understand. I understand perfectly.

There's a difference between being alone and being lonely. That much is true. Alone is a physical state. A state of separation from anything and everything that could possibly give you comfort. Alone is being proud of yourself and having no one around who loves you to say that they're proud too. Alone is having nightmares and having absolutely no one to hold you close and tell you that *it will all be okay.* Alone is the complete and utter absence of the people who love you and the people whom you love back.

Loneliness is hunger. Loneliness is a hunger for something

you can never have. Loneliness is a hunger for warmth, and compassion, and birthday songs, and love. When you haven't had someone care about you for such a long time that you think you will fall apart completely.

People come and go, here for moments and then gone, but the hunger has inched closer and closer to eating me alive. Peacoat Man does not offer love. He doesn't offer any sort of antidote to loneliness. He just exists. He is kind, and for a moment I am with someone else. Same with the other people who pass by and stop at the store. Sure, I have contact, I see people, and some of them are even friendly. But I am still lonely. There is a void in me that no person can fill by being *around.* There is a void in me that I don't think will ever be filled. It grows by the day.

The knife sits on the kitchen counter. Maeve put it there as soon as we brought the last of her stuff upstairs. She placed it there and made sure I was looking, as if to say, *See! I'm not going to kill you! I will put my artisanal knife on the counter so that I will have to walk all the way over here, in plain view, in order to kill you! Everything is all right.* Still, I know that she could make it to this knife and stick it in my gut before I even have time to react. She glowers at me from the armchair. *My* armchair. The armchair that I have eaten in every single night for the past year.

I decide to let it slide. I stare at her from my spot on the floor, slurping up a cup of noodles. One useful thing Maeve had in that ridiculous cart of hers was a supersized box of matches. Even though it's a huge fire hazard considering the amount of paper in this building, her rusted camp stove also made my dinner warm for the first time in a long time. For that, Maeve earned herself the armchair. I look back down at my noodles and swirl them, around and around and around with my fork until they've become a clump of noodles so large that I couldn't possibly fit it in my mouth. I decide to try.

Maybe I'll choke on them and die right here on the floor, Maeve not moving from the armchair due to pure stubbornness. I'll die here and fossilize, and our ever-merciful alien overlords will find my body and say ơ⊔⎍⍕⍕⍜∧! Which roughly translates to *Glutton!*

Maeve pauses and points at a photo on the coffee table, Peacoat Man's sister smiling up at us. She grins. "Who's the photo of?"

Even though I know exactly what she's talking about, my eyebrows arch. Why does she care? "Huh?"

"The lady in the photo. Is she family?"

"No." The words leap out of my mouth before I can process why I'm feeling so defensive. But why should Maeve get to know anything about my family? Why should she get to know anything about me at all? "It's a customer."

Maeve scoffs. "A customer? So you're telling me that this place is still in business? In this economy?"

"Something like that," I grumble in response. "Some people actually value the lasting power of literature." *Unlike a certain someone in this room who likes to break into bookstores and probably can't spell* Nietzsche.

"Is this what your life is like?" Maeve asks. "Plenty of food, and an open door for visitors?" Her tone surprises me. It's soft, not venomous like I thought it would be. I freeze, fork halfway to my lips.

"What?"

"Every day. Is this how you live?" Maeve repeats.

I place my fork back into my noodle cup and look up at her. "I mean, not exactly like this. Not every day. Some days are worse than others, I guess." I pause and wait for the feeling in my chest to dissipate. "But yes."

Maeve stares at me, slowly sipping her broth. "It must be nice."

Her voice is monotone, like she's reciting a well-known fact. Like it's an uncontested truth that I've had it so much easier.

"Is that some sort of backhanded jab at me? Another one? Because after this morning, I can assure you that you've gotten your point across. You don't know every—"

"I don't mean it like that." Her tone is biting, at first. But then it's not. "It just must be nice to always have people."

"I don't have people. They never last long."

And when they leave, I'm just as alone as everyone else, stuck thinking about the things I should have done. Stuck with that simmering feeling of guilt inside me.

"But at least those people exist. You have people in your life."

"Yeah, well, I can never get them to stay."

Maeve looks away, and my heart sinks. For a moment, I worry that I've ruined the conversation, not that it was a good conversation in the first place. Some part of my brain wants Maeve to like me, no matter how much I don't like her. I'm such a kiss-ass that I can't help wanting everyone to like me. I watch something flicker across her face as she processes what I said.

She nods slowly, looking down to take another sip of broth. "It's hot."

Not quite the gasp of understanding that I was waiting for. "Really? I hadn't noticed."

Maeve laughs at this, even though I don't think what I said was that funny. I think it was a laugh of relief.

"I'm sorry, by the way," she mutters, mouth half full of noodles. "For whatever you've been through."

I look at her, trying to discern if she really means the things she's saying. Nothing lurks behind her face. No bit of malice waits for me to take her bait.

"It's okay."

CHAPTER EIGHT

FEBRUARY 18: BEFORE THE FIRST STORM

It's Chinese-food night, meaning that Mom is off in the city going to some fancy lawyer dinner for people in suits. This is my favorite type of night. The type of night when I don't have to deal with her endless nagging and instead get to enjoy a nice big plate of sesame noodles.

Thea sits beside me, pushing General Tso's chicken around with her chopsticks. Dad clears his throat.

"Can I talk to you girls about something?" he asks, setting down his utensils and taking a sip from his gin and tonic.

That's probably the worst sentence you could ever hear from a parent at the beginning of a Friday-night dinner, except for maybe *I got an interesting call from your principal today* or *I've been feeling rather queasy; I hope it's not contagious.*

I stop shoveling noodles into my mouth and look up, ready to give him my full attention. Unlike my mother, he's not the type to be super melodramatic. When he's serious, he's serious. Thea, however, is unbothered.

"Sure," I reply, nudging Thea's ankle with my sneaker until she stops torturing her dinner.

"I've told you about your aunt Kathleen, right?" Dad says.

He has. Apparently we met her when we were little, at the age where you can't form full memories yet, so my only mental image of her is a woman with a blob for a face.

"Yeah," Thea murmurs. "The Alaskan one."

Dad smiles. "Yes, that one."

I pick up my chopsticks again and lift a bundle of noodles. "What about her?" I ask, before shoving them into my mouth.

"She's invited us to stay with her, if we have to. Somewhere more remote. Off the grid."

Thea coughs, eyes bulging out. Because it's not like our dad isn't . . . eccentric. But he's *Jesus Christ Superstar*–reenactment-at-eleven-p.m.-on-a-Wednesday eccentric. He's dress-up-as-an-escaped-mental-patient-and-create-an-elaborate-skit-for-trick-or-treaters eccentric. Not run-off-to-Alaska eccentric. And suddenly my Chinese food has adhered to the inside of my throat.

"Why would we do that?" she spits.

"It's not happening immediately. The whole thing is a couple of months away, once things get bad enough that we have to—"

Thea holds up her hand. "For Christ's sake, Dad. Please don't start with this again. I'm trying to enjoy my food."

She's shifted over to Mom's side in the past month. Too many newspaper articles and YouTube videos can make a person numb. And for Thea, she seems to believe that because it hasn't happened yet, it won't ever happen.

"Did you know that there was a tornado in Massachusetts yesterday? And not a small one either. There hasn't been a tornado in Massachusetts in years! And the tsunami in Louisiana.

Not to mention that pretty much all of Canada is on fire," Dad says.

"There's a first time for everything, right?" Thea replies.

I shake my head. Dad isn't always right, but sometimes he is. "That doesn't make it any less monumental."

"Thank you, Liz," Dad says. "I'm planning on leaving for Alaska in September after you girls head off to school. You could join me on breaks. Mail some of your stuff over."

Thea laughs, the sound cold, before she pauses for dramatic effect. "Oh, you were serious? That's actually insane, Dad. I mean, I understand being pessimistic. Hell, I'm pessimistic, but you've taken it to a whole other level."

"Trust me, girls. Things are only going to get worse."

"Things always get worse!"

I decide to give my input, even if it's not required. "It doesn't hurt to be prepared." And that's the truth. Sure, what if Dad's wrong and just falling off the deep end, but . . . what if he's right? I've seen the headlines, too; I've watched as my teachers have skirted around the more difficult topics. I understand what it's like to have that feeling in the pit of your stomach, like everything's about to go terribly wrong.

"This isn't just prepared, Liz," Thea says. "This is like doomsday-prepper-level shit. Next thing you know, he's going to start wearing tinfoil hats and quoting Leviticus."

"Don't talk to me like that, Thea. I'm still your father."

"I understand, Dad," I say, looking up at him. He looks tired. Too tired. "I understand what you're saying."

"Don't do it, Liz," Thea warns. "Don't join his little cult that he has going on."

I look down at my plate before murmuring, "I have to think about it."

Because maybe it would be nice to leave all of this behind and not have to worry about college or the future or whatever else comes with it. Maybe it would be better, easier, to leave the world behind. It wouldn't matter that I've got no prom date, that I've never been kissed. It wouldn't matter that I walk home every day for lunch because it's better than staying at school, alone. Maybe, in that weird way, Dad is right.

I push my food away. I'm not quite hungry anymore.

"Okay," Dad says. "That's okay. Think about it. But don't tell your mother."

I reach for the container of fried rice at the other end of the table. The food has gone cold.

CHAPTER NINE

Clouds loom in the sky, a grim reminder of what's to come. Maeve took it upon herself to create a countdown on the wall, even though neither of us has a real timeline of what's to come. But a month was a nice round number, so she wrote it down anyway. I can feel its presence, like some cursed *Mona Lisa,* as Maeve flips the open sign on the front door. I told Maeve that it wasn't helpful to have a reminder of impending doom in such a prominent place. Maeve retorted that she always works better under pressure. I can't say I feel the same.

Maeve is sketching out a plan for window repair when a woman opens the front door. I put down the rag I was using to clean the shelves and smile. I feel like I've seen her before.

Two sandy braids hang down her back, bouncing against her slightly torn baseball tee. Her face is kind, with small smile lines appearing around her eyes. Maeve looks at me, seemingly shocked as the woman walks toward the counter.

"They just come in like that?" she asks, her voice a harsh whisper.

"Yeah," I reply. They always have. I've thought of installing a bell above the door but have never gotten around to it. I've also never managed to find a bell. It doesn't seem important.

"*I* didn't."

"Ha ha, very funny." I decide to drop it there, rather than trying to explain the postapocalyptic rules of customer service. "Thank goodness the majority of the world isn't like you."

Maeve stares for a moment before leaning toward me once again. "Obviously you just haven't met the right people."

I can't help but smile, and I watch as the corners of Maeve's mouth rise. She grins back.

The woman finally makes it to the counter, shrugging a well-worn hiking bag off her shoulders. "Hi," she manages, her voice low and gritty.

Maeve moves to the side, making room for me. "Can I help you find something?" The words are practically programmed into my brain at this point.

"Yeah," the woman says, sighing. "My name is Sawyer. I think my brother left me something?"

She says it like a question. The people who come here always do, at least their first time. *Can I come in? I'm looking for a book? I have something to trade you?* Almost as if they'd told themselves that they weren't allowed to be happy anymore. That there weren't any good things left, let alone a random bookstore in the middle of suburban New Jersey.

"Yeah, of course," I answer, turning to inspect the corkboard propped up behind the inoperable register. But then I remember the crumpled photo on the table upstairs and realize where I've seen Sawyer's face before. "Wait! You're Peacoat Man's sister?"

Sawyer raises her eyebrows, her face perfectly matching Maeve's. They both look at me, staring in silence.

Sawyer shakes her head slowly. "You mean Everton? Yeah, I'm his sister." She chuckles for a moment, laughing at some secret joke. "He still wears that ragged old coat everywhere?"

"Of course. I've never seen him without it."

Maeve watches from the sidelines, her eyes bouncing from me to Sawyer back to me. I understand the look on her face. It's like we're playing a game and she doesn't know the rules.

I pluck the letter that Peacoat Man left from the bulletin board and hand it to Sawyer, who places it gently in the pocket of her pants. She lets her hiking pack fall from her shoulder and unzips it, rifling around for something inside. A few seconds later, she's found it, sliding a book of matches onto the counter.

It's one of those flimsy ones you get at the front desk of some fancy French bistro in the city, emblazoned with the faded logo of a once-exclusive restaurant. I begin to open my mouth to thank Sawyer when she adds a package of beef jerky, setting it down in front of us with a small thud. It's a bigger package than I'm used to and probably more than she should be parting with, but when she looks toward me she has this childish gleam in her eyes.

"Don't be polite," she says, a smirk appearing on her lips. "I can spare it, and I want to give it to you."

All I say in response is "Thank you." That seems to suffice for Sawyer.

She gives me and Maeve a quick wave as she walks back toward the front door, reaching for the letter resting in her pocket.

As the door shuts behind her, Maeve turns toward me, eyebrows furrowed. "Are they always so . . . generous?"

"You'd be surprised," I reply. I watch through the front window as Sawyer opens the yellowed envelope in her hands. She stands just across the street, leaning against the remains of a rusted mailbox as she reads. I watch as emotions flick across her face. First amusement, then admiration, then some small sliver of sadness before it morphs into a look of determination.

She turns, trying to orient herself in the center of the plaza as she consults the paper in her hands. Finally, she adjusts the straps of her bag and sets off, her figure growing smaller and smaller until she disappears around a set of hedges.

• • •

"This place is filthy," Maeve mutters, wiping dust off the counter with the sleeve of her flannel. "Dust on the shelves, dust on the floor, cobwebs in the corner."

"What?" I dog-ear my page in *Changing My Mind* and snap it shut.

"Do you ever clean in here?"

I turn around and pause, staring at her. She's not even looking at me. She's inspecting the floor behind the counter, which I already know could use some sweeping.

"What do you think?"

Maeve glares at me, unappreciative of my sarcasm. "I'm not here to be a maid."

"Cleaning isn't important," I reply.

"Aren't you running a business?"

I begin to walk toward Maeve, my sandals thudding across the floor. "It's not like I have very much competition."

Maeve huffs, glancing down at my to-do list on the counter. "No wonder this place is in shambles," she mutters. "You don't care enough."

I want to tell her that I do, in fact, care enough. I care more than she can imagine. I care more about this place than she's cared about anything in her entire life. But there are things that are more important than sweeping and dusting, like staying alive. And sometimes, things hurt too much for you to do anything at all. Sometimes, you feel like falling apart, and the only thing you can focus your energy on is making sure that you don't. But Maeve doesn't seem like she has any days like that. Maeve doesn't seem like she feels anything at all.

Maeve exhales, tracing the to-do list with a thin finger. "Still, this is easy stuff."

"What do you mean, *this is easy stuff*?" I retort.

"I don't know. I don't understand why you've put it off for so long."

I can't deal with her know-it-all attitude, or her coarseness, or her entitlement. I can't deal with the way she weasels into things and refuses to acknowledge the inconvenience. I can't deal with her ever-present scowl and her gravelly voice.

Maeve raps her finger against the hardwood counter. She stares at me expectantly, as if she's waiting for me to argue and say, *Shut up. You don't know what you're talking about.* That would be right. That's what I want to say, but I can't. Because if she's going to stay here until her tent is fixed, no matter how long that might take, I'm going to force our interactions to be borderline pleasant.

"Whatever you say," I manage eventually.

A small smile creeps onto Maeve's face. "I can get this done in two or three weeks."

"Yeah, totally. It's just some late spring-cleaning to make sure I'm ready for winter."

Maeve slowly rises from the stool she's been sitting on, wiping her sweaty hands on her legs.

"Is there some sort of a faucet outside?" she asks, staring up at me. "I want to make sure that the whole water problem isn't just a problem with the individual sink upstairs. Then I can figure out a game plan."

I blink slowly, staring back at her. Now that Maeve has said it, I feel completely and utterly foolish. I'll feel more foolish if she turns that spout and fresh water pours out. I can feel the heat rise to my cheeks as I nod, pointing toward the front door.

"Yeah, it's right outside," I manage. "It's one of those hose things, if that works."

Maeve doesn't answer. She walks straight past me, leading the way out the front door. I don't move. I watch her disappear around the corner of the building, no longer visible through the front windows. I revel in the quiet left by her absence before I finally decide to follow.

I make my way around the front counter and out the front door that needs a new lock and new hinges. Surely Maeve will tell me that I've been utterly idiotic and haven't been twisting the knob in the right direction. *The lock is perfectly fine; it just doesn't like you.*

I round the corner, walking along the path her boots made in the dirt.

When I find Maeve, she's staring at the slightly rusted rectangle that sits just far enough from the side of the building that a soccer ball has managed to wedge itself into the gap. She moves her tongue from side to side in her mouth, lost in thought. Her eyes are narrowed as she peers at this unassuming box, tapping her foot impatiently like she's waiting for it to do something.

"What?" I mutter after getting tired of waiting.

Maeve bites down on the corner of her bottom lip. "Do you know what this is?"

"A box."

Maeve's sharp, biting laugh rings out, and she grins. "Thank you, Captain Obvious."

I want to slap her. I want to tell her that *I am perfectly capable and have lasted this long without her.* I don't need her to save me or tell me that I don't know anything at all. Because I do know things, right? I know a lot of things, and I know now that Maeve is a *condescending asshole* that I can't wait to get out of my hair.

"Fine. Then what is it, if you're so much smarter than me? Because it looks like a rusty box." I pause, chewing on the inside of my cheek. "It looks like a normal metal box that has been here for decades and is about to crumble to dust."

Maeve raises her eyebrows at me before pointing at a small sticker on the corner of the box. "What does that say?"

"I don't really want to play detectives right now," I say, but I look anyway. The letters have almost faded, but once I squint hard enough I can see the hazy outline of a shock warning. The mysterious box shouldn't be touched by children. It can administer enough volts to knock you off your feet . . . and then some. I look back up at Maeve, who waits expectantly. "Okay, so it's an electric box. Cool. If you haven't noticed, the electricity is out. It has been for a while. I'm going to go test the hose, if you don't mind."

But Maeve does seem to mind, and she holds up her arm, blocking my path over to the spigot. "Liz, it's not an electric box . . . whatever that might be. It's a generator!" I watch as a smile erupts across her face. A genuine one, not one filled with spite. "You've been sitting on a generator for a year, and you haven't noticed!"

I furrow my brow and stare back at her. "How was I supposed to know that this was a generator?"

"You weren't. That's why you're so totally lucky that I'm here."

"What would I do without you?" I manage sarcastically. But an image pops into my head. An image of a functioning light bulb. A CD player with real live music streaming out of its speakers. Hell, maybe even air-conditioning. An image of me and Maeve on the front of a newspaper, smiling because we brought electricity back to a ravaged world. We'd be in textbooks for centuries, and they'd have textbooks in the future because we brought electricity back to a ravaged world. And saved it. Of course, Maeve would probably alienate everyone with her crappy attitude, so in the end, I'd likely get credit for everything. I don't mind that thought.

"C'mon. Let's crack this bad boy open."

I stare down at Maeve as she kneels, inspecting her bounty. As something sour blooms inside me, I realize that there's absolutely no way in hell that I'm letting Maeve open this thing up. It's *my* generator, for goodness' sake.

"You don't know what you're doing, do you?"

Maeve immediately turns to face me.

"I do, in fact, know what I'm doing. *You* didn't even know that this was a generator."

"Fine. Fair enough. I'm an idiot. But I'm an idiot who's going to get this thing running." I watch as Maeve pauses, weighing her options. Either she stays with the generator and faces my wrath or she backs off and I don't murder her in the night.

Eventually she moves backward, leaning against the trunk of the dead tree. She pretends not to care, but I can see her eyes flicking back and forth, inspecting every inch of the generator. Every gear in her brain is turning at once.

"All yours."

I move closer to the metal box, taking my sweaty finger and using it to slowly wipe the rust and dirt off the exterior. A crack appears in the outer shell, and then a pair of hinges. Slowly I uncover a door with a small plastic window, too cloudy to use. Without hesitating, I yank it open, and a cloud of dust erupts into the air, sending me into a coughing fit. Maeve doesn't do a good job of hiding her laughter, and it takes everything in me to not turn around and stare her down. Not that that would work, anyway.

Inside the metal casing sits a gas tank, the type you'd expect to see inside fancy grills in the Hamptons. The kinds that used to be featured in Father's Day commercials and Memorial Day sales at Home Depot. Those sorts of things. Beside it is a dark cylinder, attached to a small fan, both of which are supposed to be spinning, generating kinetic energy, but aren't. I stare at them, not quite knowing what to do, before biting the bullet and facing Maeve.

"What do I do now?"

She grins at me from her place under the tree. "Well, these things normally run on gas, or propane in this case, I guess. You could start by checking to see if there's anything left in the tank."

"How do you know about this stuff? Aren't you a city girl?" I ask. *What makes you think you know so much more than I do?*

"Like I said, my dad was a super, and my mom practically

locked herself in her office. I either died of boredom or followed him around as he worked. Years of exploring my apartment building's basement has led to me knowing my way around these sorts of things." She smirks slightly as she flips her hair over to the other side of her head, revealing the shaved half. "What about you? Shouldn't this be your deal, country mouse?"

Now it's my turn to scoff. "The suburbs of New Jersey are hardly a self-sufficient place. My parents couldn't even use the TV properly. I had to help them change inputs practically every night."

Maeve shrugs. "Okay."

"Okay." I turn back toward the generator, searching the propane tank for some sort of meter. A black hose snakes through the inside, connecting itself to a nozzle at the tank's top. Attached to it is a small metal disk with a red needle barely visible through a layer of dust. I wipe it clean with the tip of my thumb. It's full. So why isn't it working?

"It must be broken." I sigh, tucking my hair behind my ears. I try my best to mirror Maeve's horrible smile as I turn around. "You're a lifesaver. Thanks so much for pointing out this useless piece of metal."

"It was worth a try," she mutters back. "But they wouldn't have kept this thing here if it was broken. Right?"

"I think you're forgetting about the apocalyptic disaster that blew through last year and destroyed basically everything." I kick up a cloud of dust with the corner of my sandal. "And what exactly do we do with this generator if we somehow manage to fix it? No way the propane will last that long. Are you going to waste it on some light bulbs or something?"

"No, silly," she replies. My stomach flips, an uncomfortable sensation that I don't like. I run my tongue along my gums, stopping myself from saying something I might regret. It's only a couple of days, right? I just have to bear her until then.

I'm transported back to high school, back to a game I used to play with myself after horrible social interactions, or after one of my jokes failed miserably. Faced with crushing humiliation, I'd repeat a mantra in my head: *Only two more years and then you never have to see them again.* It later became *Stay friends with them so you won't be alone at prom.* It later became *Hold your tongue just a little longer so that you have someone to talk to at graduation.* And then graduation came and went, and shit hit the fan, and nothing really mattered in the end. Nothing really mattered at all. I was still alone. I am still alone.

I look at Maeve expectantly, waiting for her to educate me. "Think about the wonders an electric drill could do. Or a buzz saw," she explains.

"I don't do power tools."

Maeve smirks at me again. "I do." Of course she does. Maeve laughs, a low, raspy laugh that starts out small but soon boils over into a full-blown fit.

"What is so funny?" I ask, frustrated.

Maeve rolls her eyes. "I'm just imagining you using power tools. It doesn't really fit your vibe."

I might strangle her. I honestly think I might strangle this girl. And sure, she might strangle me first, but I'm starting to think that I don't really care. My fingers are starting to itch when I see her point to something behind me and hear her laughter intensify.

I throw my hands up. "Jesus Christ, Maeve. Now what?"

"You might want to check the On switch," she says, pointing

her toe at something near the bottom of the generator. I can tell she wants to add the word *idiot* to the end of that sentence, but she doesn't. She doesn't have to. She can just pretend to be nice and helpful.

And sure enough, she *is* pointing to a small black knob that I, in my infinite wisdom, somehow missed. I notice slightly scratched letters next to the knob, forming a word that looks remarkably like Off. I don't say anything in response as I reach out and turn the knob toward a tiny lightning bolt that I hope is supposed to mean On.

I wait for the motor to start moving, for this thing to hum to life. I wait to see some sign that this thing even functions, but nothing comes. I can feel Maeve behind me, getting restless. I bet she can barely stop herself from snapping at me and telling me *exactly* what I've done wrong. Then she'll push me aside and fix something, and magic! It'll work. Just like when you're having computer problems that you can't fix, but the second you ask someone else to help, they suddenly solve everything in an instant.

I stare at the motor. Maybe this has something to do with activation energy. I mean, I have a hazy understanding of what that means from my freshman-year biology class. Every reaction needs a certain amount of activation energy to get started. Once it reaches that point, the reaction starts and only an enzyme can bring that level of energy needed down. So I can be the enzyme, I think. Or at least my hand can, to get this busted-up thing running. I hate to say it, but I haven't quite kept up with my studies.

I don't ask Maeve for permission. "I'm just going to give it a little help," I murmur. If she can't hear me, she can't tell me that I'm doing something wrong.

I slowly reach my hand in, feeling the cold metal on my fingertips. I can hear Maeve say something behind me, but I don't listen. Her voice is harsh, rough. And I'm sure that if I turned around, I'd see that same spiteful grin on her face.

I feel the cold metal on my skin, and I push. All at once I hear a roar, and then I don't feel anything at all.

CHAPTER TEN

Sometimes I wonder what it would be like if a younger version of myself saw what I'm like in the present day. I used to imagine it in a more heartwarming sense, as in, *Yeah, I might not be 100 percent happy right now with my life, but nine-year-old me would be super proud.* I bet she didn't even think that she'd make it this far.

But if nine-year-old me could see what is happening at this very moment, she would have a stroke and die, right there on the spot. She would spontaneously combust like that lady in Ireland in the '70s, the one in that odd but intriguing photo of a pile of ashes and two burned feet. That's what generally happens with spontaneous human combustion, although many doctors and scientists disagree about whether it truly exists. The person leaves a foot, or a finger behind, as if to say, *I was here, whether you believe in me or not.*

Nine-year-old me would feel such a toxic mixture of confusion and pain and shame and fear that her brain would burst into flames out of pure sensory overload.

Seventeen-year-old me doesn't feel too much of anything. Time moves so slowly that I physically *can't.* I can barely hear anything over the pure cacophony of all the blood coursing through my veins. I can see Maeve's fingernails digging into my skin, leaving pale white crescent moons along my arm. I see her hair whip wildly as she pulls and twists frantically, wondering why I'm standing there and not as freaked out about this as she is.

But I'm not just standing around. My hand is being pulled, fraction of a centimeter by fraction of a centimeter, closer and closer to the generator until it disappears inside completely. The motor eats it alive, its ridges getting caught on my skin and pulling my arm through the tiny gap between the cylinder and the top of the generator. In normal times, this would be bad, but now? Without doctors and hospitals and CVS? It's so much worse. I didn't even think that this could be dangerous. I don't even know how these machines work, let alone how good they are at consuming human hands.

As I watch my hand get eaten alive by this machinery that I was so desperate to fix, I think that maybe I deserve it. Maybe the world finally got fed up with my bullshit. Maybe I've gotten so good at burying the pricks of pain that keep me up at night that the universe wants to make sure that I feel constant pain, forever. Who am I to deny the world its justice?

Maeve wraps her arms around my shoulder so tightly that I can barely breathe. I can feel her, even though I can feel nothing else. I can feel the heat of her skin, and I can feel her breath on the back of my neck. She lets go when she's finally wrestled me free of the machine, stumbling backward and pulling us both onto the ground. We sit there, huffing and puffing and looking at everything except at one another.

In an instant, time returns to its normal speed. And it hurts. In these seconds, I feel everything. Every nerve in my right arm is on fire. The whole thing throbs unforgivingly, and I can feel every heartbeat, every pump of blood, in each dull burst that erupts down my limb.

I don't want to look at it, because it hurts so badly. I try to choke down the scream that's erupting from my mouth, but I can't help it. The sound is feral. The pain overwhelms my brain, stifling any thoughts, any rational function. If my hand feels this bad, I cannot imagine what it might look like. And because looking simply isn't feasible, I turn to Maeve. I allow her to look for me. I can't meet her gaze, because it's latched on to my throbbing, bleeding hand. She refuses to turn away, as if my arm would fall off completely if she even dared to.

I can feel drops of something warm and sticky land on my feet, staining my sandals. I can't help but glance toward them, watching the red cascade over my ankle and melt into my skin.

Maeve finally pulls her gaze away from my hand. She looks scared. Really scared. Her skin is drained of color. She's biting her bottom lip so hard that I'm afraid *she* might start bleeding. I think I'm bleeding enough for the both of us.

All I can think to say is "Holy shit!" which isn't at all eloquent. I compose myself. "You know I've never broken a bone before?" I manage. My voice is quivering and weak. "Never even been to the hospital." I can barely speak. I can barely breathe.

"You're delirious," Maeve says before grabbing my left shoulder. It hurts. My whole body is on fire. Dying over and over again a million times.

I can barely hear Maeve when she says, "Liz, I need to get you inside so we can try to fix this, okay?"

I can barely think, let alone force my feet to move. With Maeve pulling me gently, I manage to hobble inside as my hand sends drips of blood spiraling toward the ground. As we limp toward the store, Maeve continues to speak, her soft voice buzzing in my ear.

"You busted yourself up pretty good, didn't you?" she mutters. "Genius idea of yours, putting your hand inside machinery. That's always a recipe for success. *Oh no! The power went out! Let me stick my hand inside the fuse box!*" I bite my tongue instead of telling her that I didn't even think that I was doing anything dangerous. She'd probably make some witty comment about my glaring lack of street smarts.

There's a small sliver of worry lurking within her voice. The feeling catches me so off guard that the only thing I can manage to say is, "I'm dripping on the floor. It's going to stain."

"You know, Liz, there are more important things than the floor. There are things that are more important than generators and broken windowpanes and rusty hinges. Like . . . I don't know . . . staying alive?" It's not a question; it's a declaration. "I heard of a place down south, in North Carolina, where the government—"

"Is there anything left of the government?" I interject, the words getting trapped between my gritted teeth.

"It's supposed to be better there. Food and shelter, military grade, all of it. Real safety."

She sits me down on the stool behind the front counter, the metal seat searing the backs of my thighs. I look up at her, woozy with pain. She doesn't understand that the two things aren't mutually exclusive. Generators and staying alive. Windowpanes and survival. They work together. She doesn't understand that safety isn't simply the government and food and shelter. It's so much more than that.

"I don't know . . . if there *is* any place safe," I manage to choke out. "This is the—" I swallow down another yelp of pain. "Best shot I've got. This is—home."

Either Maeve didn't hear me, or she's making a point to ignore my recent declaration. "Do you have a first aid kit?" A sloppy change of topic, but it works.

I nod. I suddenly have a throbbing headache. "It should be . . . over there." I point with my good hand. "Right inside that . . ." My voice trails off, but Maeve seems to understand.

As she turns, I take the opportunity to finally look at my arm and assess the damage the generator did to me. When I do, my stomach drops.

A long, jagged gash runs down the top of my forearm, still bleeding. There are grease marks in scattered lines across my skin, mixing with the deep red. My hand is in even worse shape, knuckles shaved down to what looks like bone. Fingers hang limply off, and no matter how hard I try, I can't get them to move. I can't get my hand to move.

I feel something wet well up behind my eyes as my entire world turns on its head.

Maeve returns, holding up a wad of bandages and ripped cloth, clutching them so tightly that her veins bulge around her knuckles. A look of concentration settles onto her face.

"Lift up your arm."

I do, and it wobbles in the air. Maeve gingerly places her

fingers under my forearm, lifting it slightly to glance at the gashes.

"Is it that bad?" I ask, even though I kind of already know the answer. I want to hear her lie to me. I want to believe her.

Maeve shakes her head in response. "It's bleeding a lot, but I'm going to try wrapping it. Applying some pressure. I'll wash it out first, but hopefully it doesn't need stitches, because we do *not* have the equipment to deal with that right now."

"Stitches?" I manage. I rack my brain to see if I know of any doctors who are still alive. Have any doctors come to the bookstore? Please, dear god, say they have.

"I guess we could cauterize it if it gets too bad. We don't want it to get infected, because your little first aid kit *definitely* doesn't have the antibiotics to deal with that. Also, *why* was there so much hand lotion in there?" She's not talking to me anymore. She's speaking to distract herself from the present. I understand the feeling.

Maeve throws an old decorative tea towel at me, emblazoned with the phrase *I support my local bookstore!* The tag is still on it. $15.99.

"Put pressure on the cut. I need to find some water to clean this thing out." She doesn't even give me the chance to respond before walking out the back door. She's halfway up the stairs when I hear her shout, "Don't bleed out while I'm gone."

I don't say anything, my mouth suddenly too dry to speak. I just press the godforsaken tea towel as tightly as possible down on my arm, no matter how much it hurts. I watch as my blood slowly seeps through the fabric, obscuring the letters one by one.

I SUPPORT MY LOCAL BOOKSTORE!

I SUP   T MY LOC   BOO

T MY LO

Y

Maeve walks back inside with a metal canteen. The letters on the towel are gone now, maroon overlapping with maroon.

I motion toward the blood-soaked cloth. "I need another towel."

"Here. Just give me the cloth, and I'll wash your cut out and bandage you up. Knuckles too."

I smile weakly and she kneels, carefully pouring what little water she has left over my skin. And it burns. It burns so badly that the feeling floods my brain. My vision clouds, and I start seeing little spots everywhere.

"Where's the water from?" I manage to ask.

"It's my personal supply. The last of it."

I bite my tongue until I'm completely certain that I'm going to bite it off. I bite it so hard that I can feel the blood rising to my head, my vision going from clear to red to black.

CHAPTER ELEVEN

When I open my eyes, Maeve is sitting on the counter, swinging her legs back and forth. Everything still hurts, the pain piercing the back of my brain. It creeps behind my temples, radiating from my fingertips up my nervous system. I'm on fire.

"Welcome back to the land of the living," she mutters, tucking a piece of hair behind her ear.

The comment strikes me as odd because I wasn't aware that there was another option, and so I ask, "Am I going to die?" I look down at the gaping slit in my arm, running like a ribbon across my skin and up my hand, like the crevasse in the middle of a geode. The edges of the wound are ragged like that, too, bits of stray flesh tapering off in triangles around the congealed crimson. Beneath it, in the deeper sections, there are patches of pale pink, small hints of the muscle and bone that lie beneath. I look at my skinless hand and admire the tendons stretching from my knuckles to my wrist. It's like I'm a marionette. At this moment, death seems like an appropriate question.

Maeve pauses, her chest freezing midbreath. I was hoping she'd laugh. I was hoping she'd say *of course not* and call me a fool, but she doesn't. Maeve shakes her head. "I don't know, Liz. How would I know?" She speaks rapidly, each syllable bumping into the next as they make their way out of her mouth. "I don't know."

She finally looks me in my eyes, but her glance isn't honest. She doesn't seem to believe what she's saying.

"You seem like you'd know that sort of thing," I say. "You were talking about cauterizing and stuff. It seemed legitimate." *You apparently know everything. Why don't you know this?* I wish I sounded more put together, but my brain is rattling inside my skull. I feel like I'm falling apart completely, into tiny pieces scattered across the floor.

"My parents weren't surgeons," Maeve mutters. "My mom was an entertainment lawyer and far too concerned with work to have time for anything else. As for my medical knowledge . . . It all comes from medical shows and teen dramas."

"*The 100*?" I ask, a small smile creeping onto my face. A real one.

Maeve smiles too. "God, that show was practically my entire life my sophomore year."

I can't help but laugh, forgetting my pain.

"I don't know everything, Liz," she mutters, staring off at something that doesn't exist. "Some things I do, but for others, for most things, I just pretend that I do. And somewhere along the way I tend to figure them out." Maeve looks back down at my arm, inspecting it. "Can you wiggle your fingers for me?"

I know I can't, so I change the subject. "Is this something you know, or something you're pretending to know?"

"Liz, just wiggle your fingers."

"I can't." The words sink through the air between us.

"That's not good."

Her voice cuts straight through me, tearing through my lungs and into the empty space in my chest. I hate the look on her face, the way her eyes are so empty. "Okay. What does it mean?"

"Congratulations, Elizabeth Swann. You can finally cross breaking a bone off your bucket list. That and a whole lot more."

I grimace, trying to warp the expression into something resembling a smile. "I always was an overachiever."

Maeve grabs an old ruler and begins attaching it to my arm, weaving it through the bandages.

"What are you doing?" I ask.

"Making a splint," she mutters. "I learned about it in health class in middle school."

"Okay." I don't know what else I can say to her. I'm not sure that she's even listening to me as she works, looking at everything but seeing absolutely nothing.

Maeve pauses and looks me straight in the eyes. "We've survived so much, Liz," she says. "Some generator isn't going to be the thing that takes you out. Not on my watch."

• • •

That night, Maeve lets me sit in the armchair. She decided to cauterize everything right before dinner, which is a fancy, made-up word for melting my skin with a burning hot artisanal knife. Then she made me apology soup to get me to forgive her for the pain she inflicted. I can still taste blood in my mouth. I can still smell the burning flesh, the scent hiding somewhere in my sinuses. I thought the whole limb had fallen off. Afterward, when the adrenaline faded and the pain shone through, I couldn't help but wish that it had.

"Is the soup okay?" Maeve manages, looking up at me from her place on the floor. Her features are lit by the moonlight filtering through the window. For once, she looks like she's at peace. I wasn't sure she could ever look like that. So placid. So serene.

I struggle to lift up my spoon with my left hand, haphazardly guiding it toward my mouth. "Is now a bad time to tell you that I'm right-handed?" I attempt to raise my arm out of its sling for emphasis, but it hurts too much, so I give up.

"Are you trying to tell me that you need help eating your soup?"

I grimace, trying to push that image out of my head. "Absolutely not. I'd rather die of starvation than do *that.*"

If Maeve is annoyed, she doesn't show it. She shakes her head and looks back down into her bowl.

When I clear my throat, she looks back up at me, eyebrows raised as if she thinks I've changed my mind about the soup. No way in hell.

"Thank you for today," I whisper, biting down on my lip. "I think I would have bled out without you. Or have been pulled inside a generator and sliced into teeny, tiny generator-shaped pieces."

"Don't mention it," Maeve says, blushing.

"No, I mean it." My voice is firm, unwavering. "Thank you, Maeve."

Maeve swallows another spoonful of her dinner. "We can check on the water tomorrow. There should be enough liquid in the soup to keep us going until then. For real this time. No generators involved."

"Okay." Something strange blossoms deep inside me.

Maeve smiles in response.

CHAPTER TWELVE

MARCH 21: BEFORE THE FIRST STORM

I've been sucker punched by three college rejections in a row. Maybe that's my fault. Maybe I should have sent in one early decision application, crossed my fingers for an acceptance, and then never sent another one ever again. But I knew that if I couldn't say no once I got in, then I'd spend the rest of my life wondering what would have happened if I had made a different choice.

Still, whatever feelings I might have had from being at the wrong school can't possibly be worse than what I feel right now, as I'm about to check the status of my last application.

When my parents were applying to college, they got their acceptance letters in envelopes. Thick ones meant good news, and thin ones meant bad news. You could hold the package up to the light and try to make out the letter that lurked inside.

Unfortunately, I cannot hold my computer up to the light. And so, I must click on a garishly red button in my admissions portal that reads SEE THE UPDATE TO YOUR APPLICATION. My entire life, I've been told that I shouldn't push giant red buttons, but now I have to.

My parents aren't with me right now. Neither is Thea. They're downstairs in the living room. Dad wanted to be with me, peering over my shoulders like those parents in the cheesy YouTube videos. The ones where everyone's crying and cheering and so happy for their child. I can't help but wonder what the unposted videos look like, where the kid never got in.

My mouse hesitates over the button, as if by waiting I can somehow alter my fate, but I know that I can't. And it's not like this is my top school or anything, except maybe at this point it is. It would just be nice to be wanted by someone. Either way, the decision has been set in stone as of six p.m. eastern standard time. It's six-fifteen. I click the button.

My friend told me once that confetti rains down if you get into a school, and I laughed and called her a liar. But she didn't lie. I know that now, as I watch blue-and-white confetti stream down my computer screen. I watch it settle and then disappear completely, and then I reload the page. The confetti falls again.

I don't have to read the letter to know what it says. It would be sadistic if you got confetti for a rejection. Maybe I wouldn't even want to go to that sort of school anyway.

After a few minutes, the confetti settles once again, and I feel nothing at all. I thought it would feel a bit better than this. Maybe my heart would soar to the moon and back. Maybe I would start crying and jumping up and down and screaming like the people on YouTube. Maybe I would feel a little bit more whole than I did before. But I just feel empty. Empty and numb. This is not the first time that YouTube has lied to me.

Still, I plaster a smile onto my face and open my bedroom door. I'm ready to put on a show and scream "I got in!" and pump my fists like I'm a character from *High School Musical.* But no one is here. I had hoped that my parents might be waiting for me, hesitating outside my room to hear the news, but I'm alone. No one is in the hallway or at the bottom of the stairs.

I make my way down the stairs and walk past the now-empty living room, past two half-empty cocktail glasses on the coffee table. It isn't until I start walking toward the kitchen that I hear their voices.

They're on the porch, standing six feet apart like they've each got something contagious. Their faces are red, Mom's a deeper shade than Dad's. I can hear their voices, slightly muffled through the glass windows.

"This isn't a conversation that we should be having right now," Mom yells.

"Then when would we have it, Ivy? Do you want to wait until it's comfortable for you?"

I walk toward the fridge, my fuzzy socks padding across the wood floor.

"That's not my point. It's safe here. It has always been safe here! We're in the suburbs, for god's sake."

"You really think anywhere will be safe?" Dad asks.

I swing open the fridge door and grab a Coke from the top shelf. The can is slicked with perspiration. I set it down on the kitchen counter.

"You're starting to sound like those wackos on TV, David. You realize that, right? You're being as irrational as they are!"

"Maybe they're right." A pause. "Be sensible. My sister has a place in Alaska. She has room for us there. Things are more stable there. Cooler. Safer."

"I'm not moving my family to *Alaska*. I'm not some insane doomsday prepper."

"It's less crowded up there. We can live off the land. Become self-sufficient."

Mom scoffs, her blond hair swinging wildly. "Do you hear yourself? Do you hear how you sound right now? You don't know how to live off the land, David. You can't even microwave frozen lasagna without burning it."

"You saw what happened in Texas with that hurricane. It was a massacre. They started *killing* each other over food. Over water. Over gasoline. Hundreds dead. I don't want that for my family."

The Coke doesn't have the effect I hoped it would on the empty feeling inside me, so I pull out my phone. I open my text messages and search for the right conversation.

"They have guns in Texas. People don't have guns in New Jersey. It's not like that here."

"People do dangerous things to survive. If there's someone threatening my family, that's an easy decision." Dad bites his lip. "Maybe we should have a gun. For protection. Keep the girls safe."

"We *are* safe. We had a storm cellar put in. I let you buy that *ridiculous* machine that cost half of our savings."

I see Eva's contact information pop up on the screen and click on it.

"If we have to lock ourselves down there, I'd prefer that we have oxygen."

Mom's voice is suddenly strained. "That's my point, David. That's where the difference lies. I'd prefer that we never have to go down there at all."

"That's why we need to go to Alaska! This place is a ticking time bomb. All it takes is one spark and the whole place is up in flames."

I type a quick note to Eva, my fingers trembling slightly as I do, although I don't know why. *I got in!* I add a little confetti emoji for emphasis. She told me at work that she had to be the first person to know, after my parents, of course. But, as they're otherwise occupied, she can be number one.

Three gray dots appear on the screen, and then a message.

OMG CONGRATS!!!! I knew you could do it <3

"I can't deal with you right now," Mom says. "I'm going on a walk. We can get takeout tonight."

"Fine."

As Mom slams the back door and walks past me, she doesn't say a word. She doesn't ask me anything at all.

CHAPTER THIRTEEN

Tonight, I think about Maeve, in an attempt to dull the piercing pain that radiates through my arm. I think about her cart and her knife and about New York City. I think about how even though she broke into my home, I feel a bit safer when she's around.

I sit on the edge of my mattress, the glow of the moon casting a pale white light on everything around me. I kicked all my blankets off in an attempt to get even a wink of sleep, and they sit, crumpled into a ball, in the corner. At this point, I've given up on the idea of sleep entirely. It's not going to come. Not with this heat, not with this agony, not with the number of things flooding my too-small brain.

I look at Maeve, who is sleeping on the floor a few feet away. I wonder about who she was, before The Storm. Where did she come from? When she first arrived at the bookstore, she said she had nowhere else to go. Almost like she was running from something. Hiding something. I'm not sure what.

As I ponder, I stare out the window at the night sky. A million stars blink in the dark. I once heard that they only do that on

Earth. Like, if you were up in space, up and away and out of the atmosphere, the stars would just be there. Dots of light that are so immovable and don't blink or twinkle at all. They do that only for us, as if we wouldn't be able to handle the full magnitude of them if they didn't.

I've always wanted to go to space, live in some sort of floating city. Do something cool with my life, something worthwhile. You can't have any dead weight hanging around in space. I used to tell my friends that. I'd say, *No offense, but if they offered me a place in the first civilian space community, I would take it and leave you all behind.* I think I romanticized the idea of new beginnings. I think I romanticized the idea of being alone.

"Stop!"

I'm jolted away from my thoughts by a shriek. It's Maeve, over in her corner, thrashing under her covers. She twists from one side to the other, her brows knit together.

"Please, don't."

Her voice is breathless, strained. I watch an entire universe flash across her face as she convulses in her sleep, caught in a nightmare, desperate to escape.

"It's not my fault! Please!" She's whimpering now, terrified. Whatever she's dreaming about must be terrible.

As I watch her, I don't know what to do. The Maeve I know, or at least think I know, is tough, with an ironclad exterior. This . . . this looks like fear. Pain. This is violent. This is torture. I don't know if she wants me to see her like this. But if I wake her up, I have to tell her why. And who knows how she'll react? Will she play it off? Lash out? Leave? I think of the knife on the kitchen table and remember that I don't know what Maeve is capable of.

Luckily, I don't have to make a decision. Maeve jolts awake, eyes wide, staring straight at me. Her body is drenched in sweat. As soon as she realizes what she's doing, she tries to play it off. She fakes a yawn, rubs her eyes gently. She's just about to roll over to face the wall when I stop her with a hand on her shoulder.

"Are you okay?" The question slips out of my mouth before I can stop it.

"Hm?" She raises her eyebrows like she doesn't have the foggiest idea what I could possibly be talking about. She's a horrible actress.

Maybe I shouldn't have said anything at all. "Never mind."

A second of silence passes before Maeve shimmies out from under her blanket and leans back against the wall, drawing her knees to her chest. "I'm fine."

We both know that's not true, and even if I didn't know, I'd be able to tell from the way she refuses to look at me. "Are you sure?"

Now it's Maeve's turn to laugh, her head falling back so that she's staring at the makeshift tarp ceiling. "It's not important, right? In the grand scheme of things. Like, all the shit that we've been through, it doesn't matter in the long run."

"What do you mean?"

"Look around us. Everything is crap, and it always will be. What we do is pretty insignificant, when you think about it. We have to do what we can to survive. The rest will be lost over time."

I can't help but think of the stars. About how small they look, about how big they really are. "I don't know. Like, what about space? The stars and stuff." Maeve raises her eyebrow as if to say, *You absolutely have no idea what you're talking about.* I clear my throat and try to ignore her. "They're so small, right, but you could actually fit whole worlds inside them. Looking at stars makes us feel so insignificant. But we're not. Even though we might look so tiny."

Maeve laughs a small, sharp laugh. "I have no idea what you're saying."

"If you look at the *grand scheme of things,* sure, it doesn't seem like right now matters that much. That right now matters at all. But that doesn't mean you don't feel it. That doesn't mean it doesn't hurt. It doesn't mean that it doesn't suck."

"Like stars," Maeve says, disbelieving.

"The metaphor sounded better in my head." I pause. Then a ridiculous question makes its way out of my mouth. "Do you ever wish you could go to space?"

Maeve laughs, before realizing that I'm serious. "What? No. Why?"

"I don't know. The peacefulness of it all. The unknown."

"I think I've had enough peace and unknown to last me a lifetime," Maeve retorts. "Maybe even two lifetimes."

"Fine, then what about some sort of space vacation?" I ask, the corners of my mouth tugging upward.

"A space vacation? And risk getting burned up in the atmosphere for ten thousand dollars? No thank you."

"Okay, then what about if some eccentric billionaire paid for it?"

"Boo, billionaires," Maeve says, clicking her tongue. "Where are they now, to get us out of this mess?" I can tell she's slightly delirious from lack of sleep, but I think I am too.

"Oh! Neil DeGrasse Tyson! The space guy!" She perks up

at this, and I have to admit I'm thrilled to have found in her a willing and somewhat eager conversation partner. "What if *he* invited you on an all-expenses-paid space vacation? Like *Cosmos* but on steroids!"

"Fine!" Maeve mutters, raising her hands in defeat. "You win; I'll go on the space vacation!"

A couple of seconds pass as I soak up my victory. I decide to keep going, pushing my luck to put off going to sleep and the nightmares that await Maeve when she does.

"Who'd you take, if you could take three celebrities with you?"

She groans and rolls her eyes at me. "Not this, Liz. It's too late to be bombarded with icebreakers."

"It's either that, or you go back to sleep."

The smile melts off Maeve's face as she looks down at her lap. I look down at my *Peanuts* pajama bottoms.

"I shouldn't have gone on my own. I shouldn't have left home after The Storm, with no one else who I knew. Who knew me," Maeve says. "I thought it would be easier to start fresh, you know? Explore what else was out there for me."

"I understand."

That's a lie. A white lie, but still a lie. To me, the pain of a fresh start was unimaginable. It was like having your entire support system ripped away from you. Losing the people you love is hard enough, but leaving everything behind wasn't something I was willing to try. The bookstore is all I have left.

Eva was different. Eva welcomed the unknown and that fresh start, and that was why she left. She couldn't bear the feeling of half-baked memories that surrounded her for so long. She couldn't bear the image of the ghosts that were never quite gone. The ghosts that stayed in these streets, and in these buildings, and the smells that came when each season rolled around. For her, all she longed for was something completely and utterly foreign.

I was not foreign enough for her. I was old. I held memories. I hold memories. Memories I can't give up. Memories of better times and opportunities that she no longer had. I couldn't replace the home she had lost, even though she had become home to me. Feelings aren't reciprocal like that.

Maeve seems to take my lie for the truth and nods. "It wasn't easier, though, you know?"

"I don't think things *can* be easy anymore. I'm not sure that word even exists at this point." I wish I could capture Maeve's story before she leaves. "I wish I had my notebook." At first, I don't even realize that I've said it out loud.

"What?"

"It's downstairs," I explain, looking at Maeve. To my surprise, I have her full attention. "A few months after The Storm, I got into the habit of taking down people's stories. How they made it this far, you know?" She nods slowly, not breaking eye contact. "It started as a bit of a vanity thing, I think. I didn't want to be forgotten. No one who came through wanted their lives to be in vain. But you don't have to give your story until you're ready. Until you have a version of it that you want to be remembered."

"Go get it."

"Really?"

Maeve hesitates for a moment before nodding. "Yeah, I'm sure."

• • •

I'm back in what feels like seconds, chest still heaving from bounding up the rickety steps as I tried to ignore the shocks of pain jolting up my arm. The leather-bound cover of my notebook sticks to my sweaty palm as I lay it in front of me.

"It's a work in progress, really. I've barely got half of it filled," I explain as Maeve reaches forward and flips through the pages, careful not to tear the thin paper. "But it's a good project to have. Something to keep me busy during the slower days."

Maeve doesn't say anything in response as she leans in close, reading my scrawling handwriting on the page in front of her.

Caroline Ransom

34 years old

Westcliffe, Colorado

I was working when it happened. Yellowstone, actually. I didn't even know how widespread it was for a couple of days, because I was off camping. No cell service.

People always start from different points in their lives. Some from the very beginning. Some from their high school graduation. Some from their wedding. But more often than not, it starts from the day everything ended. Only an ending can make way for a new beginning.

> When The Storm came I had been staying in a tent, riding a mountain bike every day, and taking pictures of the wildlife. My tent didn't last long in the acid, and so I stayed in a cave, night after night after night, doing whatever I could to stay alive. Doing everything I could to avoid the water and the burning feeling it left behind. Hunting, foraging. I even carved myself some weapons.

"Badass," Maeve mutters as she finishes the entry and selects a new one.

"What, more interesting than some dusty old bookstore?"

"Hardly." Maeve looks up at me, her eyes meeting mine. "It's just, imagine having the chance to actually live before everything went to shit? Imagine doing something important."

I laugh, the sound scraping up my throat, slightly shocking in the stillness of the night. "High school wasn't incredibly important?"

"Oh yeah, my barely passing grades were doing a whole lot for the world. . . ." She trails off, now focusing on the new page in front of her, her head flicking back and forth slightly as she scans the page.

Evelyn Sargent

20 years old

Cornwall, Connecticut

I got married two days after my eighteenth birthday, which my mom probably wasn't the biggest fan of, but she kept her mouth shut. And he was a tattoo apprentice, while I went to a local college. I was happy. 'Cause each day I'd go back to my apartment instead of a dorm room, and Mason would be cooking something, making the whole place smell like it burst out of Bon Appétit. I had my favorites, of course. . . .

It takes too long for Maeve to remove her gaze from the entry, as if she's savoring it. I understand why. We never made it that far. We never made it to the "normal" that we were promised.

She inches back from the journal, slowly retreating toward her bed, and I shut the cover, sliding it closer to me. "It's really just a project," I murmur. "It's not that important. It's not something earth shattering."

"It matters, Liz," Maeve whispers, so quietly that I almost can't hear it. "If you think it matters, it matters. It matters to the people who have given you their stories so far, and it matters to all the people who will read them in the future." She pauses.

I laugh at this and the melodrama of it all. I can't help it, but Maeve isn't finished.

"I don't think I can give you my story yet," she says, searching for approval somewhere inside my eyes. "I don't think my story is over, at least not how I want it to be. If this is the end of my story, then it's a bad one."

"Why?"

"I don't know," Maeve answers, gesturing loosely into the air. "I just . . . I'm not sure I'm ready. Retelling it makes it real. Do you understand?"

"Well, if it makes you feel any better, I haven't even written my story yet, either," I offer. "Kind of hypocritical, you know? To have so many but not have mine." Still, I pause. "But I wouldn't mind having yours, when you're willing."

"How about I tell you the beginning. Just a taste of what's to come?"

"Okay."

"Okay." Maeve smiles at me, her teeth still sparkling in the dark. "Where do I start?"

"Wherever you want." I've learned not to set any sort of structure for these things. It's better to wait. It's better to let them define themselves. The stories are more honest that way. Raw.

"I'm originally from the city." She's said this before, but I'll let her say it again if it gets her to tell me something true.

"New York?"

I've learned to ask that question whenever anyone calls a place *the city.* To me, it means New York City. To others, it means Chicago, or Miami, or Atlanta. Asking now saves me a lot of confusion in the future.

"I grew up there. We lived in an apartment down in Greenwich Village, over on West Ninth. Bottom floor, and we had this mudroom that my mom decided to paint mint green one day, just for the hell of it. But then we all hated that, so it ended up hot pink. Nothing in our house was ever a normal color, like gray or something. My mom said it was too boring. The worst insult you could ever give her was that something wasn't interesting enough. It was, like, a criminal offense."

She pauses, getting this far-off look in her eyes. Her mom sounds so different from mine. So spontaneous and full of life. But I don't say anything, trying to commit the story to memory so that I can write it down when I'm able. I just let her continue when she's ready.

"This one time, in middle school, we had this ugly-sweater day for school spirit. I went and told my mom, who swore she'd figure something out, like she always did. Every Halloween costume, every birthday party, my parents pulled out all the stops. Both of them. So when the sweater arrives, my mom brings it to my room and lays it out for me, and my stomach just *drops.* 'Cause the whole ugly-sweater thing? They're cute in an ugly sort of way. Like, made by your grandma with love. But this was ugly, with tinsel and ornaments and a stocking glued right onto the front. And it lit up and sang songs when you pressed a button.

"My mother loved it. My dad too. And I smiled and thanked my mom, but when I got to school, I was too embarrassed to take my coat off. Just walked around with a winter jacket zipped up to my neck all day. It was too much for me. I guess I just wasn't like them in that regard. Out loud and proud, or whatever. But as I got older, I tried to learn to be a bit bolder." Maeve bites her lip. Does she think she was successful, or is she mourning the person she could have been if she'd had just a little more time? "Of course, when all hell broke loose, I couldn't just stay there."

"Oh?"

"Yeah," Maeve says. "Too many people, just crawling all over the place. All of them had their own ideas about what to do. All of them had their own feelings to process, and most of them didn't want to do that processing alone. I needed peace. I had to get away from them. It was suffocating." She pauses, smiling a small, distant smile. "I was better off on my own than with all of them. The weight of it all, all their problems and fears and anger and danger, it was exhausting.

"So I left the city. I left it all behind. I couldn't stay there. I'd die. Either someone would kill me, or I'd die from hunger, or I'd go completely insane."

"So what, you walked?"

Maeve scoffs. "New Yorkers are good walkers." I roll my eyes, and she pretends not to notice. "I don't think I've stayed anywhere for longer than a week or two. It's like I won't allow myself to get too comfortable. If I never stay anywhere for too long, I never have anything to lose."

"Hence the tent?"

"Hence the tent," Maeve says, her eyes suddenly distant. "I guess the rest is history."

I have to admit that I'm disappointed by the vagueness of what happened to her after The Storm. And I'm not sure I believe her story, but she also has no reason to tell me the truth. Most people can go on for a couple of notebook pages at least, but Maeve seems far off when she reaches the end. Some people go on and on about what happened after. The fear, the destruction, the new beginnings that they found, but Maeve falls silent. I understand. To tell the story is to admit that it's true. To tell your story is to come to terms with what it actually means. What it did to you. How you changed.

I have secrets too. It's only fair that I allow her to have hers in return.

The moon hangs high in the sky outside my window, too-dead trees casting shadows onto the sidewalk. I hear Maeve move underneath her sheets. When I look at her, she's tucked herself back in, her blanket pulled up to her chin.

I decide to gather mine from the corner, making a poor attempt at spreading it over my body with one hand. It's too hot on my skin, but I leave it on anyway. It feels nice. It feels safe.

"Good night," Maeve whispers from across the room.

"Are you sure you don't want the mattress?" I ask. She doesn't answer, and so I roll over, facing away from the window, looking instead at my shadow on the bedroom floor. "Good night."

CHAPTER FOURTEEN

Maeve wakes me up at the crack of dawn, shaking my good shoulder gently enough to avoid causing shock waves of pain. It's days like these when I realize I used to take Tylenol for granted. When I open my eyes, she's standing over me. Her hair is pulled back into a single braid, showing off the shaved half of her head. She looks like a punk-rock Katniss Everdeen. My eyes dart back down toward her jacket, a *Fiona Apple Makes Me Feel Things!* patch colorful against a wall of black.

I sit up before she has a chance to say anything. "So you listen to Fiona Apple?" I ask.

Maeve sighs. "Liz—" She pauses. "What exactly is your last name?"

"That seems like private information," I grumble, still groggy from my rude awakening. Still, I offer it to her. "Flannery."

Maeve clears her throat and tries again. "Liz Flannery, are you judging me?"

"Maybe," I mutter. "I need to get it out of my system. I haven't been able to judge someone in a while."

She shakes her head in response. "You could have judged one of your precious customers, but you didn't. You saved this animosity for me."

There's a pause as we stare at each other, wondering what could have filled us with such sarcastically argumentative energy this early in the morning.

Maeve exhales as she eases down to a sitting position beside the mattress. I wiggle out from under the comforter to sit beside her as she turns to face me. "Yes, I do listen to Fiona Apple. What about it?"

"It just doesn't seem like something you'd be into. You give off more of a punk-rocker vibe." I gesture wildly to her combat boots and shaved head.

"And you don't seem like someone who'd be into sticking her hand into generators, but here we are."

"Hey!" I say, cheeks burning red. "That was a low blow."

I slowly make my way into the kitchen, pausing at the door. My arm still throbs and aches, but I've already started to get used to the feeling. The ache I now carry with me. A pain that never ebbs. I'm fishing through the cabinets with my good arm, looking for something to eat, when I notice an object out of the corner of my eye.

A backpack sits, fully packed, next to the front door, various supplies from Maeve's cart piled on top of it. She's ready to go.

Maeve is leaving me.

I don't know what to say. I don't know what to do to avoid the acidic bile rising in my throat. I'm not even sure why I'm shocked. I wanted her to leave, right? This was only temporary, anyway. I should be happy that I won't have to see her smug face every morning, won't have to deal with her sarcastic comments. But I'm not. All I can think about is how I don't want her to leave. How I don't know how to get Maeve to stay.

It's like Eva all over again. I didn't realize Eva was leaving until I saw the pile she'd made of her belongings in the corner of the apartment. It was well hidden, tucked behind the desk so that it wasn't visible from where I slept. I had no reason to go over there. No reason to be looking for it, and if I *did* find it, I guess she assumed I'd think it was junk. But I didn't. I noticed the way she had sorted her clothes, and the way she'd stacked the best copies of her favorite books. That wasn't junk.

I waited for Eva to tell me. I waited and tried to convince myself that I was making things up. Of course she wouldn't leave. She certainly wouldn't try to hide it from me. But the pile kept growing. It kept growing until one day it disappeared. Two months after The Storm, she was gone.

Eva told me as she was leaving. She wasn't going to, but I caught her sneaking out. She said she couldn't stand the monotony any longer. She couldn't sit around waiting for her life to change in some dusty old bookstore. She wanted adventure. She wanted freedom and exploration. And those were all things she couldn't find with me, I guess.

It didn't feel like a breakup; it felt like she'd died. It felt like an apocalypse all over again. Eva had appeared when I needed a family most, and I wasn't enough for her. As I watched her disappear down the road, I cried, and then I went back to work.

This bag sitting by the door is déjà vu. It matches perfectly. Early in the morning, not telling me until she has to. Time is so cyclical in that way, always looping in on itself until the past is indistinguishable from the present.

A part of me hates that I'm upset. Hates that Maeve's leaving feels like I'm losing someone who is important. In the grand scheme of things, a few days is nothing, but right now, Maeve is the closest thing I've had to a friend in a long time.

"When I said you could leave, it didn't mean that I *wanted* you to leave." The statement leaves a chalky taste in my mouth.

"What?" Maeve says, moving forward and maneuvering around the mattress on the floor.

"I just don't want you to think that I don't want you here." I flounder for a second, unable to understand my own emotions. "I would have probably bled out without you. Or maybe died of an infection. You saved my life."

Maeve rolls her eyes as she continues to move toward me. "Liz, I appreciate the flattery, but I'm not going anywhere."

"But the—" My hand gestures limply toward the packed bag by the door.

"I'm going out to get some food and supplies so we don't starve, if that's okay with you. I checked on the water this morning, and it seems like it's a problem with the piping, which is fixable. But it'll be a while before it's gushing, you know? I figured that it might be better to err on the side of caution and have . . ." Maeve continues talking about water and spigots, but I'm not listening.

All the air rushes from my lungs, and I feel like a puddle. I'm overcome with a strange feeling. Relief. If our future alien overlords were here, they'd say ᑯШΦ ⍋ ᑯ⍀⫯⌿ ⫽⍋[|], which roughly translates to *Get a grip, for goodness' sake.*

All I can manage to say is: "I thought you were leaving."

"You can't get rid of me that easily." Before I can react she reaches out and squeezes my hand, the good one. Her fingers hesitate slightly on mine, and I feel a momentary jolt of electricity before she quickly pulls away. As she pushes past me in the doorframe to pick up her bag, she turns. "You're coming with me, right? I don't think it's a good idea to leave you here alone with your arm like that."

I laugh, the sound bursting out of me. "Absolutely not."

"What do you mean, absolutely not?"

"I haven't left the bookstore in a year. Not since the—"

"What?" Maeve interrupts. "Like you've never left the building? For anything at all? Ever?"

I didn't think the idea was so ridiculous. In all my favorite postapocalyptic TV shows, the main characters built a safe home base and stayed put. There's a sense of comfort and protection that comes with having a place you can call home. "Why should I?" I reply. "It's safer here, and god forbid anything happens to this place while I'm gone."

Maeve pauses, as if she's judging the validity of my response. She squints her eyes. "But what about getting supplies? What about finding food to eat?"

"People will trade me the things I need for their books, and for sending letters. When I arrived, there were some supplies already here. Brought some stuff from home as well. Built up a bit of a stockpile. The rest has sort of just figured itself out."

"But what if it doesn't?"

"But it does?"

Maeve groans. "Would you leave for one day?" she asks.

I haven't even thought about leaving in god knows how long. This place is home. It is the only place left on Earth where, when I'm inside, I feel safe. This relic of a building that holds hundreds of stories, both fictional and real. It's important. More important than I am, that's for sure.

"But what if something happens?"

"Nothing's going to happen in one day," she says, rolling her eyes.

Even though every part of me is telling me not to, and that this is a stupid decision, I can't help myself. I want to see the world the way Maeve sees it. I want to understand her world and escape from mine, just for a day. Is that so bad?

"Okay, fine. I'll come."

• • •

I walk back through the bookstore, doing a last-minute check to make sure that I haven't left any windows unlatched, primed for an easy break-in. Someone came in earlier to trade a spool of twine and a bag of raisins for a copy of *The Tell-Tale Heart and Other Stories.* I shove them underneath the counter as I pass.

Maeve gave me a backpack to carry, stuffing odds and ends into a separate pack for herself. It's made of brown canvas, covered in various buttons from different comic books and bands. One reads *The Unbeatable Squirrel Girl.* Another says *Fetch the Bolt Cutters.* I make the conscious decision not to question her about Fiona Apple again.

I told myself while getting dressed this morning that Maeve is prepared and knows what she's doing. I'm sure that she's made this sort of trip tons of times before. We'll be back in a day and change, and everything here will be fine. I get a customer only once a week or so, and if I flip the Open sign to Closed, they'll understand what's going on. Anything to squash the anxious feelings fluttering around in my chest.

As we make our way toward the front door, I break off a piece of tape from the dispenser resting on the counter. Once the door clicks shut behind us, I turn around and start fumbling with the tape.

"What are you doing?"

I don't say anything as I keep working, positioning my tape along the crack in the door. I use my nail to press it down until it almost blends in with the wood. One-handed taping is much harder than it looks.

When I'm finished, I pivot to face Maeve again. She looks confused.

"The door's lock doesn't work, so I used tape," I explain.

Maeve's brows knit even farther together. "I don't think that's going to hold. Sorry to burst your bubble."

How nice it is to be the one with the upper hand, for once. "If someone uses the door the tape will break, and we'll know."

"Okay, Nancy Drew," she replies. Her lips purse together as she stares at my sliver of tape. "Aren't you supposed to use hair?"

I just shift the backpack on my shoulders. "That's unsanitary."

"Says the girl who bled all over the place days ago?" Maeve scoffs. "*That's* unsanitary."

With that, we start walking.

I'd never noticed before how disastrous the roads are. It's not like the outside of the bookstore is looking much better, but I do my best to keep it clean and free of trash. Eva and I, together, moved most of the smaller debris before she left. The stuff that remains was too heavy for two people to lift.

Covered in rubble, leftover cars, dust, and god knows what

else, the pathways are hard to maneuver through, and I'm curious how Maeve will fare with her cart. At least it's not full anymore, only an empty blue jug sitting inside next to a dilapidated backpack. Just something to help us carry whatever things we find.

As if sensing my thoughts, Maeve makes a show of dragging her cart through the streets, expertly weaving around potholes and cracks. I try, and fail, to suppress a smile.

"So did you just reference Nancy Drew? I thought you didn't read."

Maeve doesn't respond; she just keeps walking, eventually overtaking me so that I'm struggling to keep up with her. I may have long legs, but I've never quite mastered the proper way to use them.

She leads me past the hardware store. The entire facade of the building has crumbled, the once-faded concrete reduced to wreckage. The interior of the top two floors is completely visible as we walk by. On one floor I can see a clawfoot bathtub and part of a bathroom sink. On the floor above, there's peeling red wallpaper and a tattered La-Z-Boy. On the bottom floor, a "summertime fun" display is still sitting in the window, a once-black-and-white whale inflatable now faded to a solid shade of gray. The windows are smashed. The glass crunches under my Converse as we walk past.

This is the farthest from home I've been in a year. The feeling makes my heart flutter, even though it's foolish. I've depended so much on certainty for the past year. Nothing new. No changes. But today that's over, because Maeve decided to wake me up at an ungodly hour and drag me out of the store. I guess it's better than sitting behind the dusty front counter, unable to do anything at all.

Yet that still doesn't take away the stinging feeling I have, deep inside me, as I finally take in all the sights I couldn't see through my dusty front windows. It's all gone. The places I grew up in, spent my afternoons after school, frequented with my parents on weekends, they're gone. The people who inhabited those spaces are gone too. I'm all that's left, and do I really deserve to be? Or perhaps it's my punishment to inherit this destroyed Earth.

I don't know what I expected. It would be ridiculous to expect anything else, right? To emerge from the bookstore and for everything to be just fine? Maybe a part of me was hoping that there'd be someone here, someone else who remembers what this place used to be like, holding on to whatever strands of normalcy that they can in their own little corner of the universe, just like I have in mine. But there's no one here. Just me. Me and Maeve.

It's ironic, now that I think about it, to still be stuck in New Jersey. Even worse to be stuck in the same four blocks of suburban New Jersey. I've become a hermit. A recluse.

Maeve continues to walk, unaware that I am currently crossing my own invisible barrier. We pass a row of identical houses in various states of disarray. Mold crawls up the once-white exterior of a Tudor-style home. I carefully dodge part of a children's play set that lies discarded in the road.

"Have you always moved around like this? Since The Storm?" I ask, although I'm not sure why I'm so curious. I'm not sure if her answer will make me hate myself for never leaving.

Maeve pauses, as if weighing options in her mind. The sound of her cart's squeaky wheels fills the air. Does she tell me the truth, or does she say what makes her feel better? "Yeah,"

Maeve replies slowly. "I never stay in one place for too long. To create some sort of false 'normal' only sets you up for failure in the long run, right? If you get too comfortable, then you become sloppy. You start putting your hand into generators." I stick out my tongue, and Maeve laughs. "I'm joking, of course."

"Of course." My cheeks are red, but for the wrong reason. I'm not upset with what she said; I'm more embarrassed for being so ridiculous. "What about the new Storm, the one that's supposed to be coming?"

"If I'm not with you, you mean? I'll figure it out, though. I always do."

If I'm not with you. She says it as if it's a given, as if the thought of her riding out The Storm with anyone else is ridiculous. I am suddenly aware of every vein in my body.

"But what about staying put?" I ask. "I came back here because it was all I knew that I still had. I spent two weeks at home, with ghosts, eating the remains of the rotted food in the fridge. Everywhere I walked, I had reminders of *them.* But I needed it, I think. I think I needed the reminder that things were once okay, normal, and that things would be that way again someday. I couldn't leave. I couldn't go far, so I came here."

Maeve chews her lip for a moment, running her free hand through her dark hair. "But why here? Didn't it feel stifling? Like you were being haunted or something?"

"Haunted by good memories?" I reply. "Why wouldn't I want that? And when I got here, it was like nothing at all had happened. Sure, the place looked like hell, but it felt familiar. And the books on the shelves were familiar. And the stories within them were familiar. I couldn't let that go. I don't think that feeling is false, right?"

One of the cart's wheels squeaks as it bumps over a twig. "Do you still have that feeling?" Maeve says, her green eyes looking deep into mine. "Now that we're together here."

I nod.

I think long and hard about what *together* means as we walk, quiet once again filling the air between us. I don't think I've had a *together*—the type of together that I took for granted—for a long time. The together of doing my homework at the kitchen table while my mother cooked dinner, listening to Ella Fitzgerald. Those rare summer nights when I'd sit with my friends in the middle of the football field, gossiping and shouting at random passersby. Going to work and being surrounded by people. Not even having to speak to them, but knowing they were there and that you weren't alone.

There is a difference between being alone and feeling lonely. I've said it before, and I'll say it again. But right now, walking with Maeve, I realize that for the first time in a long time, I am neither.

CHAPTER FIFTEEN

We stop at an old Target off Route 46. It takes us a few hours to get there, weaving through abandoned cars with Maeve's cart. The building is in better shape than anything else I've seen. I guess concrete and cinder blocks will do that for a place. As we make our way through the automatic doors, which have been pried open by prior visitors, I turn to Maeve.

"Have you been here before?"

"Once or twice," she admits as our eyes adjust to the darkness. "It's not as good as hunting, but it does the job . . . and hunting isn't always an option." She fishes around in her cart for something as we move forward, enveloped by the darkness that consumes every aisle. I hear a small grunt of satisfaction as Maeve pulls out a camping lantern and clicks it on, casting a green glow over our surroundings.

"It's battery powered," she explains, turning at the end of the aisle and entering the grocery half of the store. "I nabbed some double-As from a bin under the counter."

"Those were mine!" I protest, although I only half mean it. "Someone gave them to me before you even got here."

Maeve laughs, her eyes glinting in the dark. "You snooze, you lose."

We make our way into the canned-food aisle, and Maeve slowly pivots, taking in our surroundings. A few cans lie on the shelves, filled with creamed corn and the least appetizing varieties of soup. Broccoli cheddar, cream of mushroom, and a couple of cartoon-shaped chicken noodles. I nab the latter and pile them into the cart haphazardly before looking back at Maeve.

"How is there even anything left?"

"I don't know," she mutters. "Maybe people grew tired of all this canned stuff after eating it for months on end with no variety—I know I did. It was the monotony. It drove me insane."

"You can't just starve in the name of variety," I say, moving on to a Styrofoam cup of instant noodles. "I have this stuff all the time."

"Not all of us had doting customers who were willing to make those kinds of trades with us. Anyway, it's not like the stuff on this shelf is the best of the best. It's not home cooking." She smiles, lost in some distant memory. "I'd rather grow something or kill something or harvest something than eat this junk every day."

I swallow down the lump rising in my throat as I remember Maeve's bloody knife. "You kill things? And eat them?"

She nods in response. "Do you think I've been grocery shopping?"

I guess that this makes sense. People had occasionally traded salted meat or some dried beans for a book, or a story, or a letter, but I never thought about where it all came from. Is everyone who comes into the bookstore like Maeve? Have they all done what they needed to stay alive? Am I really so different?

Maeve continues moving down the aisle, grabbing a can of black beans in one hand and some pickles in another. "If you could have any meal right now, what would you have?" The question comes out of the blue. Maeve has never struck me as the type to partake in small talk, but I indulge her anyway.

I stare at the cup of instant ramen in front of me and imagine that it's something else, anything else. "A burger," I say. "A burger fresh off the grill with a chocolate shake that's so thick you can barely drink it. A ripe peach and a lemonade filled to the brim with ice, maybe a sprig of mint on top." I pause to think before continuing. "And some sort of potato, and maybe a Caesar salad." A smile creeps onto my face as I imagine that meal, the way it might smell, the people I might share it with if it were only a different time. A different place. A different timeline completely.

Maeve laughs behind me, softer than usual, as she tosses her cans of beans into the cart. "I'd have something made by my mother, of course. Maybe lamb, maybe some steak too. A cold Coke and a whopping slice of chocolate cake. I want so much frosting on it that it outweighs the cake, you know?"

I nod knowingly. "Of course. The frosting is the best part."

"Glad we're on the same page."

Maeve disappears down another aisle. I follow her, suddenly surrounded by outdated kids' toys made from the most blindingly neon plastics in existence. Maeve doesn't seem to notice, so I do the honors, reaching for a bright blue Nerf gun and fumbling with its cardboard packaging. The motion sends a shock of pain up my arm, but I do my best to ignore the feeling.

Maeve pauses at the noise, slowly pivoting. She glances at the foam bullets in my hand as I carefully load the orange clip and slide it into my weapon.

She shakes her head. "What could you possibly be doing with that thing in your hand, Liz Flannery?"

"My parents never let me have these when I was little," I tell her. "My mom was too into pacifism, and my dad was too distracted with work to argue with her."

"So what? Is this your childhood dream coming to fruition?"

"There's no time like the present," I reply.

I carefully aim my weapon at a stack of trading cards sitting on a dust-covered shelf. I'm a terrible shot, and that fact is only confirmed as my foam pellet pings off the aisle's metal siding and drops to the linoleum floor rather unceremoniously.

"You're horrible."

"What? Like you could do any better?" I pause. "No, wait, you're the incomparable Maeve who is so good at everything."

"You're not usually right, but I will say that you're right about this. I'm a whiz at carnival games."

She selects her weapon of choice from the rack on the wall and peels off the plastic, inspecting the revolver-like barrel with a furrowed brow. "They make these things terrifyingly realistic. No wonder my cousins turned out so badly. They had a room filled with these things when they were little."

"You sound like my mother," I say.

"Well, look how you turned out. . . ."

Maeve cocks her weapon and aims it at the trading cards before pulling the trigger. The boxes come tumbling to the ground with a loud thud. Of course, Maeve is better than I am at this as well. What isn't she good at?

She grins at me as she playfully blows on the tip of her weapon. "Bull's-eye," she croons, suddenly adopting a Southern accent.

"You're insufferable," I mutter, aiming my toy at her. "It's a shame it had to end this way."

"Oh, the betrayal!"

Maeve takes off running through the darkness, carrying her lantern with her. My Converse slap against the linoleum as I run, my legs churning, my arm throbbing with each step. She turns a corner, running down the next aisle, and I scramble to change my direction and follow.

I'm stopped only when a stuffed toy bounces off my forehead.

"What the hell?"

Maeve beams at me through the darkness, her Nerf gun held out in front of her. The lantern is on the floor, a stuffed dalmatian in her free hand, ready to be launched in my direction.

"What, you thought I never got caught in a Nerf war with my cousins?" she asks. "Do you surrender?"

Summoning my bravery from deep within, I straighten my back and look defiantly into her eyes before shouting "Never!" Then I stick out my tongue for good measure.

"Big mistake," Maeve says in a low, gravelly voice that sends shivers up my spine. Not wanting to wait around to face her wrath, I sprint down the makeup aisle, pausing at the end only to glance behind and make sure I'm safe. There's no one there. I double over, catching my breath, and try to listen for the sound of Maeve's boots thudding against the linoleum floors. I hear absolutely nothing and let out a sigh of relief, thinking I'm safe.

Wrong.

Out of nowhere, Maeve runs up and collides with me, sending us both tumbling to the ground. I make contact first, my tailbone striking the floor, my good arm underneath me in an attempt to break my fall, my other arm throbbing from the impact. Maeve falls forward, her hands slapping against the linoleum as our chests slam into each other.

She stops herself, her nose mere inches from mine. I can feel her breath on my skin as we stare at each other, unsure of what to do or say.

Maybe I'm all right with that. Maybe it feels nice to be close to someone again like this. Maybe it feels nice to feel Maeve, even if her touch is unintentional.

Eventually, she laughs and rolls to the side, her hair brushing over my skin. We lie there, side by side, in the darkness.

"Did you ever think you would be here?" I ask.

"You mean Nerf battling in an abandoned Target in New Jersey? Scavenging for food with a relative stranger who practically got her arm ripped off a day ago? No," she scoffs. "I can't say that this was included in my life plan."

"Me neither."

Maeve leans in closer, her head resting on my shoulder.

I hear her exhale, air escaping through her teeth. "Still," she says, "I'm glad I'm not alone."

"Me too," I whisper.

Cameron Fraizer

67 years old

Horsham, Pennsylvania

Part of me thought that surviving the rain would be the worst of it, but I guess I should have known from our shared human history that destruction often causes more chaos. I'm not young, but I'm not dead yet. Sure, it was quiet for a day or two after the rain and the death, and a naive portion of my brain was telling me that was how it would stay. But that was just the floodwaters keeping people from coming out, moving around. And once people left home and saw the full scope of the destruction around them, that was when everyone started worrying about resources. You know someone shot me in the foot over a box of stale Mini-Wheats? Yeah, we were doomed from the start.

CHAPTER SIXTEEN

We begin our return to the bookstore that afternoon, our cart now filled with cans of food and a trap that Maeve took from a nearby hunting-supply store. She said we needed it *just in case,* and I didn't have the energy to argue.

Maeve stops by a hiking trail about fifteen minutes away from my home territory. I'm not sure why we've stopped, because I certainly did *not* sign up for hiking and am by no means wearing trail-appropriate clothing. She pauses at the sign designating the trailhead. Small symbols dot the edge. 8 MILES. WATER VIEWS. PETS ALLOWED. I look over at Maeve.

"If you make me walk the full eight miles, I swear to god that you won't make it off this trail alive," I grumble. My throat feels like sandpaper, making me annoyingly aware of how thirsty I am.

"Nah, no hiking, princess," she replies. "There's a water source nearby that can be accessed only via trail. We'll fill up, turn around, and be back on the road in no time."

I shake my head. "Why couldn't we just get some at the

store? I'm sure they have some sort of bottled beverage for you to steal."

"I like to make you walk." She pauses, waiting for a reaction. "Kidding. Did you see anything left back there? We'll get some naturally occurring water. It'll be good for you to take a little hike."

Maeve starts down the trail, boots smacking against the rocks and roots. For the first time in a long time I wish I were wearing adequate footwear instead of a pair of Converse with absolutely no arch support. I'm beat up enough already as it is. I'm not sure how much more I can take.

Maeve pushes forward, avoiding every single root and rock that attempts to take me out. She doesn't even stop to take in the leaves and the ferns and the green that surround us. I haven't been out in woods like this in over a year, not since an ill-fated family camping trip right before everything went wrong. I forgot the way it makes your lungs feel, like they're fresh and new. The way the air tastes crisp.

Maeve moves constantly, even though the sun is high in the sky and the trees aren't offering as much coverage as I hoped. Rays of light beam through the gaps in the branches and land on my bare skin. I can feel it starting to burn.

We make it to our destination in less than twenty minutes, stopping about a mile in. There's a small stream no more than a few feet deep, and the sight of natural water stops me dead in my tracks.

"Isn't it acidic?" I ask, my voice wavering slightly.

"Not anymore," Maeve responds. "It's been slowly watered down for the past year."

Even though that makes sense, I don't move any closer. I can't. Instead I watch, doing nothing, as Maeve slowly wades in. As the water rises above her ankles, my breaths become shallow, something solid sitting inside my chest, right above my ribs. Blood rushes to my temples, my heartbeat thudding in my ears, and I seal my eyes shut. Everything inside me is screaming that this is how it happened last time, something harmless turning deadly in mere seconds. Everything inside me is certain that I'll hear Maeve's voice soon, terror rippling at its edges. And when I open my eyes, I'll see the blisters forming, the blood bubbling up beneath her skin.

But the seconds continue to tick past, and my eyes open, and Maeve is fine, staring at me with a look on her face that asks a million questions I don't want to answer. Instead, I choke down the bile at the back of my throat and force a smile. She's fine. Everything's fine. Deciding to trust her, I tentatively dip a foot into the running stream, the water seeping through my shoes. When that feels fine and not flesh eating, I wade in, being careful to keep my bandaged hand dry.

The water is freezing cold, like plunging straight into ice, but I don't mind. I allow my feet to lose feeling completely, the water up to my knees. I'll get it back eventually. The water is so clear, it's as if I'm staring through glass at colored stones. It feels so good, so clean, and so real. For the first time in a long time, my surroundings truly feel alive.

Maeve takes my backpack from me and clomps out of the water, tossing it to the side by her cart before returning, a canteen gripped in her hand.

"Will that be enough?" I can hear the sound of the river trickling through larger stones.

"We'll get the jug too. Don't worry," Maeve explains, gesturing haphazardly as she leans down toward the water. She slowly fills up her canteen, air bubbles escaping frantically to the surface. When she's done, she holds the metal bottle out toward me. "Drink."

"Is it safe?" I might not be some rugged survival expert like she is, but I did go to summer camp. The most important camping rules were don't wipe with poison ivy, leave no trace, and don't drink unpurified water. Maeve just looks at me expectantly, still holding out her bottle. "Aren't we supposed to boil it?"

She rolls her eyes, a small smile forming on her lips. "Liz, when was the last time you had cold water on a hot day?" I say nothing at all as I wiggle my toes around in the river. "One sip won't kill you; you'll just have horrible stomach problems for a while." Maeve laughs. "And if it does kill you, your ghost can haunt me for all eternity."

"Don't think that I won't," I grumble, before taking the canteen. I relish the feeling of the freezing surface, cooling my fingertips. The icy water travels down my throat, and I swear I can feel it as it moves, snaking down my intestines, reviving my body. Pure bliss. I hand the bottle back to Maeve as I slosh my way out of the water, retrieving the blue Culligan jug from the cart. I can hear Maeve snickering as I struggle to get a proper grip on it with one hand.

"I swear to god," I mutter. "You better not be making fun of me, Maeve." She neither confirms nor denies this.

I'm finally able to wrap my arm around it, clutching my right shirt sleeve with my left hand. I hug the bottle as tightly as possible, keeping it close to my body so that it doesn't fall. As

I turn back to the stream, I'm met by a jet of water to the face. The blue canister tumbles from my arm as I stare at Maeve, her hands soaking wet. Her shirt sleeves are pulled up, revealing her tattoo.

"Oh, no, you didn't."

"What are you going to do?" she taunts. "Splash me? You can't get your right hand wet."

"Touché," I mutter as a childish grin forms on my lips. "It's a good thing I have two hands."

Maeve just keeps laughing, as if daring me to follow through with my threat.

And I do. My good arm slaps the water, sending a spray of liquid straight at Maeve. When the surface settles I stare at her, dumbfounded. Her shirt is soaked through, clinging to her skin, revealing the outline of her body beneath. She makes a vain attempt to wring out her shirt, while I try to force my eyes to look anywhere else. It's hard, though. She's lean and strong, and when she lifts her shirt to squeeze out the last bits of water, she looks like something out of an epic. Like Botticelli's Venus, if the goddess of love were known to wear cargo pants and maroon boots. She doesn't seem to care that her shoes are soaked. I'm sure they've been through worse. I can feel my cheeks burn as I stare, stopping only when Maeve makes her declaration of war.

"Oh, it's on."

Her boots slosh through the water as she half jogs toward me, attempting to tackle me.

"Whoa, there!" I exclaim. "Careful with the merchandise."

Maeve pays no heed, wrapping her arms around me and

sending me tumbling down into the river. The only thing I can do is raise my bad arm in an attempt to keep it dry.

We resurface and I laugh, swiping the wet hair away from my face with my functional hand. I spit out a mouthful of water in her direction.

My spine comes to rest against the stream's rocky bottom, Maeve on her knees by my side. We pause there, just breathing, as Maeve looms above me. It's so quiet, no sound except for the faint trickle of running water. For an instant, everything else fades away, and all I know is how *right* this moment feels.

"Oh no! It looks like you might have gotten a little wet."

I shake my head. "You don't look so dry yourself."

"Hey, I did what I had to, to take you down. You have to be humbled sometimes, Ms. Flannery."

I'm about to dip my hand into the water again when I see a shadow in the woods, dashing past the shoreline on the other side of the stream. I blink quickly, just to ensure that my mind isn't playing some dirty trick on me. It tends to do that.

Maeve pulls back her arm for another splash but hesitates, seeing the flicker of worry that passes across my face. Just a brief moment. But Maeve doesn't miss it. I watch as her muscles tense, and the playful mood of the past few minutes slowly dissipates.

"What?"

I scan the woods. Suddenly I'm wishing that we weren't so far from the main road. So far from home. Maybe we shouldn't have left. But I shake my head. "It's nothing," I reply, turning back toward Maeve's cart. "Just my brain playing tricks on me. I'm just tired. It's fine."

But Maeve doesn't seem to buy it. She pauses, staring at me, scanning me for some sort of clue about what's going on inside my head.

With my functioning hand, I reach for the blue canister and force it underneath the water. "I told you, it's fine."

Maeve narrows her eyes before carefully lifting my full canister out of the water, her arms straining. Her boots splash through the stream as she makes her way back toward the cart. With a thud, she drops it back in, the paint chipping from the force of contact.

I'm about to turn and make my way back toward the trail when I see it again, out of the corner of my eye. A blur, barely visible through the cover of the trees. The sound of a single twig breaking sends a shiver up my spine. I whip my head around to Maeve, but it doesn't seem like she's heard anything. The sound of the rushing water is too loud. I must be making this up, right?

"Are you sure you're okay?" she calls out.

I'm about to nod, about to tell her that *of course I'm fine, could you stop asking that?* when Maeve's eyes go wide. Her mouth opens, ready to say something, shout something, but nothing emerges.

And then, I feel cold steel on my neck.

Maeve moves quickly, but the figure behind me is even faster. Before Maeve is even able to unsheathe her hunting knife, the blade at my throat is digging into my skin.

"What the hell do you want?" Maeve asks, her voice hoarse. The figure behind me doesn't answer, and instead clamps a sweaty hand over my lips. "What are you doing?"

I'm forced to watch, silent, as two more people emerge from the woods behind Maeve. She notices the fear on my face and spins, blade outstretched, before they're able to approach.

"What the hell is going on?" Maeve asks.

The man and woman wear all gray. At least, it's gray now, dulled over time by dirt and sheer sunlight. I'm not sure what I expected people to be like. Things end up like this in the books I read, but my people, the ones who come through the bookstore, they aren't like this. They haven't been turned into this yet. The man has a patchy beard and long hair, halfway down to his shoulders. He's younger than the woman, maybe midthirties, while she has to be over forty. Her hair is pulled back in a series of intricate braids, the type of thing you might expect to see on a Viking. In her hands she holds a well-worn pistol, her finger hovering over the trigger. Suddenly, Maeve and her small knife don't seem so tough.

The person behind me finally drops their hand from my mouth, but they don't loosen their grip.

As Maeve scans the faces of our attackers, her posture changes. She stands up straight, and the hand holding the knife steadies out. She's no longer shocked or confused.

She knows who these people are.

It's unmistakable, the look of recognition in her eye. She must know what they want. Why they're here. I'm just wondering why she didn't fill me in before she persuaded me to leave home. I feel my anger start to rise as I try to meet Maeve's gaze. Did she know that she was putting me in danger when she was trying to get me to come with her?

"What do you want?" she growls.

"We have nothing to give you," I add. "We haven't done anything!" I'm unable to muster the same strength that Maeve does.

The man speaks first. "We can never get rid of you, can we?"

"I've never been in these woods before, I promise," I offer.

The woman shakes her head, advancing closer to Maeve, who just grips her blade harder. "We were talking to *her*."

Of course—this altercation isn't about me in the slightest. I'm caught in the middle. Collateral damage.

The figure behind me, a young man by the sound of his voice, laughs harshly. "Just a few weeks ago we caught you hunting in these woods, didn't we?"

I'm about to deny everything when Maeve steps forward, nodding, her face full of indignation. "And so what if I was? I have no choice. You know that."

"You managed to weasel your way out of your punishment last time," the woman says. "We can't afford to be kind this time around. We were clear about the terms of your banishment."

"You don't own these woods," Maeve barks back. "Where else was I supposed to go?"

The man behind me finally releases me from my choke hold, pushing me into the center of the triangle. My neck hurts from the pressure of his blade, and I can't help but rub my hand across it, the skin now raw.

Maeve looks at me, her shoulders shaking. "I'm sorry," she whispers, her voice barely audible. "This is my fault. I shouldn't have brought you here."

I don't say anything in response; I just stare into the eyes of my assailant. He looks like a ghost as he peers at me, unmoving. Something looks familiar about his eyes. His nose. Like

I've met him before. Maybe in the bookstore? But this teenager doesn't seem like the type of person to come to the bookstore. Maybe before, but not now.

His hair is long, just like his companion's, but he's clean-shaven. He squints slightly as he looks at me, staring me up and down. He knows me too. I'm sure of it.

Behind us, Maeve continues to argue with the man and woman, but I can't hear her clearly. Their words float into one ear and out the other. The teenager in front of me doesn't seem to be listening, either, his knife hanging limply from his arm.

"I know you," I mutter, the words getting stuck in my throat. I'm not sure if I'm even talking to him or trying to convince myself. "I know you," I repeat. Then, in an instant, it all comes together. With a better haircut and less dirt on his face, he's unmistakable. How many times had I seen him sitting on my couch, canoodling with Thea?

"Benji?" I ask, my voice breathless. My sister's boyfriend. He made it. He's alive.

"Liz." It's clear that he recognized me first. He looks down at my heavily bandaged arm. "What happened?"

"Generator," I murmur, trying to hear the conversation between Maeve and the woman.

"A generator?" Benji asks, eyebrows raised. "You have a generator?"

"Yeah. And I'm not so happy with it."

"And it works?" He pauses before adding, "How's Thea? I tried to come back and find her after everything, but you all were long gone."

I swallow, wondering how I could possibly explain what happened, when our conversation is interrupted.

"We should have killed her the first time!" the woman sneers.

I spin around. "What?"

"Becca," Benji says, a hint of desperation creeping at the edge of his voice. "You know that isn't protocol."

One thousand questions whirl around in my brain. "Protocol? What protocol?"

"What about your little friend?" Becca asks, striding past Maeve. "Would that send you a message?"

It takes me a second to realize that *I'm* the little friend that Becca is referring to, but I don't realize it fast enough. She quickly wraps her arm around my chest and shoves her pistol against my temple. I try to lift my arm and break her grip, but a shock wave of pain shoots up my side. Once again, I'm useless.

Maeve lunges toward me but is quickly caught by the man, who grabs the back of her jacket with his fist. She struggles against his grip.

"Let her go."

"Whatever you think she's done, I promise you, she hasn't," I choke. Whatever anger I had has dissolved into distress. Maeve has her secrets. I've known that since I met her, just as I have mine. But nothing that bad. She wouldn't be capable of that. She couldn't be.

"You don't know anything about her," Becca replies.

"She's a good person."

The man sneers. "Good people don't exist anymore."

Becca tightens her grip around my chest, forcing the air out of my lungs. "Since Benji is so keen on protocol, I say we kill the girl and bring Maeve back with us."

"No," Maeve growls. "Just take me instead. She didn't do anything wrong."

"You should know that I'm not the one who is gonna get your friend killed," Becca says. "This is all your fault, Maeve." She pauses before whispering in my ear, "You might want to close your eyes. It'll be easier that way." Maeve struggles for a moment, thrashing as the man holds her tight, before Becca adds, "Tristan, keep her quiet."

The pistol is pressed even harder against my temple, and I can hear her fingers fumbling with the trigger. She doesn't want to shoot me. None of them *want* to shoot me. They just think that they have to. We all *think* that we have to do horrible things to survive.

"You don't have to do this," I say, and yet I can't bring myself to fight against Becca's grip.

Tristan laughs as he shifts his hold on Maeve, restraining her in a choke hold with one arm and using the other to fish for something in his pockets. Something to bind her hands. But the transition is all the time she needs. She lunges toward Becca, blade in hand, and grabs for the pistol, forcing it away from my skin.

Becca loosens her hold on me and takes a stumbling step backward, sending me falling toward the ground, a shock wave rippling up my spine, blood pooling in my mouth. Everything is moving too quickly. Maeve is a blur, almost feral, as she slashes her blade at Becca. Tristan takes a few steps forward, trying to look for an opening in the scuffle, but Benji stays put. He doesn't do anything to stop Maeve or protect his friend. He's afraid. I understand the feeling.

Maeve pulls her arm back as Becca raises her gun in front of her. My gut clenches, threatening to wring itself apart. But Maeve doesn't hesitate.

Instead, I watch as Maeve's knife plunges into Becca's torso, twisting slightly as it cuts through the fabric of her shirt.

My heart leaps up into my throat, blocking any air from my lungs, as Maeve's face contorts into something pained. As she realizes what she's done. *What has she done?* For a moment, my mind doesn't even begin to process, each muscle in my body suddenly unmoving. It's like I've lost all autonomy, my soul floating out and staring at the scene from above. *What has she done?*

I watch as Becca falls backward into the stream and Maeve backs away, each motion slow and deliberate, leaving her knife embedded into the woman's skin. Becca gasps, her voice garbled, as if she's drowning before she even hits the water, her pistol slipping from her hand. Red seeps into the running stream, dying the liquid crimson. I don't need to look down at Becca to know what has happened. There's only silence. Silence, punctuated by the sound of running water.

Finally, Tristan staggers toward Maeve, no weapon in his hands, but he's too late. Maeve scrambles to the ground, her hands searching for Becca's discarded gun. She holds it out, arm shaking. She shoves it in his direction, finger hesitating over the trigger.

"Come closer," she snarls. "I dare you." She stands in front of me, crouched on the ground, blocking them from moving closer. Her nose bleeds, staining her teeth red. Once again, she's protecting me. Once again, I'm useless, left staring at the body in the stream, Becca continuing to take shallow breaths. *The body.* I am reminded of what death looks like. I am reminded of the toll it takes.

Tristan continues forward, but Benji places a hand on his back, halting his advance.

"Stop," he mutters, hints of acid in his voice. "She's not worth it."

I glance at Benji, but he's not looking at me. He leans in close to his friend and whispers something in his ear, pausing for a second to gesture to Maeve. She grits her teeth in response. He's making some sort of bargain, but I don't know what the terms are.

Tristan pauses, as if holding back a tidal wave of rage, before turning back to Maeve, still standing in the stream, pants soaked through.

"If we catch you in these woods again, you're both dead."

Maeve wipes her nose and glares at the man. "You won't." She rises slowly, stalking over to me. When she offers me her hand, I hesitate to take it. But Maeve needs me right now. She did this to save me.

"I'm sure we'll see you again," he replies.

The man grimaces as Maeve pulls me away, tossing the gun into her cart and pulling it behind us. I watch as the man rushes toward Becca, her chest rising and falling as the blood begins to seep. She's alive. For now. He stoops down, placing a hand on her shuddering stomach and watches, as we continue to inch away.

As soon as we're far enough away, Maeve abandons her cart, turning toward me. My breaths are ragged and uneven.

"Thank you for not letting me die," I whisper as she pulls me close. Her hug is desperate and tight. We stand there, breathing together, our heartbeats blending into one. Our bodies melting into one.

"I'm so sorry, Liz."

"Don't be sorry." I'm not sure if I mean what I'm saying.

I'm not sure if I'm afraid of her or grateful. I'm not sure how I should feel at all.

"I shouldn't have brought you here. I shouldn't have done this," Maeve whimpers, burying her face into my shoulder. I flinch, unable to control the response. "I should have found another way."

I want to reassure her, but I can't bring myself to. Does she deserve that? She *stabbed* someone right in front of me. A million questions want to burst out of me in response. Who were these people? What did she do to deserve this? I want to run. I want to hug her back. I don't know what I want, so I just force the words out. "You did what you had to."

Maeve chokes out a sad laugh. "We never have another choice. That doesn't make our actions any better."

I don't know what to say in response.

CHAPTER SEVENTEEN

MAY 14: BEFORE THE FIRST STORM

It's not like I was expecting senior prom to be the best day of my short life, but maybe Mom had spent so much time talking about hers when we were little that I expected it to be at least somewhat life changing. The whole thing is just so symbolic that I figured once the day actually arrived, something profound would have shifted in my soul and made me excited to go. Excited to put on a tight-fitting black dress and don a pair of too-high heels and hobble my way through a bougie New Jersey event space with tickets that cost over a hundred dollars.

But my stomach is filled with insurmountable dread as I hike up the hem of my dress and slide into the back seat of a Jeep that belongs to someone I've never met before. This isn't how I imagined this going. This isn't how it was supposed to go at all. My friend Mia is sitting shotgun in front of me, mooning over Finn, her newly acquired boyfriend, who can't manage to find his car keys. He has one of those boy band–esque swoops of wavy brown hair, and his navy-blue suit fits him well. He also doesn't seem all that peeved that I'm third wheeling on what might have otherwise been a romantic prom date, even though he definitely has the right to be.

Mia was supposed to be my date tonight. We were supposed to complain about the lackluster dating scene that our high school has as we ate extra desserts and watched people dance. And then we were supposed to head out early and go get ice cream before spending the rest of the night watching movies. It was supposed to be fun, until she deserted me for this guy I'd never heard of until last Thursday.

Through the windshield of the Jeep I can see Thea getting into another car with her boyfriend. Benji runs around his convertible to open the door for Thea. It's a fumbled attempt at chivalry, but she smiles anyway and sweeps her hair away from her face. It's not actually his convertible, but apparently it took a lot of persuading to get his dad to lend it to him, and that's all that counts. Thea emptied an entire can of hair spray trying to make sure that the drive to the venue wouldn't ruin her updo.

Benji grins at her, cracking some joke as he puts his key into the ignition and the car rumbles to life. Thea smiles in response. In our Jeep, Mia is turning up the music in front of me until I can feel the bass vibrating through the car. Her date says something I can't make out, and she rolls her eyes, turning to look out the window. Young love.

As Thea and Benji pull away from the curb, our car finally starts to move. Thea disappears around the corner, her hair stiffly flying out behind her, despite her vain attempt at defying physics.

Mia turns to me, mouthing something that I don't hear over the pounding bass.

"What?"

She purses her lips and turns down the volume a few notches before repeating herself.

"You okay?"

I nod quickly. "Of course I am."

• • •

Thea and Benji descend on me while I'm holed up in a corner consuming my third chocolate cupcake of the night. My sister walks over with a cocked eyebrow and a *I-don't-know-what-words-are-going-to-come-out-of-your-mouth-but-I-already-don't-believe-them* look on her face as Benji follows her. In the distance, I can see Mia's and Finn's heads bobbing up and down in the throng of people on the dance floor. I tried to stay with Mia for as long as I could, but then my feet started to hurt, and I didn't know the song that was playing, and I remembered how horrible I am at dancing in any situation, but especially in a form-fitting black dress.

"I told you that you could sit with us," Thea says once I put down my half-eaten cupcake and acknowledge her presence. "You didn't have to do . . . this."

And that's true, she did, and sure, her friends are nice, but I didn't want to intrude or feel like I'd been hastily wedged into another social situation where I don't actually belong. But Thea cares, even though she doesn't have to tonight. I feel like prom is the one night where all sisterly responsibilities are forgotten, even if Thea doesn't seem to have gotten the memo.

"I know," I reply. I think about lying and saying that I got hungry, or that Mia is in the bathroom, but I know that Thea would see through that, and then Benji would probably offer to go find Mia for me, and then everything would unravel. It would be even sadder to lie than to just accept my embarrassing existence. "I didn't want to bother you."

There are a few moments of silence as Thea processes this, wondering whether to state the obvious—that I wouldn't have bothered her—or just ignore the statement entirely. "Do you want to leave?"

"What? No. I'm fine." I'm not going to ruin this for her. "Mia's still gallivanting with Mr. Wonderful. I'll wait until she's done."

But Thea shakes her head. "You don't have to. We can drive you back." She stares straight into my eyes, hammering in the sincerity of her offer. "We want to leave anyway."

Benji nods at this, a grin appearing on his face. "I should probably return the car. It's getting late." He pauses. "We can just watch some movies or something. Whatever you want."

I think about the convertible and their romantic car ride and how I might be ruining another couple's romantic evening if I accept. I think about how they probably have plans for the rest of the night that don't involve me. But I also think about Mia and Finn and the Jeep and the three cupcakes I've already consumed. I think about how prom technically isn't over for another hour and a half and how my toes hurt and I forgot my Converse at home.

"Yeah, that makes sense," I reply, rising to my feet. I leave my cupcake wrappers on my plate and follow Thea around the dance floor.

She lets Benji lead the way as she walks by my side. As we make our way out the front door, she leans toward my ear and murmurs, "You know it's my job to take care of you, right?" Like she's sensed the guilty feelings swirling in the bottom of my stomach.

"But you don't have to."

"I want to. You'd do the same for me."

CHAPTER EIGHTEEN

We pause by the side of the road after almost an hour of walking in silence, sitting down on a rusted barrier, blocking the sidewalk from the long-gone traffic. Maeve retrieves Becca's gun from her pocket, rubbing the tarnished metal with her thumb. I've never seen a real gun before, I realize. Only in crime thrillers and action movies. Never in real life.

I have too many questions I want to ask, most of them containing expletives. They ring in my ears and hide in the crevices of my brain. I wonder if she wanted to kill Becca. I wonder what would have happened if she'd been successful. Part of me is angry. Angry with her for lying. Angry with her for putting both of us in danger. But another part of me wants to say: *Thank you for not leaving me alone. Thank you for staying. Thank you for saving my life.*

"You could have told me" is all I say. "About those people."

Maeve stiffens slightly. "I didn't want you to think I was dangerous."

"You broke into my house. I already thought you were

dangerous." It's meant as a half joke, but it doesn't sound like one when I say it.

"I know; I'm sorry," she says, her voice so deflated that I'm not sure that I can be angry. Maybe now it's my turn to take care of her. We've both done things that we regret. We've both hurt people—that's one thing that we share.

"It's okay."

I think about what Becca said. That I didn't know Maeve at all. That Maeve had managed to weasel her way out last time. And I think about how it ended this time. Maeve didn't hesitate to stab Becca when it came to saving my life. I can't help but wonder if she's done it before.

Maeve continues to fumble with the gun, pausing only when the magazine slides out. A breath escapes from her throat as she inspects the part, peering into it. Her face pulls taut as she holds it out toward me, showing the nothingness that lurks inside.

"It's empty," she murmurs, not daring to look me in the eyes. "There was never anything in it."

I don't know what to say. I don't know how to fix this for her. "You didn't know that, Maeve."

"I didn't have to hurt her."

"You couldn't have known."

With shaking fingers, she slowly slides the magazine back into the pistol, handing the entire weapon to me.

"I didn't have to do anything. You would have been safe either way."

She doesn't wait for a response, slowly standing and moving back toward her cart. She continues down the road, not looking back to see if I'm following. I look down at the gun in my hands and swallow before tossing it into the grass beside the road. Maeve doesn't need this weighing on her conscience. She doesn't need to be haunted by this object.

It takes me a few moments to catch up to her, but when I do, I pretend that nothing has happened at all, guiding our conversation in a different direction.

"Is this what it's always like?" I ask as we pass a deserted football field, a jersey and water bottle still sitting on a bench. The field is completely overgrown, weeds up to my knees with moss and ivy strangling the bleachers. A scoreboard looms in the distance, a few degrees from falling over completely. Maeve looks ahead, like she's trying not to acknowledge what happened. Like maybe, if she doesn't move her gaze, she won't meet my eyes, and I won't be able to ask her anything about Becca. "Is it always this empty?"

Maeve grips the handle of the cart tightly. "If people left home, they didn't take someone else's. If you're lucky, you'll find mold and the smell of rot in the buildings that are left. If you're unlucky . . . you find death. Nobody wants to encounter a dead body, halfway rotted. They come up with other solutions for shelter. Away from the leftovers of society."

"So it's all just hidden away?" We round the corner and pass a deli that's a block from the bookstore, the Open sign still hanging in the window. The rest of the building has all but crumbled to dust, the front wall the only one left standing. It looks like a poorly made stage set, dull and one dimensional. Behind the shattered glass door, an ice cream freezer lies on its side, mold blossoming inside. I don't get a sense of the outside world from my patrons. I'm too busy focusing on their past, their stories, to understand how the world functions now. And sure, I know that there are groups, but Becca and the man in the woods talked about protocol. I didn't think anything that organized could happen in a year.

I think about the bookstore, about people lurking outside. Hopefully no one has run off with all seventy-eight copies of *The Giver* that we have left. One of my coworkers accidentally ordered three hundred copies instead of thirty when preparing for a school order, and we've been stuck with oodles and oodles ever since. I haven't managed to get rid of a single copy in the past year. Surprisingly, people don't seem to have an appetite for dystopian literature after the end of the world.

"There are things that still run," Maeve is explaining when I snap back to reality. "Like your bookstore. There are groups. Like the one in the woods. Some are more dangerous than others. You just have to know where to find them."

"Do you know where to find them?"

"I used to," she manages.

"Used to?" But Maeve doesn't respond. She looks away, picking up her pace.

"I don't want to talk about it."

A pang of realization passes through me, and I stop, waiting until Maeve looks me in the eyes. I realize I never actually saw Maeve's broken tent. And I understand. I know what it's like to be left behind. *Banished.* That's what the man had said. "Maeve, tell me the truth. Did your tent really break?"

I watch as conflicting emotions flick past on her face. "No," she finally admits. "I was alone, and I didn't know where else to go. I couldn't keep running from them. I needed shelter, and when I saw the bookstore, it seemed like as good a place as any. I didn't know anyone was living there."

I don't know what to say in response. I've never known what to say in situations like these. I've never known how to properly comfort anyone, except to give a lackluster hug. I look at Maeve's clenching jaw. She stands there, tense, like she wants to run the last block to the bookstore. I understand the impulse, but I don't let her.

Instead, I shrug off my backpack and walk over to her, wrapping my good arm around her neck and holding her close. She doesn't pull away. I stay in this position, not knowing if I should stop, but then I feel two hands around my back, hugging me tight. She exhales, her warm breath filling my ear.

"You can stay as long as you need," I say. It's the least I can do. She's saved my life, twice.

She speaks so quietly that I can barely hear her. "Thank you," she whispers.

• • •

Eventually we continue down the block, making our way back home. Maeve tugs her cart over the asphalt carefully, trying to avoid spilling any of the water we collected. Her pace is slow and deliberate as she plods toward the bookstore. Each step seems to take just a bit more energy than it should, like she's running on an almost empty tank. Something about the way she carries herself tells me that this is the true Maeve. No overwhelming energy, no grating confidence, no biting humor.

Although I want to ask if she's okay, I don't. I know she

won't tell me the truth. No one ever tells the truth when asked that sort of question.

But then Maeve stops short a few feet away from the curb, sucking in a jagged breath.

"You good?"

"It's not me," Maeve replies, dropping the cart handle to point at the side of the building. "It's that."

At first, I don't even notice. At first, I knit my eyebrows and wonder what Maeve is going on about. But then I see it. The dead tree beside the building has fallen, taking down most of the wall with it.

CHAPTER NINETEEN

I am completely and utterly screwed. I keep repeating the sentence over and over again in my head. When I was younger, I begged Dad to let me get a tree house. This isn't what I had in mind.

Maeve keeps looking back at me, double- and triple-checking to make sure that I don't turn to dust in front of her eyes. I'm not 100 percent sure that I won't. A part of me, possibly the worst part of me, wants to laugh right now. Wants to laugh at the utter absurdity of the past couple of days because shit keeps piling up on top of me like the universe thinks it's funny. It's the part of me that occasionally lets out a chuckle when I see someone wipe out on the sidewalk. I know it's a horrible impulse, and maybe that makes me a horrible person, but it sometimes makes things a little bit better.

I slowly sit down on the trunk of the tree.

"We're royally screwed," I manage. Maeve stares at me from her place at the corner of the sidewalk.

"I think *royally* might be a bit of an exaggeration." She's not being honest; I can tell by the way she stares at the tree trunk, the grass, anywhere but me.

"Maeve, there's a hole the size of a Mini Cooper in the side of the building. What do you want me to do? Pretend that I always wanted a second entrance?"

I wait for her to respond, but instead she walks straight up to me and, before I can react, wraps me in a hug. And I let her. I let her hand gingerly glide under my right arm and around my torso. I let her fingers press into my back with a firmness I haven't felt in a long time. Three hugs in one day—scratch that, a couple of hours—when I haven't had one in years. And sure, when I hugged Maeve it felt nice, but *being held* is something entirely different. Her grip around my waist is strong and sure.

But still, I feel the tension swimming in my stomach, tears moments from tumbling down my cheeks. I let my lip tremble as I bury my face in Maeve's shoulder, taking heaving breath after heaving breath. This was the place that was supposed to be safe when everything else wasn't. This place is supposed to stay solid for me, because it was here when my home was gone. Now, with another Storm approaching, it matters more than ever.

A tear comes, just one. Hot and salty, slowly inching down my face, dripping onto Maeve's shoulder. She senses it.

When she pulls away, she doesn't let go completely. She keeps her arms wrapped around me and loosens up just enough so that she can see my eyes and look at my face.

"Liz," she says, her voice heavy with sincerity, "let's go inside. Assess the damage and make a game plan."

She leads the way toward the front door, not the hole-in-the-wall door, pulling her cart behind her. She hesitates before entering, moving to grab the blue jug and bring it inside with her.

"We don't have to bring that stuff in now, do we?" I ask, and Maeve crosses her arms.

"Our future selves will thank us if we do." She stands by the front door and picks off my piece of Nancy Drew tape, which thankfully hasn't been broken.

From inside, the damage looks worse. The tree branches stretch from the wall to the edge of the front counter, knocking over every shelf and rack of birthday cards in its path. I'm thankful that the tree wasn't tall enough or close enough to the bookstore to do more damage. Still, the gaping hole is much more than I can handle. Maybe four feet across. Five, if I'm being generous. It's a middle schooler–sized hole, trapped somewhere between elementary school and puberty.

Maeve vaults over the curved front counter, making her way to the other side of the trunk and inspecting it carefully.

"Expert diagnosis?" I ask, afraid of the answer.

"For once, I'm no expert," she admits. That's a first. "But we have two options."

"And they are?"

"One: We get to work. We remove the tree. We patch the hole. Two: we remove the tree and then head somewhere else to wait out The Storm, just in case."

"What?" I scoff. "I'm not leaving, Maeve."

She turns to look at me. "But maybe that's the safest option. We'll come back later when there's no looming threat."

"Really?"

"Yeah."

I shake my head. "That's not an option. That's not even on the table in the slightest."

"But could it be?"

I pause. Leaving this all behind? Opening this place up to the threat of looters? It was hard enough for me to go on our recent expedition. The idea of abandoning the bookstore to the elements is a bit too much. I could lose the one place I have left to call a home, just for a marginally better shot at survival. And who knows? The next place we go to could have an even bigger hole in the wall.

"Not a chance."

Maeve hesitates as if she wants to argue, but she stops herself. "Fine. We can talk about this later."

Maeve begins to rip branches off the trunk, sending them flying back out toward the street. The snap of each branch is deafening, but she doesn't seem to notice. She works furiously, using her whole body weight, every muscle tense and in motion. I feel useless as I pick off the smaller pieces with my good arm. The tiny branches that never quite made it. My arm is healing, I can feel it, but it'll be a bit longer before it's fully operational. I stare out the front window as I work, allowing myself to be distracted by the *nothing* that sits outside the door. If this were a spaghetti western, I'd expect a tumbleweed to come flying through right about now.

I stare at the railroad bridge that hovers at the side of the square. It's rusted and unsightly, and when you walk under it, mysterious liquids tend to drip from overhead. I remember running to the train station on hot summer Friday nights with Thea to meet my dad coming home from work. Everyone would wait on the other side of the bridge until the train disappeared down the track to avoid the strange substances that would drip from the train's undercarriage. Then, once the train was gone and the passengers began to approach, it immediately turned into a competition to see who could spot Dad and his well-tailored suit first. We'd stand there, sweating slightly in the sweet summer air until he smiled at us, giving us permission to race into his arms.

As I stare at the bridge a figure appears, hesitating in the shadows. It's too far away for me to make out any specifics, but from where I'm standing I think it's a man. Possibly someone headed to the bookstore for a trade or to deliver a letter. I'm not really in the right headspace for human interaction right now, but I figure a conversation with a random person has to be more exciting than picking twigs off a tree. So I fix my posture and walk toward the door, ready to greet the new arrival.

But the figure doesn't move. They just watch, any discernible features concealed by shadow. I stand there, waiting for this person to do something, anything. But they remain, as motionless as a statue.

"Are you seeing that?" I ask, turning to Maeve.

She'll confirm my suspicions. She'll laugh about how odd it is and tell me that there's nothing to worry about. It's just some stranger, nothing less, nothing more.

"What?" Maeve walks toward me, the floorboards creaking. She wipes her hands on the fabric of her pants.

I turn back to the window, ready to point out the figure underneath the bridge, but when I do, they're gone.

Maybe I am going insane.

• • •

I don't sleep well, and not because of the heat this time. An unseasonably cool breeze wafts in through the open window, and I clutch my quilt in my hands, pulling it close to my chin.

I wanted to tell Maeve about the person under the bridge. I wanted to prove to her that they were real, but she has deep circles under her eyes and calluses on her hands. Every breath seems to take its toll. She doesn't need my inane ideas making things worse.

I continue staring at the ceiling, even though I can hear something rustling behind me. I only sit up in bed when I hear the front door creak shut, my quilt bunching up around my waist. My eyes glance around the room, bouncing over various objects before I realize that Maeve's spot on the floor is empty. I wait, wondering whether to follow her. Maybe she wants to be alone. Maybe she forgot something in the cart and just remembered it right now, in the middle of the night. I always remember the most ridiculous things at the most ungodly hours. But then I hear the front door slam shut and the faint sound of gravel crunching under feet.

I don't want to be alone right now. Not in this darkness.

• • •

Maeve sits on the front step, her feet extended out in front of her. She doesn't look back at me as I carefully make my way through the door, my leg brushing against her back.

"Hey," I whisper, attempting to preserve the peace that hangs in the air. I sit down beside her and tuck my legs underneath me, the tips of my Converse drawing lines in the dirt. "Couldn't sleep?"

"Not a wink," she replies, smiling weakly.

"When was the last time you slept?" I ask. "Like, actually slept peacefully. No crazy dreams or anything like that."

A sharp laugh bursts from her lungs, echoing through the emptiness. "Would it be horrible if I told you I couldn't remember?" A pause. "Jesus Christ, I feel like I've turned into a zombie."

"Generally, zombies do come with the end of the world."

"I always thought I'd do well in a zombie apocalypse," Maeve says. "You, on the other hand, would be the first one dead."

I feign an arrow shot through my heart. "What are you talking about? I'm essentially a teenage John Wick. I'd be a zombie serial killer. Zombies would teach their zombie children to fear me!"

Maeve laughs. "Okay, Elizabeth Swann."

We sit in silence for a while, and though I don't want to ruin the pleasant air between us, I know I'll burst if I don't ask the question that's been festering in my mind for hours.

"Do you want to talk about it?"

"About what?"

"What happened before?" My cheeks are turning bright red, but I continue. "What happened to you before you came here?"

Maeve shakes her head. "I'm not sure that I want to talk about it." I nod, expecting that to be the end of it, but then she clears her throat. She looks out, straight ahead, and takes a deep breath, as if preparing herself to give an impassioned speech. "I used to live with a group that I found about ten miles north of here for seven or eight months. It seemed almost too good to be true, you know?"

And I do know. I know how it feels to be so certain that nothing good will ever happen to you again. I understand what it's like to believe that the only thing that's waiting for you in the future is pain.

"I was the youngest in the group by a few years," she continues, staring at something hiding in the darkness. "That boy that they were with yesterday hadn't arrived yet, and it became clear very quickly that they judged me for my age. Everyone except one of them, who'd stand up for me when things got too tense. Who'd check in on me whenever I hid out on my own for too long. She was a friend, a good friend, but everyone else? They judged me. Everything I could do, someone older could obviously do better. They never gave me the chance to prove I was more capable than all of them combined." I watch as she bites her lip, threatening to break through the skin. "Obviously, I didn't take that well. I wasn't the most gracious guest, and I didn't take kindly to being ordered around. And one day I decided to prove my worth. I set out to go hunting on my own, took Becca's knife with me. Didn't tell anyone. I left early in the morning, so that no one would be able to stop me, so that no one would be able to tell me that I shouldn't go.

"I found a man in the woods, all bloody and bruised. He said that he had been attacked and needed help. He said that his daughter had been taken by his attackers and he didn't know where she had gone. And so, I abandoned my hunting trip to save the man. I guess I figured that by helping him, the others would see that I was better than they were. Stronger than they were. To take a life is one thing, but to save a life is worth so much more."

Maeve pauses. "I should have known that he was lying. I should have known as soon as he hesitated when I asked him his daughter's name. Or when he said no when I asked him if he needed bandages. I should have realized, but I didn't. Instead, I brought him back to camp with me, just like he wanted me to, and let him walk right through our walls. He was gone again in less than two hours, taking most of our weapons and food with him. Anything he could use to survive. And I was left with the blame.

"They said that it was the last straw. A last strike. They set it to a vote, and my friend? The one person I thought would stick up for me and understand why I did what I did? She was the deciding vote. And so they banished me. From their woods too. It didn't matter to them that those woods are the only place nearby with clean drinking water, or any real wildlife."

I know I shouldn't be asking questions right now, but I do anyway. "Then why did you stay in the area? Why not move on to another town?"

Maeve laughs a small laugh. A desperate laugh. "I would have gone far away from here. I would have stayed on my own, would have kept moving, but when the opportunity presented itself, I figured it was safer to have shelter now. Nature doesn't always adhere to a strict schedule." She pauses, her brow furrowed. "I was going to loot the bookstore and get back on my feet, but obviously that's not how it worked out. At the end of the day, I thought the store was far enough away from the woods that it wouldn't be a problem. I'd worry about defining *home* later." She pauses.

"This place became home for me," I say, my chest suddenly tight. "After The Storm, this became home. I had this coworker with me—a friend—and that was nice too."

Maeve pauses. "Really?" I realize I've never mentioned Eva to Maeve before.

"She was here with me for a while, but then she left."

"And you cared about her?" Maeve asks, even though she doesn't look like she wants to know the answer.

"More than she cared for me, I think."

A few seconds tick by before Maeve finally says, "Oh." She purses her lips. "Why stay if you have bad memories here? In this town?"

"I'd like to think that the good outweighs the bad. At least by a little bit."

"But after all of this don't you . . ." Maeve's voice trails off before she finishes, saying, "Maybe we should leave."

The sudden shift in her tone hits me hard, and it takes a couple of seconds to realize what she's saying. "What?"

"There's a Storm coming, and we both have too much history here."

"We've both made it through a Storm before too."

"But not like this," she argues. "Not with a hole in the wall and a missing roof."

"Then we fix it. Like you said."

"I know. But we don't have any way of getting more water. I don't think it's safe anymore."

I laugh slightly, like she's joking. I know she isn't. "You've been hunting in the woods before, right? Even after the banishment?"

But Maeve shakes her head. "We can't risk it again. I won't risk your life again."

I reach out and grab her hand, surprised by my own actions.

I lace my fingers around hers and look into her eyes, my insides fluttering as I do.

"Leaving isn't an option. I'm sorry about everything that happened to you, but now isn't the time to run. I can't run again." A pause. "People like that are the reason we can't leave. It's safe here." Because here, people come and go, but at least they're alive. Here, it might get lonely sometimes, but now there's Maeve. And there's food, and some water. There's part of a roof over our heads. Away from here, who knows?

I'm not sure if she believes me, but I hope she does. I hope she realizes that she isn't alone.

But she doesn't say anything in response.

CHAPTER TWENTY

I stare at what's left of the tree, and it stares back at me, the knots in its bark beginning to look like eyes. Maeve stands behind me, practically breathing down my neck, and I tap my foot impatiently.

"Do you have a saw?" Maeve asks, massaging her chin with the tips of her fingers.

"Maeve, this is a bookstore. What would we possibly need a saw for?"

She cocks an eyebrow, not surrendering to the power of my poorly delivered jokes. "What about the hardware store?"

An image of empty shelves lurks in the back of my brain, dark dust gathering on beige metal. "They won't have one," I say. "There's nothing left in there."

"Fine." Maeve exhales, turning to meet my gaze. The circles under her eyes have only deepened, the irises' once sharp green color now dull. "Then give me a solution." She pauses, brushing a strand of hair away from her face. "And a place where we can get some wood, too, in order to patch up this hole."

I want to fire back *What's your solution?* But I don't. This isn't her home turf. It's mine. My town, my responsibility, right?

As that thought enters my brain, it's immediately followed by another. I know where to find a saw, and wood, and whatever the hell else Maeve might need to work her magic. It sends an uneasy feeling through my bones, but it's the best option we have. It's probably the only option that we have.

"Okay, I have a solution," I announce, and an ounce of life makes its way back into Maeve's face. "It's a house, a ten-minute walk from here, but we should be able to get what you need." Even though the idea of leaving this place again makes my stomach turn. Even though I remember all too well what happened the last time that I did.

Her lips press into a straight line; a small crease forms on her forehead. "Liz, we're surrounded by acres of suburbia. I don't want to come face to face with the bodies of anyone who wasn't as fortunate as the two of us, and I sure as hell don't want to be waltzing through a house that smells like rotting flesh." I nod slowly, about to explain myself, but Maeve isn't done. "And we can't just go and grave-rob someone's home. I mean, it's different if no one lived there, like a store or a school, but someone's house?"

I just shake my head. "We wouldn't be stealing from anyone," I clarify. "We'd be going to my house."

• • •

We leave the next morning, a headache pounding at my temples from the moment I wake up. The gravity of the situation hits me in the chest like a ton of bricks as I tie my Converse and head downstairs, Maeve by my side. *My house. My. House.*

I smile at Maeve, as if to say, *Everything is okay. I promise. I'm okay with this.*

I'm not okay with this. The truth of the matter is that I haven't been back since it happened. I've tried not to think about it, the way the house used to look, the way it used to smell when my mom would cook dinner. The feeling of the front doorknob in my hand. The way my voice echoed around the drafty halls whenever I called out, *I'm home!* The sound the floorboards in my bedroom would make on the rare occasion I decided to dance. I've tried to leave my home in my memories, build a barrier, and start a new life. I haven't been that successful.

I've often thought about what I would do if someone offered to reset my memory. It sounds implausible, but then so did the end of the world at one point. I've thought about starting fresh with nothing left to hold me back. Being content in my present because I had no past to reference. I wouldn't be able to think about things like school or air-conditioning or family, because I wouldn't remember their existence. I would start at the present, alone and surviving, and maybe I'd have a real fighting chance at happiness. This existence of sheer survival, day after day after day, would be all that I would know. There would be nothing at all to miss.

But sometimes, the memory is worth the pain. It's like watching the saddest episode of your favorite TV show again, even though you know how badly it's going to hurt. It's like looking through a photo album at pictures of people who are gone.

We set out after our "customer" for the day departs, trading a bottle of antiseptic spray and a bag of rice for an old pack of batteries that I forgot that I even had. That and a copy of *The Miraculous Journey of Edward Tulane.* The antiseptic spray might have been more helpful a few days ago, but beggars can't be choosers.

"Are you sure you're okay with this?" Maeve asks quietly. "We don't have to go. *I* haven't even gone back since . . ."

I don't let her finish. I don't want her to have to think about that. "It's fine," I promise. "I wouldn't have offered it if I wasn't okay with it."

Maeve seems to accept that as an answer, though I suspect it's more because she doesn't want to argue, rather than because she believes me. She follows me out the front door, the busted lock jingling as it slams shut. We tape the door like we did before hiking through the woods. We'll be back in two hours, and then we can attack the tree again, full force.

I lead the way, walking away from the bookstore on a path I haven't traveled in almost a year. I keep my breath steady, staring firmly ahead. This is fine. Everything is totally fine.

I take another turn as Maeve walks a few paces behind, her boots thudding on the stone as she pulls her cart behind her. We pass through a park. The park where I went on my first date with a boy from my band class. It was my first and last date with a boy, and it ended abruptly after he talked about boxing for two and a half hours straight. Last I knew, he was headed to Harvard. I wonder if he's still alive. This is the park where I used to go sledding on cold winter days, racing up and down the hill in a frenzy, knowing that a comforting cup of hot chocolate would be waiting for me when I got home. The park

I used to walk through on my way to work, where I used to sit on Fridays after school with my friends, letting the grass graze my ankles as I drank Pepsi and munched on whatever flavored chips were the cheapest.

We pass Holland Court, which used to be the best street for a bike ride, with a slight hill that sloped enough to let you pick up real speed as you went down. The houses at the bottom of the hill gave out full-sized candy bars on Halloween, and one of them had a tabby cat that would appear on our back porch during the summer. It smells like summer, too, that tangible scent of hot asphalt and too much pollen. It feels fresh and heavy at the same time. And with the slight breeze comes seventeen years of memories.

Bike rides wearing sweatshirts even though I was sweating like hell, because the sweatshirt was new and made me look cool. Headphones on, the ones that cost fifteen hours of minimum-wage labor because they blocked out every background noise, which was definitely not safe on the road, but I didn't care. Violent Femmes and Woodkid and Harvey Danger and Radiohead blasting into my ears like I was standing in the middle of a concert hall.

It washes over me, like a thousand little hailstones raining from the sky, almost knocking me off my already unsteady feet. If Maeve notices my fugue state, she doesn't acknowledge it. Yet the memories keep coming, pummeling me with gut punch after gut punch. Birthday parties in the backyard, hitting tennis balls against the garage door, cold Cokes from the gas station three blocks away. At this moment, the mundane is beautiful. The mundane is rare and precious and gone as quickly as a breeze, depositing me back in the present.

The front gate stands ajar, and when I see it, my heart drops. I stop in the middle of the road, my Converse suddenly glued to the asphalt. Maeve tenses up beside me, and I feel gentle fingers wrapping themselves around my arm.

"We don't have to do this," she whispers. "We can find some other way."

"I'm fine," I say. I am not.

The gate is purely decorative, a little bit over knee height with white paint chipping off from lack of care and certain weather-related apocalyptic events. A part of me hurts as I look at it, wishing I'd done more to fix it up before I left. To keep it the way I want to remember it. But then I remember what a *great* job I've been doing with the bookstore. Maybe if I had stayed here there'd be a tree through the roof by now.

The actual house is covered in peeling yellow paint, shutters hanging off like something from a poorly made Halloween movie. And sure, I've never seen an *actual* haunted house, but I'd say this qualifies, even without my life-sized cutout of Emma Stone peering down at me through my bedroom window. The roof is almost entirely gone; moss grows on the sides of the building and on the dark gray asphalt sidewalk. I climbed onto that roof once, believing that I could fly like Wendy Darling from *Peter Pan*. Luckily Mom spotted me before I was able to jump. I refused to talk to her for a week after that.

The whole building looks overgrown and unwanted. I remember that I'm the reason that no one was left to give it the love it deserved. It's my fault that this building is empty.

I make my way up the front walk, stepping over various weeds and wildflowers that have sprouted from the cracks in the cement. My dad would have a stroke if he saw the state of the yard, considering the number of hours he spent expertly cultivating it.

"I'll just be a minute," I say, trying to plaster on the biggest smile I can muster. I don't think it's very convincing, but she nods anyway. "You can come in if you want, or you can wait out here."

"I'm not letting you go in there alone." Her eyes search mine, but I mask my reluctance well. Still, she stands by my side as I open the front door.

The entire house smells musty, and there's dust clinging to every surface. As I step onto the carpet in the hallway, a cloud erupts in front of me and I can't help but sneeze. My shoulders shudder, and I wince from the shock of pain it sends shooting down my arm.

"Are you okay?" Maeve asks.

"It's just a sneeze; I'm not dying." I can hear a half-hearted chuckle and feel relieved.

The whole house is dark, except for columns of sunlight that come through the broken windows. I start heading up the stairs, the wood creaking under my feet.

"You keep your saws upstairs?" Maeve jokes.

It's enough to get me to laugh, or rather exhale through my nose in a sort of half laugh. I turn to face her. "Yeah, right under my pillow." I point at a door on the ground floor. "There should be wood in the garage from the time when I tried to build a shed in the backyard. You only have to take the pieces you think you can use. The saw should be there as well. It's right through there. I'll just be a minute."

Maeve rushes through the opening, closing the door gingerly behind her. I continue my ascent, managing to put one foot in front of the other even though each step feels like it weighs a thousand pounds.

My bedroom is the first room at the top of the stairs. The door is slightly ajar, and I hesitate in front of it, wondering if I want to go in. I'm not sure if I want to see this world, this place that served as my safe space for so long, in shambles. I'm not sure if I want to walk in and smell the air just to realize that it no longer smells like me. But my curiosity eats at me, so I push on the knob gently with the pads of my fingers.

Part of the outer wall has crumbled away, yanked off my house by some ungodly force. I knew that there had been some structural damage during The Storm from the wind, but I hadn't stayed long enough to find out what or fix any of it. The entire room has been exposed for the past year, allowing in rain and snow and who knows what else. The white bedsheets have turned a faded shade of beige, so moth-eaten in some places that you can see the mattress. Mr. Frog, a childhood favorite, sits on top of my comforter, fur matted and one button eye hanging off by a thread. The sight makes my insides turn, but I still step inside, taken over by some sort of macabre fascination.

I sit down on my desk chair, which feels as firm as a rock. The metal has been corroded, but I can still swivel a bit in the seat. It's weird, but this feels normal. This feels the closest to normal anything has in a long time, and so I close my eyes. I close my eyes and don't look at the moth-hole-ridden covers. I don't look at the peeling paint or the dust that surrounds me. I imagine that this *is* normal, just for a moment. For as long as I can maintain the illusion.

I'm transported back to another time, one and a half years

ago. I'm hunched over my laptop typing away some nonsense about *Frankenstein,* nattering on and on about Pandora and Prometheus and the metaphor of it all. The sun sets outside, slowly replaced by twilight, but I don't notice, earbuds in as I listen to Interpol and tap along to "Evil" with the tips of my boots.

The light on my desktop flickers, perched atop a pile of books I've yet to read, no matter how many times I promise myself that I will *get to them eventually.* I am happy, or happy enough. Somewhere between happy and content as I write my essay and listen to music about murderers, pretending to be more rebellious than I ever will be.

In my imagination, my dad taps on the door gently with his knuckles, even though it's open. I pull my earbuds out of my ears, setting them down on my laptop keyboard. I can still hear the pulsing bass notes of the song, now small and insignificant. As he looks at me, I smile, and he smiles back.

What are you working on? he asks, his voice warm.

Just an essay for Thompson. I know what I'm going to write but . . . it's not flowing as well as I might have hoped.

Is it any good?

It's good enough for me to turn in, I reply.

He smiles, lines appearing around his soft blue eyes. *I know you too well. I'm sure it's fine. You've always been such a good writer.*

I know he's just saying that, in the same way that all parents do. It's their job to tell little lies sometimes, just to make you feel better. But I decide that in this memory, he believes he's telling the truth.

Have you eaten today? he asks.

I had soup. And that much is true, because I ate soup every single day during my senior year of high school. It was my main food group.

Dad groans. *If you keep eating so much soup, you're going to turn into soup!*

I know, I know. But what can I say? Don't mess with a good thing.

Dad reaches behind him, grabbing something off the table in the hallway. A mug sits in his hand, dotted with images of golden retrievers.

I made you some tea.

I can feel warmth rise to my cheeks as if this were real life and not just a figment of my imagination.

You're too good to me, I tell him.

It's my job.

Before he leaves I turn to him, swiveling in my desk chair and breaking away from the path of my pre-lived memory.

I love you, you know.

I love you too.

I let the sound fill my ears. I let it encircle me, suffocate me. When I open my eyes, I'm transported back to real life. The illusion is over.

The essay still hangs above my desk, haphazardly thumbtacked onto my bulletin board, torn mostly to shreds but still distinguishable. Its yellowed pages have curled up into themselves, and I stand to take a closer look.

With a shaking hand I push the pages down. The 8/8 grade is barely there, almost faded into obscurity. If I didn't know it was there, I wouldn't be able to see it. I am the only one who still remembers that I got an 8/8 on this assignment. It will die with me.

I hear a door slam downstairs and footsteps across the wooden floor below me.

"I found the wood," Maeve yells up to me. "And the saw, just in case you were still looking."

"Awesome," I tell her, my voice breaking on the last syllable. Her voice reminds me that I'm not alone, no matter how lonely I might sometimes feel. And for that, I'm grateful. "I'll be down in a second."

Something warm and wet falls onto my face, and I realize I'm crying. I wipe the tear from my cheek and take one last look at the room, my room. I try to remember it as it once was. I try to remember Dad and the tea and the essay, not the moth holes and the peeling paint and the smell. Not the horrible things that happened here. Before I head back out the door, I pluck the frog from my bed and hold it close, clutching it with the crook of my elbow.

Maeve waits for me at the bottom of the stairs, saw in hand, standing in front of a carefully stacked pile of wood.

"I have some nails in my pockets, too," she says as she passes me the saw. I struggle to hold it without losing my grip on Mr. Frog. Maeve looks from the frog to me and then back to the frog. "What's with the toy?"

"A friend."

• • •

It's hard to sleep tonight. Well, it's hard to sleep any night, but especially tonight. Because going back forced me to remember. It brought all those locked-away memories to the front of my mind. They roam around my brain with nothing left to stop them.

After we got back to the bookstore Maeve immediately fell asleep in the armchair by the kitchen window. She sat down, just to rest her feet, she said, but in an instant she was out like a light. I didn't want to move her, and even if I did, I probably wouldn't be able to with only one hand. The bedroom feels empty without her. Too quiet. There's no sound of rustling sheets in the corner, or snores, or the occasional twisting and turning. There's just quiet.

I stare out the window at the street below. Only the smallest square outside is even visible from my position in bed, but I look anyway, staring at a crumpled-up poster advertising a coding summer camp as it flutters around the street. It reminds me of a lyric from a Fiona Apple song, which just reminds me of Maeve.

I don't notice the figure at first, creeping in from down the street. No one stays outside long at night anymore. There's too much to be afraid of. But this figure—this person—seems totally unaware of the fact that they're being watched. Totally unaware of the fact that there's someone awake inside to be looking at them. It's the same person from the other day who was lurking underneath the railroad bridge. I can tell from their hunched posture.

The figure moves closer to the bookstore, bending over to look at something that I can't make out from this vantage point. They pause before walking toward the side of the building, disappearing from my view completely. Maybe they've noticed the giant tree poking out of the wall. It would be hard for them not to notice, figment of my imagination or not.

It's a few minutes before the shadowy figure returns to my field of vision. I scoot out from under the covers and tiptoe across the floor to get a better look. It's a man, I think. Or a very tall woman. They stand on the sidewalk across the street, hand in their pocket, fumbling for something.

When they withdraw their hand, they are holding a small square of white. A slip of paper. After pausing and scanning the page, they pull out a pencil and begin to write.

My heart flutters as I continue watching. Who are they? What are they writing? A message? A warning? What do they want? Maybe I'm being ridiculous. Maybe they're drawing a cute little portrait of the building and I'll wake up tomorrow to find it sitting on the front step, a gift. Maybe they've been struck with artistic inspiration and absolutely had to write a poem about the stillness of the night and the weeds growing through the pavement. Both of these theories are highly unlikely, but I'd rather pretend that the mysterious person stalking the house is really just a nocturnal poet, rather than a dangerous interloper.

I creep toward the window, as if the extra foot will give me a better view. All it does is cause the floorboards to emit a ghastly groan. Shit.

I hear Maeve rustle in the other room as I stumble back to my mattress. "Liz? You okay in there?"

Maeve has woken up in the kitchen, her voice making its way through the closed bedroom door.

I want to tell her to look out the window, but I know what will happen if I do. I don't want her to think I'm crazy all over again. I can play it off once, but twice? That's pushing it.

"I'm fine!" I reply. "Just headed to the bathroom."

And sure enough, when I look back out the bedroom window, the figure is gone.

Tobias Browne

42 Years Old

New York, New York

I swear I was right on the cusp of the rest of my life, you know? I mean, I guess I'd spent a couple of years in that state, just about to accomplish everything I'd ever wanted. But I mean it. Two days before the Storm I received the final callback for this feature film. A stage-to-screen adaptation of a musical—you remember the one about Greek mythology and that cult?—yeah, that one. They wanted me to play Dionysus, this really rich baritone role. I finally felt like I'd found a part that was written for me. And sure, it wasn't mine yet, but it was going to be. But I guess that doesn't matter anymore. Things can fall apart more easily than they are put together. And poof, the role was gone, and everything else with it.

CHAPTER TWENTY-ONE

The next morning, I wake up before Maeve and rush to throw on a shirt, unable to shake the memory of the stranger outside. It's like I've been possessed by the spirit of Nancy Drew as I make my way down the stairs, careful to put my weight only on the sides of each step, where the foundation is strongest. (I did, in fact, learn that from a Nancy Drew book, although I can't remember which one. There are ten thousand of them.)

I'm not sure what I'm looking for as I step outside. Maybe some reassurance that I'm not totally insane. Maybe a weed with a broken stem, trampled by the figure from last night. Maybe muddy footprints by the side of the building, even though it hasn't rained recently.

I pause by the front door, just to make sure that my wild ideas about poetry and portrait drawing weren't somehow correct. Maybe it's a letter for me. Maybe it doesn't all have to be horrible. But no slip of paper waits for me. Nothing at all.

I walk toward the center of the street, peering up at my bedroom window as I try to approximate where the person was. And as I get closer, I notice something trapped in the gap between the road and the sidewalk. So wedged in that I might not even notice. But I do notice.

A small, wooden pencil.

I've circled the perimeter of the bookstore enough times to know that pencil wasn't there before. I'm not making this up. There *was* someone out here last night. I feel relief that my suspicions have been confirmed, though any triumphant feelings are soon cut through with dread. I was right. The figure watching the store was real. That then leaves me with the question: Why were they here?

Before I can think too hard on that question, I hear Maeve call to me from upstairs. I stoop down and pick up the pencil lying discarded on the road. After glancing at it one last time, I slip it into my pocket and return inside.

• • •

That night, Maeve and I sit across from each other at the kitchen counter, both of us perched on stools as I thumb through a copy of *The Penderwicks.* There used to be only one stool up here, and one was enough for me, but I trudged downstairs and grabbed the metal one from behind the desk. It belongs up here, I've decided. The days of sitting on the floor and perching on the armchair are over.

"What do you want for dinner?" I ask, even though I'm a lousy chef. It's not like I need to be a young Gordon Ramsay right now, but I just wish things tasted a little better. I'm also secretly trying to get a conversation started so that the reveal of my early morning discovery seems less abrupt. I've held the news in all day, and the pencil is beginning to burn a hole into my pocket.

Maeve pretends to be deep in thought as she slowly rises from her seat and opens the cabinet to reveal our freshly stocked pantry.

"Hm. Looks like our options are soup, noodles, or beans."

"Oh, the variety!" I muse.

"I promise I'll lay out that trap before The Storm," Maeve replies. "We can salt the meat and dry it and keep it with us once we leave the bookstore. Have some good food for once."

She's trying to goad me, but I won't take her bait. I don't want to argue with her about leaving. Not right now. Not when she just mentioned it a couple of nights ago. There are more important things to think about, so I nod.

I riffle through one of the kitchen drawers, looking for the book of matches I could have sworn I saw Maeve drop in there yesterday. This is one of those drawers that exist in every house, filled with the stuff that doesn't fit anywhere else. Old wine corks and broken pencils with the erasers that barely work and leave behind streaky messes. Some scrap paper, but it's already been used, and the takeout menu for every single restaurant in a thirty-mile radius.

As I stand there, leaning over the drawer, tendrils of reddish hair sweeping over my face, I can feel two hands and ten long fingers spread across my back. Maeve leans closer, mouth by my ear, her breath tickling my face.

"It's a little hot for a warm dinner, don't you think?" she asks.

"And you want us to eat this cold?"

She laughs. "C'mon. I'll make it appetizing, I promise." She pushes me to the side, practically herding me into the bedroom. "Go, keep yourself occupied while I whip something up."

I pause, unsure whether now is the right time to tell her. But I have to tell her. There might never be a right time, right? I reach into my pocket and wrap my fingers around the pencil, just to make sure that it's still there before turning to Maeve.

"I think someone's been watching us," I say matter-of-factly.

I half expect Maeve to laugh and tell me that I'm ridiculous. She doesn't.

"Really?"

"I thought I was making it up, but they came back last night. They dropped their pencil too." I place it on the kitchen counter for emphasis. "And unless we're both hallucinating the same pencil, that means that they're real."

"Shit," Maeve murmurs, forcing a laugh. "Just another tally on the side of *Let's get out of here.*"

She says it like it's a joke, but I know what she's getting at. It's like she's not even listening to what I'm saying, purposely missing the point so that she can back up her own beliefs. It's not quite the reaction I was looking for, if I'm perfectly honest. I frown. "Who do you think they are?"

"I—" She pauses, thinking of the correct way to phrase her sentiments. "I don't know. Let's talk about this later, okay? Once I've had time to think. But for now, let me focus on dinner."

"What?" Her nonchalance is dumbfounding, and my mouth hangs open slightly. "Don't you care?"

Maeve huffs. "I do care, Liz. But let's talk about this once we have food in our stomachs, okay?"

That doesn't make sense. I would have expected Maeve to get angry or leap into action, coming up with the perfect plan to get to the bottom of everything, but her reaction is foreign. No part of my mind can make it compute.

"What has dinner got to do with anything?" I ask. "No, Maeve. I've waited too long to talk about this. I've kept it to myself all day, and I'd like to talk about it with you. Can you spare five minutes?"

"Fine, Liz," Maeve says, not turning to face me. "You want to talk about things? Then we can talk about leaving, too, right? If we're talking about *big, pressing issues.*" She says it like I'm a child, which then makes me feel like a child, a sense of elementary-school playground indignation rising up inside me.

"That's not fair, Maeve."

"It sounds perfectly fair to me. We talk about what you want to talk about, and so we talk about what I want to talk about too. Even Steven."

I press my lips together and glare. We're not talking about leaving. Not now. Not again, because it's not happening, and Maeve should know that. She should understand by now.

Eventually, Maeve crosses her arms. "Now let me get dinner ready, please."

With no other choice, I shuffle back into my room as Maeve shuts the door behind me. I sit down on the mattress and fiddle with the bandage on my arm, carefully pulling it out of its sling. I slowly unwrap it, one piece after the next, uncoiling it like I'm some deranged mummy. I've done this before, checking on the wound when I can, but that doesn't make it any less unsettling. I slide the stick out as my skin starts to appear, puckered and scarred from where Maeve pressed her hot metal knife. I can still hear my muffled scream echoing in my ears. I think about how I buried my face in an old T-shirt, until all I could smell was sweat and must. I think about Maeve's hand on my back, doing everything and nothing all at the same time. I think about the stranger outside. Does Maeve know who they are, or is she just worried like I am? She has to know them, I think. There's no other way to explain her reaction.

I tell myself to wait until she has time to think, and not to let the distrust in the back of my mind melt into something else. She needs a moment to process before she comes clean. Everything will be better then.

My knuckles are healing slowly, even though I still can't move the fingers attached to them. I feel removed from it all as I stare at my hand. It doesn't look like it's mine. It doesn't feel like it's mine. It's like the way people say they know something like the "back of their hand." Now I don't know the back of my hand at all. I used to know the curves, the valleys, the places where my veins pushed up slightly against the barrier of my skin. The shape of my nails and the angles of my thumb. The way these fingers cascaded over piano keys, and clutched a pencil, and strummed a guitar. I wonder if this hand will ever play, or write, or touch again. And I need it now, even more than I did before.

After inspecting my lump of arm meat for long enough, I carefully wrap it back up, positioning the ruler in the same place. I check one last time for signs of infection, even though I don't know what I'd do if I found any. Then I slide my arm back into its sling and try to forget about it completely. I look out the window at the glowing sun, almost disappearing beneath the tree line. It's a pretty view. I'm always surprised to find beauty these days. The aesthetics of the apocalypse aren't always appealing, but this sunset is gorgeous. It's Pinterest-board-worthy. A Pinterest board for the end of the world.

I'm jolted back to attention by a knock at the door.

"You better get out here, Liz!" Maeve shouts. "Hurry up! It's not going to last that long!"

I want to ask her what she could possibly be talking about, but then the door swings open and I see it, sitting on the kitchen counter.

A can of beans sits there, open and hardened enough for a matchstick to stick out of it, all lit up. At first, I'm confused. Beans and a matchstick? Is this some sort of inside joke between me and Maeve that I'm too preoccupied to remember?

Maeve beams at me as she stands beside her handiwork. Her smile is almost brighter than the flame.

"Happy birthday," she says, her voice strong and hopeful.

It's my birthday. It's my birthday? Already? Somehow it doesn't feel right that a whole year has passed, and I'm now a whole year older. We've officially slipped into August without me even realizing. I watch the matchstick, the flame getting smaller and smaller, on the cusp of extinguishing completely.

"How?" I ask, not managing to complete the sentence.

"It was on a calendar in your kitchen. I hope you don't mind that I—"

"No," I interrupt, forcing a smile onto my lips. "This is great. You—" My voice breaks off as I realize that I don't know how to explain the way I feel. I'm not even sure that I truly know how I feel. Maeve doesn't seem to mind, though. "I forgot about it," I admit at last.

She nods in response. "It's hard to celebrate when you're alone, right?"

"I can hardly remember what day it is, let alone keep track of my birthday." But it's so much more than that. I can feel a typhoon of acid welling up inside me, reminding me of what happened. Reminding me why I'm alive, and why I don't deserve to be. It's like there's a time bomb etched into my bones, and it's only a matter of seconds before I explode. Dear god, I need to explode. I need the shame and the tiredness and the desolation that weaves through my brain to overwhelm me and then finally dissipate. I need to feel normal again and quiet the ever-present voice in the back of my head whispering that it's all my fault.

"Blow out the candle," she urges, and I move closer, sliding onto the nearby stool. She follows suit, sitting down across from me.

I stare at the makeshift birthday candle, flickering ever so slightly as the wooden shaft chars, the match evaporating before my eyes. It's like when I was a kid, sharing a cake with chocolate frosting and trying to beat Thea at blowing the candles out. Her small smile visible through the warm glow, my mother trying to capture it all on camera.

Maeve smiles expectantly, nodding her head as if she's nudging me along. *That's it, you're almost there! Just blow.*

With a huff, the flame is gone, phantom-like smoke slithering up and up, fading into nothingness. I'm left with Maeve's eyes boring into mine.

"Are you okay? Did I do something wrong? I swear it was just supposed to be nice." She puts her hand on my shoulder, and I flinch. It's so small, barely even noticeable, but Maeve still curls away, her arm retreating to a comfortable, safe place in her lap, her tattoo still visible in the darkness. The moon stares up at me from her skin.

"I'm fine," I say, even though I feel like my bones are being hollowed out.

"It's okay if you're not." And just like that, every ounce of energy I have is sucked out of me. Something I didn't even realize was there in the first place.

"I—" I can't speak. No matter how perfectly my thoughts line up in my brain, they won't come out. So I take a shaky breath and start again. "I had a sister."

The truth hangs in the air between us, sucking every ounce of energy out of the atmosphere. I wait until Maeve clears her throat.

"Oh."

"Her name was Thea." I realize that this is the first time I've said her name out loud since it happened. I can feel something warm, something weak, lurking behind my eyes, ready to burst forth. Not yet. "I had a sister, a twin sister." With that, a gasp springs forth, and the tears start rolling down. "She was better than me. And stronger than me. People cared about Thea, you know?"

"I care—"

"She's gone and I'm here and it's my fault. It's my fault that she's dead." I curl my legs in, trying to disappear entirely. "Today is her birthday too."

I shouldn't be here. It hits me like a punch to the gut, sending vibrations all the way up my body. I shouldn't be here if she isn't. I shouldn't be here if my parents aren't. I shouldn't be here if so many other people aren't. And my sister was so good. So much better than me. She deserved so much better than this.

Maeve places her hand on my thigh, a soft and encouraging touch. Her nose wrinkles from the smell of smoke.

"I'm glad you're here," she says, voice firm. "I know it hurts. I know how this feels, this drowning feeling. I know how suffocating it is."

All I can do is nod, gulping down air as tears stream down my cheeks. I must look like a fool.

"But you're here. With me. Okay? And I wouldn't trade that for the world. Or what's left of it."

I run my hand under my nose, attempting to pull myself together.

"Thank you." I pause, wondering where this should go next. "You know I'm eighteen? We would have been eighteen." Laughter erupts from my lungs, and it feels right. It feels like I might spontaneously combust if I don't laugh right now. "I should be getting lottery tickets, or something. I should be going skydiving. I should be, I don't know, legally purchasing fireworks."

"Sure," Maeve replies, moving her hand and reaching out toward mine. I feel a jolt of electricity as our fingers touch. "I know."

It's a slow approach, each move a hesitation, but when our lips touch, the warmth radiates through my body. As her lips press into mine, they feel soft. They feel familiar. They feel like something I never knew I was missing. It feels like home. She places her hand on the back of my head, pulling me in closer, her lips parting around mine. When we finally pull apart, something electric wavers between us. I've never kissed someone before.

I'm blushing and realize that Maeve is too. "I'm sorry," I mutter, not sure what else to say. "I just thought that . . ."

"No. It was fine!" Maeve interrupts. "It was good!" Her

voice breaks off as she pauses, searching for the right thing to say. I watch as heat rises to her cheeks. Maeve, embarrassed? Never. "What I'm trying to say is I liked it."

When she says that, a weight is lifted from my chest and I can breathe again. "I did, too," I manage.

"Okay."

"Good."

We stare at each other for a few more seconds before Maeve lets go of my hand and plucks the matchstick out of the can of beans. The awkwardness is palpable, but for once it feels good. It feels real. It feels right. All I want to do is kiss her again.

"Bon appétit," she offers.

"I thought you were going to make it appetizing."

"That's what the matchstick was for."

I nod as Maeve fishes around in a drawer for two spoons.

"So," she says. "Tell me about your sister."

A small pang ripples through my chest. "Are you sure?"

"I wouldn't be asking if I wasn't."

I decide to start from the beginning.

CHAPTER TWENTY-TWO

"I pushed my sister into a radiator when we were little." This is what I start with. It's an odd choice, but it feels appropriate. It feels like the beginning, because as far as I know, that's the first memory I have of my sister. Pushing her into a radiator at the age of three.

"We had this chalkboard in the corner of the dining room, and it was winter, so the radiators were on full blast. It was our old house, not the one you saw—and it was from the Victorian era—so there weren't really any safety features on it," I explain. "She was using the chalkboard, and I wanted to use it to draw something pointless, so I pushed her out of the way and right into the radiator. She had burns all over her leg. My parents thought she'd be scarred for the rest of her life, and even though they eventually went away, she never let me live it down. She always reminded me. She could hold a grudge; that's for sure."

I hesitate, but Maeve stays silent. She's given me the floor.

"We were always sort of an odd pairing. No part of us really fit with each other. Everything she was good at I wasn't, and the things I was good at she didn't like. I mean, there was some overlap, but for the most part . . . She never read The Hunger Games because I was so obsessed that I basically spoiled the whole thing for her. She was a field hockey star, and I was completely inept, even though my mom enrolled us both every season.

"We weren't the sort of siblings that went everywhere with each other. Some twins we knew were inseparable, wearing matching clothes and hanging out with the same friends. We weren't like that. We always gave each other space. She had her friends and I had mine, and we'd bump into each other sometimes in the halls at school. We were individuals, and we liked it that way, but we were still close.

"We told each other our deepest, darkest secrets. We complained about our parents. We'd do each other's homework in middle school. When I came out, she was the first person I told, and she told me that she'd known for years. She probably knew before I had even figured it out. I think we knew each other better than we knew ourselves.

"She just cared so immensely about me. No matter what was going on, she always made sure that *I* was all right, and yet there I was pushing her into radiators."

I pause, feeling the tears welling in my eyes once again. "I didn't deserve that sort of love."

"Don't be ridiculous," Maeve finally murmurs. "She cared about you for a reason."

"She was just so *good*" is all I can manage to say. "She was so good, and I was just . . ."

"You're good, too," Maeve whispers, grabbing my left hand and holding it tight. "You're the best person I know."

I don't know what to say in response, so I don't say anything at all. She doesn't know half of it. If she did, she might hate me. She might leave me, too, and I don't know what I'd do then. I'm not sure how I'd keep going.

CHAPTER TWENTY-THREE

JUNE 21: BEFORE THE FIRST STORM

We've never had a storm drill before. At least, I don't think we have. Sure, we've had fire drills, and lockdown drills, and shelter-in-place drills, and evacuation drills, but never a storm drill. There was never any need for it. Maybe in Florida there could be hurricane drills, but in New Jersey we never really get weather horrible enough to require a drill, and if we ever do, it normally travels up the entire East Coast before making its way to us.

But I suppose this is always how it happens. You don't need a drill until you do.

We didn't need lockdown drills until we did, and now they're mandated. At least twice a month. We crouch in the corner, back against the wall, and wait. We wait as the school security guard makes his way down the hallway and jiggles the doorknob. We sit in the dark and wait for the loudspeaker to come on and let us know that we can go back to whatever it is we are learning in calculus.

Ms. Carey is standing at the front of the room, flicking through a PowerPoint presentation half-heartedly. It's filled with stock photos of menacing clouds and fallen trees and big yellow Caution signs. It's all going in one ear and out the other.

The shooter drills started in third grade. Either that, or third grade was the year that I was finally able to understand what it all meant.

I remember my teacher sat us down on the rug and told us that we'd have to hide in the corner of the room, between the dots that she had stuck to the classroom's cabinets. That way we wouldn't be seen from the hall.

I remember she let us ask her questions afterward, but I'm sure she regretted that decision almost immediately. I raised my hand and asked her what would happen if a shooter broke the glass on the window. She said that the glass was reinforced with wire. Another kid asked her what would happen if a shooter made it through the classroom door. That was when my teacher decided to send us out for recess.

Ms. Carey looks stressed, her cheeks flushed as she gestures wildly toward her presentation. Any change is scary, but this sort of change is terrifying. Knowing that *this is just how life is now* is terrifying.

When I was in third grade, I didn't think about what implications a lockdown drill would have on my life. On society. But now, I understand this means that things have gotten bad enough for this to be necessary. And, judging from the papers my dad leaves scattered on the kitchen counter, it only continues to get worse. There's a storm coming; the papers seem sure of it. And it'll be bad. They keep testing emergency-alert systems on our phones and running simulations on TV, but the truth is, no one knows what it'll look like when it comes.

"Sometime during this class period they're going to announce a weather-related emergency on the loudspeaker," Ms. Carey says as she pauses on the last slide of her presentation. There's a picture of smiling stick-figure students on the screen. I fiddle with the eraser of my mechanical pencil. "I'm letting you know now that this is a *drill.* There's no need to be alarmed." My history teacher looks very alarmed. "You are going to line up in single file and make your way into the hall—"

"And I thought that our days of single file were over once we made it to high school."

I turn around and see the boy in the seat behind me beaming, pleased with himself. The girl beside him leans closer.

"C'mon, Dawson," she whispers. "I would've thought that you enjoyed being bossed around by powerful women."

I roll my eyes and turn back to the whiteboard at the front of the room.

"Now, it'll be crowded in the hallway," my teacher continues as she closes her laptop. "I know that the presentation provided by the school said to sit with your backs against the lockers. Unfortunately, there isn't quite enough room for that."

There's only one high school in town, and it doesn't take a genius to realize how overcrowded it is. Kids are packed in like sardines, even though the school board claims that there aren't more than twenty-five students in each class. I count thirty-seven.

"Just try to find a place on the floor, and if you can't, then stand in an open doorway."

A hand shoots up in the front of the room. "Should we go inside the lockers if there isn't enough space? It might be safer."

Ms. Carey lets out an exasperated sigh. I can't say that I

blame her. "I'm just going off what it says in the memo I got from administration, okay? And in there, it doesn't say anything about lockers, so *please* stay out of them."

The loudspeaker crackles to life above us, right on cue. *"Attention, faculty and staff. Attention, faculty and staff, this is a weather-related emergency. A weather-related emergency."* And then, the voice disappears.

It takes a moment before any of us move. It takes us a moment to remember what our teacher told us to do literally ten seconds ago. But then we stand and shuffle across the linoleum floor toward the hallway like a herd of lemmings.

I grab my phone from my desk and slide it into my pocket. I learned the hard way to never leave anything important in the classroom during any type of drill. Once, I left my laptop inside during a fire drill only to discover that it wasn't actually a drill. Someone had lit a bottle of hand sanitizer on fire in one of the bathrooms. It wasn't until the fire trucks pulled up that I discovered my error. I had to wait two hours to rescue my computer.

Once we make it into the hallway, I realize that my teacher wasn't exaggerating. It's a zoo out here, with too many students pushing and shoving against each other, trying to find room to sit. I can barely see Thea at the other end of the hall, chatting with her friend on the floor as she avoids getting trampled by three members of the football team. It's not like I see her very often at home either. With Mom and Dad spending more and more time away from each other, working late or seeing friends, she's taken the opportunity to spend her afternoons and evenings at her boyfriend's house.

I find a spot by the boys' bathroom and slowly lower myself

into a squat, trying to distance myself from my neighbors. My teacher stands by her classroom door, struggling to get a head count as if she could have somehow lost a student in the three feet we walked from the classroom to the hallway.

A Spanish teacher cups his hands around his mouth. "Remember what we said in the presentation," he bellows. "Hands over your head!"

We all pause, whispers rippling through the crowd. A few kids look around, waiting to see if their friends will obey the instruction, not wanting to be the only one who looks stupid. Eventually, everyone falls into line, and we follow his directions.

I clasp my hands around my head and brace for nonexistent impact.

CHAPTER TWENTY-FOUR

I stare at Maeve as she hands me a sawed-off piece of wood. We've got a system going: she cuts and I throw, sending each part of the tree through the hole in the wall. Teamwork makes the dream work, or whatever.

She pauses to wipe a drop of sweat from her brow, the slight breeze coming through the hole doing nothing to stop the might of the summer sun. I can feel the heat, too, making my arm itch underneath its slightly dirty bandages. I'll have to change it out later, and I'm sure Maeve will insist on helping.

Part of me squirms inside from the floating feeling she gives me. A smaller part of me wishes I'd never let myself need her. Because I do. That's the truth and it washes over me, like it will drown me and leave me for dead. I need Maeve, even though I swore I would never need anyone ever again.

I've been down this road before. Waking up every morning and knowing someone will be there, until they aren't, and they leave like everyone else does, and you're alone. Eva left because I couldn't get her to stay, and now I've gone and let Maeve in. I can only hope that she needs me too.

In a sudden moment of weakness, I move toward her and give her a peck on the cheek.

Maeve turns to me, a small smile on her lips. "What was that for?"

I don't know what that was for. It just felt necessary. So I tell her the truth. "I don't know. It sorta felt right."

"Sorta felt right." Maeve laughs. "Is it possible that I've made the unflappable Liz Flannery tongue-tied?"

"I'm hardly unflappable."

Maeve blushes before turning back to the remnants of the tree and the hole in the wall. I want to say something else, do something else, to make this last longer, but I don't know what.

She pauses as she reaches down toward another log, ready to pass it over. Then she straightens her spine and turns back toward me.

"I liked it, you know," she says.

With that, she's back to work, as if she hasn't just dropped a major revelation on me. I lean against the counter so that my legs don't turn to jelly beneath me.

"We're practically domestic," Maeve says as she hands me another piece of wood.

"Domestic?"

"Yeah," she confirms, wiping her brow with the back of her hand. "I bring home the bacon, and you wait on me hand and foot like a good wife."

"Wife?" I say, my voice slightly strangled. "I think that mentality is slightly toxic. I'd like to believe we've moved past the 1960s as a society."

"Don't knock it till you've tried it."

"I *am* trying it," I retort.

Maeve finally turns toward me, her eyebrows raised.

"You're telling me that you don't enjoy this?"

"What, being your dutiful assistant?"

"You're doing more than assisting," Maeve corrects. "You're boosting morale. That's equally important."

"It's not the same."

A grin appears on her face as she takes a step toward me, hopping onto the counter beside me. She rests her head on my shoulder. I'm the perfect height for that sort of thing.

"Fine. If you want to be in charge, then you should teach me something."

"Like what?" I ask, wondering what I could possibly teach Maeve.

"Teach me to shelve books," she responds, gesturing at a pile of books at the end of the counter. "I'm sure you have an incredibly complex system."

Maeve wiggles off the counter, landing on her feet and striding over to the pile to give it an inspection.

"It's all alphabetical," I mutter. "It's nothing groundbreaking."

"Hey! For our ancestors, the alphabet was pretty darn groundbreaking."

The way the sun filters in through the front window makes the room glow with golden light. And it also makes Maeve look even prettier, even though she's sort of sweaty and her hands are covered with sawdust.

I'm the type of person who avoids going near water at the beach because I hate it when sand sticks to my feet. I'm the type of person who avoids getting into a pool because I don't want to be wet later in the day. But with Maeve, I'm okay with the sweat and the sawdust, especially because I also probably don't smell the best. How good can either of us smell if we've gone days without a proper bath?

So I lean in just a little bit as Maeve continues monologuing about the alphabet and carpentry. She sounds like me, ranting about minuscule facts from the books on the shelves.

She pauses, eyebrows raised, but doesn't ask a question. I don't give her an opportunity, kissing her once again before she has a chance. She doesn't pull away, wrapping her sawdusty hand around my waist and pulling me close until I have to break away to take a breath.

"You know, the word *alphabet* comes from the first two letters of the Latin alphabet," I offer.

"Is that your version of a romantic comment?"

I smile. "Alpha and beta."

"I guess that makes sense," Maeve replies. "Where did you find that nugget of wisdom? *100 Ways to Romance Women*?"

"Nah. The eleventh volume of *Fun Facts for Kids!* Naturally. You should read it sometime."

"You know I don't do that sort of thing."

I grin. "One day I'll find something on these shelves that'll float your boat. I swear."

"Sure you will."

Now it's Maeve's turn to lean toward me, cradling the back of my head as our lips touch. I wrap my good arm around her torso and return the favor.

The front door slams open with a gust of wind, no doubt the fault of the busted lock, but I ignore it, pulling Maeve even closer to me.

Eventually, we break apart, Maeve giggling at some nonexistent joke. I'm just about to make some witty comment when I hear a voice.

"I didn't mean to interrupt."

Maeve's cheeks turn bright red as we both turn to face our unexpected visitor. It takes a second for my eyes to adjust to the bright light streaming in through the front windows, but then, I realize who I'm staring at.

Her blond hair in a braid down her back. The tattoo next to her ear of ivy, just barely visible. As I take in each detail, my heart twinges.

She breaks the silence for me.

"Hi, Liz." There's that voice. That all-too-familiar voice.

"Hi, Eva," I manage. "Long time no see."

CHAPTER TWENTY-FIVE

Eva is here. Eva is *here.* The thought races through my mind on a loop, along with about a million other thoughts all colliding and falling over each other in my messed-up brain.

Maeve is just confused. And shocked. She raises an eyebrow and leans in closer to me. *"Eva?"*

I don't respond. I can't respond. I've forgotten how to speak.

She came back, just like she said she would. Sure, it took a little bit longer than I might have wanted it to, but she came. And she's here. I want to run toward her. To hug her and tell her how much I've missed her. To tell her everything that's happened to me since she left. A part of me wants to stare and get used to the feeling of seeing her again. The sound of her voice. The color of her hair. The gleam in her eyes. But I also know how things ended, and I know that things are different now. I decide to let her make the first move.

But Maeve moves first, reaching out with her left hand. "Maeve," she offers.

Eva takes her hand.

"Eva." Her voice is hoarse. Hoarser than I remember.

"I know."

Eva looks toward me, as if for approval, before turning back to Maeve. "I used to work here, before I—"

"Before she left," I finish.

"Were you fired?" Maeve quips. But Maeve knows the truth. I've told her the truth. And Eva does too.

Eva grimaces before responding. "Something like that."

I want to interject. Say something smart and witty that'll ease the tension and make this feel familiar. But I can't think of anything, so Maeve just keeps talking.

"So why are you back?" she asks. At first, it seems like an innocent-enough question, but then she adds, "She doesn't need you anymore, you know that?"

My mouth drops open as I look at Maeve, shocked by her audacity. She doesn't apologize. She doesn't even look remotely sorry for what she's said. Instead, she cocks an eyebrow, challenging Eva to disagree. But Eva says nothing.

"Absence makes the heart grow fonder, right, Eva?" I offer her a smile. An olive branch.

Eva takes it gladly. "If you say so."

• • •

Maeve is taking a nap in the bedroom upstairs as Eva and I talk. Alone.

I can't help but inspect her face. She seems different. She has smile lines now. They were never there before. Has she been smiling more than she used to? Or has she just gotten older?

Stray wisps of hair frame her face, doing little to hide her icy blue eyes. She seems older. Different. I'm not sure how I should feel about it.

"So. . . . Maeve?" she says, attempting to gently slide into conversation.

"She's a friend. Her tent broke, and she needed a place to stay, so she's here for the time being." Eva doesn't need to know everything. Not yet.

Eva nods. I can tell by her expression that she doesn't believe me, but she doesn't question me.

Instead, she says, "You seem happy."

"I am." And sure, that's not the whole story, but it's a general summary. I'm happy right now, or at least happier than I've been recently, and that's all that matters.

"How's the old bookstore holding up?" Eva asks, mockingly rapping the counter with her knuckles.

I laugh, trying to signal to her that it's all right that she's here, and that we can leave the past behind us for one conversation. She lets out a half-hearted chuckle as well, absentmindedly running her fingers through her hair.

"What, besides the hole in the wall? Pretty good. I mean, Maeve's been helping. For a second there, I thought that I'd lost my running water, but she got that squared away."

"And your arm?"

I look down at it, disdainfully. "You should have seen the other guy," I quip.

Eva's eyes widen. "Did you get into a fight?"

"No, nothing like that. It was a generator. I may have done something stupid."

"Somehow I don't doubt that," Eva murmurs. "Does the generator work?"

Of course she still cares about me, and this building. "I'm sure that it does. Although I kind of busted it up with my hand, so it'll take some supplies to get it humming again. Maeve will fix it once we have what she needs."

Eva just nods before asking, "How do you know her?"

And for a moment, it's just like old times, the pair of us chatting about mundane things like girls. It feels nice. It feels right.

"It's actually a funny story," I start before realizing that Eva might not find it funny at all. I don't think break-ins really count as funny for most members of polite society. But it's funny to me, so I continue. "She actually sort of broke in while I was—"

"Broke in?"

"Yeah." The worried look on her face means that she does not, in fact, find it funny.

"You have to be more careful than that, Liz. You can't just trust anyone who walks in through your front door."

Something tightens inside me. I'm glad to see Eva, of course, but it feels strange for her to be telling me off for letting people in when she left me in the first place.

"I trust her."

"I doubt you know very much about her," Eva grumbles.

"She saved my life."

Eva looks like she's ready to make another comment, but she bites her tongue, her chest heaving. A few seconds pass. "I wanted to tell you that I'm sorry."

"It's fine," I reply. "It's okay. I forgive you." And I do mean it. I think. What matters now is that Eva is here. She's back. And I'd rather focus on the present than rehash the past.

"But you shouldn't. I should have talked to you before I left."

"You didn't. And that's okay. You're back now, and that's all that matters."

Eva doesn't try to argue. Instead, she places her hand on my arm. It's an awkward maneuver, her fingers shaking slightly as they make contact. I don't brush it away. And even though it's not a hug, not like the one she gave me when she thought I was leaving for college and would never return to New Jersey, it has to count for something.

"I have to tell you something too," Eva murmurs.

"So you didn't come here just to ask for my forgiveness?"

She looks offended, like she's about to defend herself, but she doesn't. She chews her bottom lip.

"I hate to be the bearer of bad news," she mutters, so softly that I almost can't hear her.

I steady myself preemptively. *Bad news* has a new meaning nowadays. Bad news used to mean *I lost my wallet* or *I got a parking ticket on Sunday; isn't that crazy?* Now bad news could be *I got my arm eaten by a generator* or *I've run out of food and water.* Still, I don't know what she's going to say. It might not be that bad. Whatever she has to tell me could be the new equivalent of not-so-bad news, as in, *I haven't run out of food and water, but all I have to eat is creamed corn; doesn't that suck?* But the look on Eva's face tells me that it isn't.

"Another Storm is coming," she says, her voice hoarse.

I roll my eyes, releasing a shuddering breath. "I know that

already." That's not bad at all. Nothing that I wasn't already dealing with.

But Eva's not finished. "It will be here in a week. Maybe less, maybe more, but it's coming."

That can't be true. Fear wraps around my brain as I glance around the room, from the hole in the wall to the broken door to the missing windowpanes. "No, it's not. We still have a month." Peacoat Man didn't say anything about it coming a week and a half from now. He said we had a month. Maeve said the same thing. I was planning on us having a month. Maybe more if we were lucky. So who's right? Eva or Maeve?

Eva's face is solemn as she looks at me, her skin almost gray. "We had until the end of August last year, sure, but that's not reliable data, right? I mean, you should know that."

And I do know that, no matter how much my heart might try to contest it. I can't rely on last year to determine this year. That's just not statistically sound. As my AP Stats teacher would say, it's not a large enough sample. As our alien overlords would say, ⊬O̲ՈϞɯ ՈՈᘏ⚲ɯ[|], which roughly translates to *You're royally screwed.* But I'm not quite ready to give up just yet.

"How do you know?"

"A friend of mine," she says, and the words sting a little, the feeling only made worse by the fact that she paused before saying *friend.* Maybe I forgot that she could have friends outside of here. That life went on for her after she left, and that I could be replaced. "He's an amateur storm chaser—or used to be. Meteorologist adjacent. He eats this stuff up. He's right about these sorts of things ninety-five percent of the time, from drizzles to thunderstorms. If he says it's coming, then it is."

"Are you sure?" I ask, my voice quivering just slightly. There's still a chance she's wrong, but as I start playing the facts over, I start to realize we might have less time than we thought. I think about the birds, and the deer, and the rabbits. They weren't gone until mid-August last year. And the wind has been picking up, the temperature getting cooler than it should be at this time of year.

"Would I have come all this way if I wasn't?" Eva replies.

The question stings at first. How could I be so thoughtless? Of course, she wouldn't just come here unless she had some important reason. She wouldn't come back here if she didn't have to. She made it very clear that she left for a reason. But then, realization sets in, and it's like a stone has been dropped on top of my head. The Storm might be coming in less than a week, and I'm not prepared. I look down at my useless hand. I have so much work to do.

"I had to tell you," Eva says solemnly. "I wasn't just going to leave you to die like that. I can't have that on my conscience."

The thought of that makes my heart skip a beat. She still cares. I knew she still cared.

"I've made it this long. This Storm won't take me out," I reply. "I can promise you that much."

CHAPTER TWENTY-SIX

We sit together in a lopsided triangle, sipping on room-temperature soup. I'm not sure I have the stomach for it. The quiet that exists among us is deafening, and every time I look up from my bowl there are two sets of eyes staring at me. Maeve turns to Eva, glaring, but Eva refuses to look up, for reasons I've yet to discern. Maybe she's jealous.

I feel like the connector of two different friend groups. Like when it's your birthday party and you sit at the head of the table with a dozen other kids looking toward you for guidance. You act as the bridge between the kids from your art class and the kids from your soccer team and try to make awkward conversation about how much you all love Skittles and hope that they don't wonder what they're doing there.

I look between Maeve and Eva, who both peer back at me expectantly. Eva looks ridiculous, three years older than me yet waiting for me to tell her what to do. I'm not sure whom I should look at—Eva or Maeve? I keep glancing between the two of them, feeling as though any time I turn my attention to one, I'm somehow offending the other.

"We'll be fine," I tell them both, trying to hide the fear from my voice. It still breaks, but both Maeve and Eva don't notice, or they pretend not to. "Remember that time a raccoon got loose in the store? And you and Laurel both totally freaked out, and it tried to eat the limited edition of *The Brothers Karamazov*? It was a hellish ten minutes, but the raccoon ran out, and we fixed the damage it did, and everything was all right in the end."

"Sure. I remember," Eva murmurs, although it doesn't really sound like she wants to at all. She purses her lips, her eyes scanning the space between me and Maeve. "Have you seen this place lately? It was bad when I was here, but now . . ."

Maeve just sits there grimacing, so I decide to defend the both of us. "We have the supplies." I look toward Maeve, who just slowly nods, as if to say, *We do. That is true.* I wish she would look at me. I wish she would be my conversational cheerleader. But she stays silent. So I continue on alone. "It shouldn't be that bad. I mean, easy for me to say when I'm not the one doing hard labor, but . . . we have the supplies, right? We can fix that hole in a week." No one corrects me or says that we might not even have an entire week at this point.

Maeve turns to Eva, her jaw clenched. "We don't need your help, Eva. If that's what you're asking."

Her tone catches me by surprise, solemn and grating. She hasn't been like this since I first met her, and even then it wasn't this bad. This isn't some wry, biting sarcasm. This is animosity, an anger that I can't even begin to grasp. She stares at Eva, as if daring her to break, and Eva stares back, her jaw clenched. I ignore them and instead try not to think about the other things on my to-do list. I don't have time for their weirdness right now. The windows. The roof. The front door. Maeve's voice echoes through my head. *I'll go on a real hunting trip before The Storm comes.* We didn't even stop to think that there would be no animals to catch, even if we did have a trap.

We're in a time crunch, a ruthless countdown that was just shortened by weeks, but I'm stuck pretending that it's okay. I think back to an essay I wrote before I graduated from high school, about the five stages of grief. Denial, bargaining, anger, depression, and acceptance. Not always in that order, but I'm feeling the first one right now. Some part of me won't believe that this might be how it ends. For real this time.

"We'll be fine," I tell Eva, trying to give Maeve's statement a friendlier sentiment. "You don't have to worry about us."

She shakes her head as she looks back down at her bowl of soup. I'm feeling a lot less hungry than I was before.

"If you're fine, then you're fine," she says.

This isn't like Old Eva. The old Eva would have questioned me for longer. She would have continued talking to me until she drilled into my head that I wasn't, in fact, *fine.* Old Eva would have gone on and on about acid rain and how "fine" doesn't cut it in these situations. Old Eva would have pestered me until I admitted the truth, but New Eva seems resigned. She's done her job, cleared her conscience.

I can't help but wonder how Maeve feels, sitting next to me, even though it feels like we're miles apart. If Eva weren't here, she'd just tell me if I was being foolish or ridiculous, or she'd make fun of me like she always does. But she sits there quietly, hardly saying anything at all. She refuses to speak to Eva any more than she has to. I never took Maeve to be a jealous person, but people can be surprising in unprecedented situations.

I reach underneath the kitchen counter slowly, tentatively, until my fingers touch Maeve's. She doesn't squirm away. She waits, allowing me to wrap my hand around hers. I squeeze it gently as if I'm never letting go.

I turn toward Eva. "So are you back, then?"

Maeve puts down her spoon and turns to look at Eva fully, for the first time since we started our meal. "I'm sure that you can't afford to stay very long." Her voice is cold.

Eva nods. "Yeah, I've got to head home. But it's pretty far away, so I was planning on staying the night and leaving in the morning, if that's okay with you guys." She looks from Maeve to me and then back to Maeve. "The trip is dangerous in the dark."

"Where are you headed?" I ask.

"I've got a group of my own," Eva replies. "It's not much, but it's something."

"Oh." I can't pretend that the news doesn't hurt just a little bit, but what was I expecting? That she would come back and stay and we'd all live happily together? She's not cool enough to cultivate the totally awesome loner vibe that I have. Used to have. "Are they as groovy as I am?"

Eva looks down at her lap. "We don't have to talk about them." Then she looks up, shaking her head. "Sorry. It's just that I'm boring. You're more interesting than I am."

I feel the heat rising to my cheeks, and I look away. Still, some part of me senses that her words are insincere, no matter how much I might want to believe them. She's just trying to humor me.

"I *will* say that Maeve certainly makes things more interesting. Things have been nonstop here recently, for better or for worse."

I turn to glance at Maeve, who bites her tongue.

"Well, I don't want to ruin what you've got going on here."

"You could stay longer," I offer, although with Maeve acting like this, I'm not sure that would be in any of our best interests. Why does she refuse to just play nice for a few hours? "If you wanted to, of course. I'd love to have you here."

Eva shakes her head. "I wish I could."

"That's probably for the best," Maeve interjects, her voice hard. She still doesn't look back at me. Maybe if she looked back at me, she'd understand. Maybe if she would just talk to me, she would realize that Eva is a friend. Not an enemy. But Maeve remains oblivious, trapped in her own head.

• • •

Eva sleeps out in the living room.

Maeve and I share the bedroom. We share the mattress too, which is an exciting development, except that I'm not sleeping. I'm staring at Maeve, who is trying to pretend that she's tired.

"Why do you hate her?" I ask.

Maeve finally gives up the act and rolls over to face me. "What?"

"Why do you hate Eva?"

"I don't hate her," Maeve murmurs after pausing for a couple of seconds.

All I can do is laugh. "You haven't said more than one word to her the entire time she's been here. You're cold. You're distant."

"Because I know that she hurt you," Maeve grumbles. But that doesn't make any sense, because I never told Maeve that.

"That's in the past."

Maeve huffs, her eyes narrowing. "That doesn't mean anything."

"But I forgave her," I reply. "You don't have to hold a grudge, because *I'm* not holding a grudge. You can't be more upset with her than I am."

"Yes, I can."

Maeve rolls over once again, and I'm now looking at her back.

"Will you be nicer to her, for me?" I ask, unsure if Maeve is going to even respond.

"Liz, please don't do this right now." Her voice is tired and well worn.

"Just think about it, okay?"

Maeve doesn't respond.

• • •

I can hear them whispering in the kitchen when they think I'm asleep, even though I'm sure they think they're being super quiet and stealthy. I don't know when Maeve was able to sneak out of the room without waking me, but I mentally add *ninja* to my list of things that Maeve is inexplicably good at. Still, they're doing a good enough job that I can't make out every word from my bed, just the important ones.

It's odd that they're talking, and talking without me, sneaking around in the middle of the night to talk about god knows what. Especially considering Maeve's hostility and Eva's reluctance to return in the first place. And maybe it makes me self-centered to think that they shouldn't have anything to discuss without me in the room, but it's true. What could Eva possibly have to say to someone she knows nothing about? Why wouldn't they include me?

But as their voices rise, I can't help but wonder if there's something I'm missing. A dimension to this situation that I can't even begin to understand.

"Go to hell, Eva," Maeve snaps. Something slams down on the kitchen counter, and I'd like to think it was her hand rather than something more menacing. "You can't pull the wool over my eyes like you did—"

The end of her sentence is too quiet to hear as wind whistles outside, muffling whatever's going on in the kitchen.

"You don't know—don't pretend like you know what's going on."

"Then tell her. Tell her about—and how—came here to—do you think that she'd be proud of you? Do you think she'd still—?"

There are too many gaps in their conversation for me to understand what's going on. It leaves me with more questions than answers, but I try to remember each one.

As I roll over in bed, staring at the ceiling, I try to fill in the blanks, trying to solve a puzzle that I might not want to know the answer to.

Kat Delgado
16 years old
Morristown, New Jersey

My mom swore up and down that the National Guard was going to come. That they'd fly in with choppers, guns blazing. It was like she was counting down the hours. She'd walk down the stairs and take a look at me as I watched the water swirling outside, and she'd announce her best estimate for when the government was going to show up and save us. "Just forty-eight hours!" she'd say, or sometimes she'd be more specific and say, "It'll be only twenty-seven hours from now." I don't know where she was getting those numbers from. But she kept saying it because we both thought that this was something that had happened only here. Not across the entire country. Not so widespread. And we still don't even know about the rest of the world. But as the days passed, and no one came, we started to understand. No one was coming to save us.

CHAPTER TWENTY-SEVEN

JULY 19: BEFORE THE FIRST STORM

Thea was busy kissing her boyfriend on the living room couch, so I decided to walk to work today. She has the car keys, and I'm not eager to interrupt. It's not far, but Mom prefers if we drive because I have a bad habit of walking with earbuds in at all times and almost getting run over by cars. I like to think that it's worth it. Mom disagrees. Mom is away for the week, staying in upstate New York with some relatives because she needs some time away. Away from Dad. Away from us. Away from all of us. So the house is silent, except for Thea and her boyfriend, and I am alone.

My earbuds are in as I half jog across the street. One thing I've always appreciated about the bookstore is the fact that there's no dress code. I used to work at a local pizzeria where all the employees wore matching shirts, and by the third day of the week it smelled so strongly of smoke and garlic that I couldn't bear it. The bookstore is much more casual. Still, I'm kicking myself for not putting on a sturdier pair of sneakers this morning, since I'll be spending my afternoon standing behind a register.

A little bell rings above my head as I step inside. My

coworker Laurel spots me from the back of the store. Eva is nowhere to be found, meaning she's probably downstairs scarfing down the rest of her lunch.

"Can you get the register?" Laurel asks, her voice carrying throughout the tiny store. I nod and acknowledge the woman standing by the checkout.

I slide behind the front counter and plaster on my best and brightest customer-service smile, tucking a stray strand of hair behind my ear. I decided to give myself an impromptu haircut last night, and I'm afraid that I may have cut the front pieces a little *too* short.

"Would you like a bag for these?" I ask as I begin scanning the woman's books, one by one.

"I'm fine, thanks," the woman says, smiling back. "Save the trees."

I want to tell her that one paper bag isn't going to save that many trees. I want to tell her that even though she refuses the bag, the tree has already been killed and chopped into tiny pieces and turned into a bag. The journey is over for the little tree that later became this bag.

"Your total is going to be thirty-six-oh-eight," I tell the woman, nudging the books toward her.

The woman says nothing in response as she shoves her credit card into the fancy little machine. She squints slightly and scribbles a hasty signature with her finger. Then she pauses and looks up at me, as if performing some sort of inspection. I'm suddenly very uncomfortable, so I train my eyes on a stack of Shirley Jackson books on the shelf just above her eye level.

She clears her throat, and I muster yet another customer-service smile.

“Do you go to Middlebury?”

“What?” And then I realize that she’s looking at my shirt. My shirt that very clearly reads *MIDDLEBURY COLLEGE*. “Oh. Yeah, I am. Next year.”

“I went there!” She beams. “Loved every second of it!”

I don’t quite know what to say, so I say, “I’m so glad.”

“You’ll love it,” the woman promises, although I’m not sure how she could be so sure. She knows absolutely nothing about me.

“I’m very excited,” I say, even though I haven’t yet figured out how I feel about leaving home. Sure, leaving high school was exciting. It was fantastic, actually, but leaving the bookstore seems a whole lot harder. Leaving home feels a whole lot harder.

“Well, congratulations,” the woman says. “College is the best four years of your life!” How depressing must her life be that the four years she spent broke and stressed were the best four of her life? I don’t think she means for the statement to sound threatening, but they cut through me like a knife.

And with that, she scoops up her books, and I’m alone with my thoughts.

• • •

At first, I don’t notice that Eva has stayed late. Sure, she normally leaves early on Mondays, but I figure that she has some extra shelving or filing or receiving to do.

I begin to wonder only when Eva asks me to shelve in the kids’ room. The kids’ room is spotless. I know this because I shelved in the kids’ room at the start of my shift. When I make my way back there, of course, I find that everything is mostly in order, with only a couple of picture books scattered on the floor. I'm offended that they would even dare to question my meticulous organization.

I pick up the books from the floor and check my watch. It's almost seven. Closing time. Eva shouldn't still be here, right?

But I decide, once again, not to question it and turn instead to the picture-book shelf. I sing the alphabet song a few times in my head as I put away the copies. I always joke that I forget the alphabet on a regular basis. Eva laughs, but it's not a lie. I actually can't tell what letter comes after which without singing through the entire alphabet song. It's a fatal flaw . . . my Achilles' heel.

It's a few more minutes before I hear Eva call my name from the other room. There's one picture book left, and I slide it into place before jogging back toward the front of the store.

Eva and Laurel stand side by side, a cupcake in each of their hands as I approach.

"Surprise!" Eva says.

"What?"

Laurel just laughs. "Happy almost last day!"

"Oh!" I say, like I forgot. But how could I forget? I take the cupcake in hand and pick idly at the waxy pink liner. At least the frosting-to-cake ratio is just right. The more frosting, the better. A cupcake without enough frosting isn't even worth it.

Looking at Laurel and Eva, at their wide, beaming faces, I feel sick. In the glow of a single lit candle, I feel the warmth of the gesture radiate around me. Things are a mess right now, in the world and at home. But here, I feel safe. How can I leave this place that I love? Suddenly the cupcake feels like a hand grenade. One wrong move and everything will blow up in my face.

Eva hands me a card.

"Open it later."

I nod. "Thanks, guys. You really didn't have to do this."

"We wanted to," Laurel replies. "We're trying to persuade you not to leave us."

I force a half-hearted smile as I look at them. "I wish I didn't have to."

CHAPTER TWENTY-EIGHT

By the time Maeve and I wake up in the morning, Eva is already ready to leave. I can hear her rustling about in the kitchen, trying unsuccessfully to be quiet.

Maeve looks at me as I roll over, our faces inches from one another, her leg resting on top of mine. I used to hate sharing a bed with Thea on family vacations, but this is better. This feels right.

She raises her eyebrows as if to say, *Why in god's name is someone up this early*? I don't ask her about their conversation last night. If I ask, she'll know that I know and she'll shut down. I might get more information if I wait it out. If I'm a little bit gentler. But I've never really been the gentlest person in the world.

I glance out the window, and my breath catches as I do. Sure, the sun has just risen, but that's not what my eyes gravitate toward. Clouds dwell on the horizon, so small that I can barely see them, but I know that they're there. Everything outside is darker than usual, the blue sky faded into a sad gray. It just makes me want to get working on the downstairs wall even sooner, and I wiggle out of my blankets. Maeve pretends not to notice, although I can see her biting her lip as she steals a quick look outside. She can sense it too.

I pull on a fresh T-shirt over my tattered sports bra. My arm is still too sore to lift, so I fumble with the fabric, trying to gently guide my arm through its sleeve. It's not clean, but it's been rinsed recently, and I can't find any stains on it as I inspect the fabric. Emblazoned on the front are the words *DWIGHT D. EISENHOWER MIDDLE SCHOOL SCIENCE FAIR CHAMPION.* I have never won a science fair, nor have I ever participated in one, but the shirt is a hand-me-down from a cousin, and so I wear it with pride. I also wear it in a vain attempt to erase my horribly embarrassing science demonstration from freshman year. Neither Maeve nor Eva needs to know about my shoddy history with physics.

I slowly rise from the floor, using the edge of the desk chair to steady myself, and walk toward the living room.

I knock on the door hesitantly, attempting to avoid startling Eva. I have a bad habit of doing that. I tend to move silently and appear behind people when they least expect it. When I was five, I thought it was cool, almost like I had some top secret superpower, but most of my family and friends would beg to differ. If I recall correctly, Eva found it "unnerving."

"Can I come in?" I ask. I shouldn't be walking on eggshells around Eva. She should be used to me.

I don't hear anything except for the faint rustle of sheets as Maeve creeps out of bed behind me.

Then the door creaks open in front of me. Eva is standing there, her hair neatly braided.

"Did I wake you up?" Eva asks as I walk past her into the kitchen. She already has her backpack in her hand, her shoelaces knotted. I know what she was going to do if she'd had a few more minutes alone. She's done it before.

"Not at all," I reply before pausing. "Why? Were you trying to sneak out again?" She looks embarrassed before shaking her head. "I'm joking, I swear."

Maeve appears in the kitchen, her hair also braided down her back, although slightly messier than Eva's neat plaits. I feel like I've been left out of a club.

"I've got some walking to do," Eva says finally. "I should probably head out." She glances tentatively out the window, and I follow her gaze. She's noticed the clouds too. My blood curdles as I stare at them, looming.

"Unless you want to stay," I reply, offering a small shrug. Maeve says nothing.

Eva takes a slow step forward, and at first I don't understand what she's doing, but then she reaches out and wraps her arms around me, holding me close. It's warm, if awkward. I've grown an inch since we saw each other last. It's different, she's different, I'm different. Still, I can't bring myself to pull away, can't bring myself to let go. This is the goodbye we never got. Last time I was too tense. Last time I didn't hug her and then spent the next month wishing I had.

There's a part of me that wants to beg her to stay. There's a part of me that's wishing I didn't have to. But I've spent so much time waiting for Eva to return and make my life work again, I didn't realize it was functioning without her. Time has gone on. I have gone on. And Maeve is here now, a factor in the puzzle I never imagined would exist. I cannot beg Eva to return to a life that no longer exists.

It's not that I don't want her to stay. It's not that at all. I just can't do that to myself again. I can't spend my life waiting for Eva to choose me.

Maeve and I walk Eva down the stairs and out the front door, moving in awkward silence past the remainder of the tree and the hole. We pretend not to notice it, but I know that we all do.

Eva walks out the front door, stopping as she reaches the sidewalk and turning to me. I watch as her eyes flick up toward the tarp covering the roof.

"Good luck," she says, her voice steady.

"You too," I reply, hoping that she picks up on all the things I can't say out loud.

Eva turns to Maeve, who gives her a quick nod.

"Remember what we talked about?" Eva asks, still gazing at Maeve. Maeve just nods, slowly, before Eva turns and walks away. I don't even have a chance to ask her what she means. I don't have time to question her about what I overheard.

I watch her leave, disappearing down the road and behind the hedge. Heading toward home. It feels weird for me to not know where home is for her. It feels weird for me to have known her so well, and for so long, and then suddenly feel like I don't know her at all. She has a new life. She has a new group. She has a new home. And so do I, right?

I turn to Maeve, who grimaces, trying unsuccessfully to make it look like a smile. I reach out and hold her hand, somewhat surprised that she doesn't pull away. But she didn't pull away last night, and she didn't pull away the night before. She won't leave me like Eva. The cycle won't repeat itself. Not this time.

"Are you okay?" I ask, half hoping that she'll spill whatever secret she's keeping from me now that Eva's gone. But she's not ready to.

Maeve nods and says, "Of course." She pulls me back toward the tree and the hole and the pile of wood. Sawdust still litters the floor, a reminder of the work to be done before The Storm arrives. "C'mon. We better get started."

"Of course."

• • •

Maeve positions herself carefully. "Nail," she mutters, reaching her hand back toward me.

I scramble slightly, rustling through the container and handing one to her. She grips it in her free hand and then turns to me once again.

"Hammer," she commands, and I pass that to her as well.

I watch as she prepares her supplies with expert precision. She gestures to me wildly and I move forward, placing my good hand on the wood to hold it in place. She steadies her nail, pinching it with her pointer finger and thumb. Then she brings the hammer down with a slam, narrowly missing her fingertips.

"Another," Maeve says, reaching out behind her. I hold out a nail, but as Maeve reaches for it, I pull it away, concealing it behind my back. "What?" she asks, raising her eyebrows and finally turning to face me.

"What did you talk about with Eva?" I ask, my voice suddenly firm. I need to know. "I heard you last night."

"What?" A pause, before her face hardens. "Nothing important."

"Don't bullshit me," I warn.

"It's none of your business."

"It's totally my business!"

A few seconds of wordlessness float between us before Maeve finally caves.

"She wanted me to persuade you to leave."

"What?"

Out of all the people left in the world, Eva is the one person I thought would remember what this place used to be. The one person I thought could comprehend how much this place means to me and why I can't just let it go so easily.

"She told me where her group is headed and said that we could join her. We might make it if we leave today. Then, once The Storm passes, we can head down to North Carolina. Be safe for once. Stop fighting so hard to survive."

"Why would she tell you?" I ask. "Why wouldn't she just come to me?"

Maeve shakes her head. "She doesn't quite have the best track record of persuading you to leave. She thought I might have more sway."

I brush off the feeling of betrayal that festers inside me. There will be time for feelings later. "Do you even know how to get there?"

"I do, Liz. We're not going to make it through The Storm as is. There's too much work to do, and I can't do it alone. I know you have some shit to sort through, but surviving is more important than anything."

"And what makes you think that they've got it so much better?" I ask, ignoring the way her words sting. "We don't even know who they are! They could be just as screwed as we are. And we've put so much work into this place already. . . . Do you really want that to go to waste?" I pause before adding, "Please, Maeve. I wouldn't be asking you if it wasn't important to me."

"You don't get it," Maeve says, her voice rising. "It's so much bigger than what you want and how you feel. I've said it before: Staying here is a horrible idea. It'll kill you."

"I've already told you that I'm not leaving."

Maeve scoffs, putting down her hammer on the counter. "And I'm telling you that staying isn't an option. What do you think it's going to look like when The Storm actually gets here? That we can huddle in the cookbooks section and ride it out? Acid rain and debris will tear this place apart, Liz. We'll end up burning together."

"We can do the repairs!" I protest.

"Don't you trust me?" Maeve whispers, reaching for my hand. I retreat, evading her touch. "We can't be together if we're dead."

"And do you want to be together?" I ask, my throat suddenly dry. "What do you think is the mileage on this thing? The two of us."

Maeve stops short, her mouth hanging open. Then she swallows and looks down at her feet. But I don't look away from her. I hope she can feel my stare boring through her skin.

"I do, Liz. Don't be ridiculous." She pauses, searching for the right thing to say. "That's why we need to leave. I don't want this to end before it even starts."

"I bet you wish that you'd never come here," I mutter, my spit tasting like venom. "I bet you wish that you had stayed far away from me, and this place."

"I don't. Never. Because I *do* care about you, Liz. I cared about you two days ago, and I care about you now. We wouldn't be having this argument if I didn't care about you. No matter how this ends, I won't regret coming here."

"And how will this end?" I ask, unsure if I want to know the answer.

"That's up to you," Maeve replies, turning back to look at the hole in the wall. She extends her hand toward me. "Nail."

• • •

I sit at the counter, watching as Maeve adds a few finishing touches to our new wall, pounding in nail after nail *just in case.* The whole thing looks like a patchwork quilt if I'm being generous and Frankenstein's monster if I'm not, but I force myself to hope. It will work. It will have to. And then we can deal with the roof.

Maeve wipes her brow with the end of her sweatshirt sleeve and turns to me.

"You're incredible," I say, miming a one-handed round of applause. "You're a lifesaver. Literally."

Maeve laughs, finally, and pushes her hair behind her ear. "I'm going to head upstairs," she says, looking toward me for approval. I nod in response. "Just a quick nap, and maybe a change of clothes, just to clear my mind."

"Absolutely. You deserve it."

"And we can talk about next steps in about an hour or two, okay? Think about what I said."

I nod again and Maeve disappears. I can hear her boots pounding up the stairs before the door to the apartment slams shut behind her. I don't tell her that I don't have a watch. I don't tell her that I'm scared. I don't tell her that I wish we had more time. I don't have to say anything.

CHAPTER TWENTY-NINE

Maeve is waiting for me in the kitchen when I finally make my way upstairs after another hour of work. She sits on one of the stools by the kitchen counter, fiddling with her matchbook. The only light in the apartment is her camping lantern, casting a slight haze over the room. Her eyes are practically glazed over, looking at nothing and everything all at once.

"Are you okay?" I ask. It hits me now how many times I've spoken these words in the past few days. The number of times I've had to ask. The number of things that we've both experienced that allowed for the possibility of either of us being *not* okay.

Maeve doesn't answer. She pushes a lukewarm can of soup toward me, half-eaten. "Are you hungry?"

"That doesn't answer my question."

Maeve looks up at me slowly. "I can't do this, Liz," she says, her voice hard. "I can't keep doing this."

"Look, we'll make it through this," I murmur, trying to catch her eye.

Another minute of quiet passes between us. It reminds me of a first date, of the horrible pause in conversation when you both know you'll never go on another date with the other person again. Not in your wildest dreams. I don't know what I can say to ease the tension. I don't know if I should even try.

"You're not listening to me, Liz. I can't live like this," she whispers, her voice barely audible. "I don't know what to do."

This is the first time I've heard her say that, and I was beginning to think that I never would. Is this the same Maeve that pushed me out of the way to work on the generator? Is this the same Maeve who had so many solutions and fixed the hole in the wall when I couldn't?

What's changed? But then I remember the hushed conversation from last night. That's the only variable that's shifted from yesterday.

Maeve looks away before adding, "I don't know what I can do to stop them."

Them? At first, Maeve doesn't realize what she's said. I can tell by the way her jaw tenses as her brain works out what just came out of her mouth. Then the color drains from her face as her eyes flick around the room, searching for something to say to explain away her slip of the tongue. But it's too late.

"Who are you talking about?"

"It's nothing. I phrased that weirdly. I don't even know what I was trying to say," she quickly fires back.

But I call bullshit. This all must be connected. Their hushed conversation last night and the fact that they had to leave me out of it. Eva knows something. Something bad. Something dangerous. This is about so much more than a Storm.

Maeve quickly rises from her seat and moves toward the bedroom, refusing to look me in the eye. "I'm going to pack, okay?" she mumbles.

"What did she say to you, Maeve?" I step in front of her, blocking her access to the door. "Tell me."

Maeve takes a step back, looking at me. "I'm not afraid of you, Liz."

"Then I'm not leaving."

Maeve stares straight at me, shaking her finger in my face. "You don't understand. You leave, or you die."

"I'm not going to die," I grumble.

"Fine," Maeve growls. "You want to know what we argued about? It's the people from the woods. They're coming here. They'll kill us both."

"What?"

"They're coming before The Storm, which is why we need to take this opportunity and leave while we still can."

"What? Why here? Why now?"

Maeve shakes her head. "Apparently you blabbed to that kid in the woods about the generator? This place wasn't even on their radar until you decided to tell them about it. I didn't want to tell you, because I didn't want to frighten you but—" She pauses for a moment before continuing. "You need to know."

It's like the blood has been drained from my body, every inch of my skin growing cold. It didn't seem so major when I was whispering to Benji. I thought I was just talking. Connecting with someone from my old life. I didn't know that everything was so much bigger than I imagined. My head is swimming, and all I can manage to say is, "This is your fault. Not mine. I didn't have these sorts of problems before you arrived."

"This isn't my fault," Maeve replies, her voice choked. "Don't say that."

"If you hadn't attacked Becca . . ."

"If I hadn't attacked Becca, they would have done god knows what to us. Remember?" And I do remember, but I don't care. But Maeve isn't done. "They're not coming here because of that. They're coming here to take the bookstore. In and out before The Storm even arrives."

I take a staggered step back. "Why would they want the . . ."

Maeve laughs a harsh laugh. "Why wouldn't they? You have a trade system set up here. There's a generator collecting dust outside. And when Eva arrived you opened your mouth once again, talking about fresh running water!"

"This place is falling apart!"

"You're inept!" Maeve barks. "You're not capable of taking care of a place like this! Not like it needs to be. They are. You're just a kid who's too sentimental about an old building. We're both just kids!"

My heart pangs, but I ignore the feeling. "Why did you lie, then? Why not just tell me? Why hide it?"

"I didn't know before Eva came. I only found out after I questioned her. I know Eva too well to trust her," Maeve spits.

"What do you mean?"

Even though my brain can't make Maeve and Eva compute, I know that this makes sense. The whispering. The angry glares. The harsh words. Maeve was never jealous of Eva. It was something more. The two of them, conspiring together. Against me.

"My friend from the woods? The one who got me banished? That was Eva. Your Eva. I've known her for months, ever since she arrived at our camp in the woods. Coming from here, I guess. She was my friend, and she hurt me just like she hurt you. I knew she wouldn't be here to play happy family." She pauses. "I didn't tell you, because I know you too well. I know that you want to stay and protect this place. And I know you don't want to believe that Eva is anything but the friend you once knew." She stares straight into my eyes. "Tell me that's a lie."

All of this, she hid from me. It was secrets and lies, no matter the intentions. All I can say is "Who *are* you?"

Maeve scoffs. "You're being ridiculous!"

"You lied to me. You lied to me, and you had the gall to be upset with Eva for leaving. You're so much worse."

Maeve opens her mouth, searching for the right rebuttal. "This was all Eva's fault!"

"Don't blame her!"

"Why do you think she came here? To say hello to you? She came here to case the joint, just like that stranger you saw through the window. To confirm that their efforts will be worthwhile, which, might I remind you, you did for her."

"You're lying."

"Eva isn't as innocent as you think she is. This world changes people, Eva included," Maeve says. "She's part of that group in the woods. She's *hurt* people." She pauses. "I knew something was up when she came here. There was no reason she would show up here randomly. It was too much of a coincidence."

"That's not true."

"I hate to break it to you, Liz, but I think I know Eva better than you do. I lived with her in those woods for *months.* At least, I can see the real her. Not the person she used to be.

That's why I questioned her. That's why I found out what she was actually doing here."

Suddenly, this perfect memory of Eva comes crumbling down. The person who was always there for me, who always listened, turns into something else entirely. The person who did what she had to, to ensure that she made it out alive; the person who forgot about me; the person who left to save her own skin.

And with it comes my understanding of Maeve, whom I let into my home. Whom I allowed myself to feel for, to care about, to kiss. The person who made me feel like I was home for the first time in a long time. I let myself care, and this is what happens. Maybe Maeve never cared at all. Maybe I was just the means to an end, nothing more.

"*You've* hurt people!"

"I did that to save your life!" Maeve protests.

"But that wasn't your first time, right?" I spit. Then, slightly softer: "Tell me that was your first time."

Maeve doesn't say anything, her silence enough of an answer in itself. She shakes her head. "We did that to survive. Only when it was necessary." But that doesn't mean anything. I didn't need to hurt others to survive. "I'm trying to be better. I'm trying to do the right thing. The good thing."

"Some of us never made those mistakes."

"Eva made those mistakes!" Maeve protests.

But that's not true. I don't care what she says. "Eva isn't like that."

"You don't know anything about her anymore."

"I don't know anything about *you* anymore!"

I pause, letting the silence simmer between us. Maeve stares at me, her eyes boring holes into my skin. I don't look back.

"Where would we even go? To Eva's group? The group that banished you?" I ask.

Maeve looks down at the floor before shaking her head. "I made that up," she says. "She didn't invite us anywhere."

"You lied about that, too?" I burst out, flames rising to my cheeks.

"I knew you would only leave if you knew where we were going to go."

"So what was your plan?" I refute. "If I left, were you just going to let us die somewhere else?"

"I was going to come up with something! Something better, I don't know!" Maeve slams her hand down on the counter, the stress showing as her forehead creases. "I would have figured it out, I swear."

"So you just expect me to leave? After everything? You want me to leave and go to some made-up place that you aren't even sure exists? You want me to leave so we can die somewhere else, away from my home." I pause. "You're telling me that you're trying to save me, yet all I'm hearing is that you have absolutely no plan and absolutely nothing to show for yourself."

"Please, Liz. Leave with me. No matter what you might think, I do care about you. I did all of this because I care about you."

"Don't say that. You only care about saving your own skin." I pause. "I can't abandon the bookstore." The thought seems comically small as the words escape my lips, but I pretend not to notice. "It's kept me alive for so long. I can't just leave it to die."

Maeve shakes her head. "You don't get it, do you? You're talking about this building, this crumbling building, as if it's a person. As if its survival is worth as much as yours. But it's not. To me, it's not. Not a chance in the world that I'd pick this place over you. That I'd pick this place over us."

"I'm not doing it," I say, my voice firm. "I'm not leaving, even if I *do* die. Not for Eva and not for you either." Though my voice wavers, I know that this is the honest truth. I can't go anywhere with Maeve. Not right now. Not after this.

Maeve glares at me. "I had a sister, too," she spits. "I had a sister, and a mother, and a father, and people who I cared about, too, Liz. You weren't the only one. And when they died, I left them behind. Sure, it hurt to leave, but I did it to survive. I did it so that I wouldn't be suffocated by their memory. I did it so that I wouldn't starve. Maybe if you could take a second and finally get a fucking grip, you'd realize you aren't the only one who has lost someone. Allowing yourself to die here? Accepting that? Thea would have wanted better." She pauses as she shakes her head. "You've dug a grave for yourself here, Liz, and there isn't enough room for the both of us."

I don't say anything in response. I listen to the wind whistling against the window. I don't look at her, either, opting to trace the lines of the wood floor.

I can almost hear the gears turning in Maeve's head. I can almost read her thoughts. *Get a grip, Liz. You've screwed everything up. Why won't you say something?*

What she actually says is, "I understand why Eva left." And that hurts more than anything else could.

My mouth is dry. So dry that my voice barely makes a sound. "You don't understand," I mutter, even though it feels only half-true. "You don't understand at all."

"No, I do, Liz," Maeve retorts. "I understand perfectly.

Maybe you need to realize that you just don't have what it takes to survive. Maybe you need to realize that you wouldn't be so damn alone if you had a backbone."

It all comes bubbling up. The betrayal. The hatred. The lies. The memories. It all comes swirling into my brain. Maeve is selfish. Maeve doesn't understand. Maeve is a liar. So I clench my jaw and say the only thing that I have left to say.

"I need you to leave. I need you to go away."

Maeve turns to me, her animosity melting away. "Liz."

"Leave. Please," I whisper. "When I wake up, I want you to be gone."

She hesitates, swaying just slightly, before turning and disappearing through the bedroom door.

CHAPTER THIRTY

AUGUST 22: BEFORE THE FIRST STORM

Family dinners have become few and far between. It's not my fault, though. Mom says that she's tired of cooking all the time if we're not going to appreciate it. I also think she's tired of our nihilistic dinner conversation. Dad is working longer hours, although I'm not sure if it's for the money or so that he can avoid Mom. Avoid talking about Alaska. I think it's a combination of both.

I know that Dad is going to go to Alaska anyway, with us or without us. He'll let us make our decision when it's time to come home for winter break, assuming the world hasn't gone to shit before then. He left the email chain with his sister open on his computer once when he went to the bathroom. I had come in to steal some of his printer paper, and I saw his screen. I don't think it's snooping if the person leaves it out like that.

Mom insisted on having a family dinner tonight, however, because she wanted to do something special before we send Thea off to college in Ohio. Still, the special occasion doesn't change the fact that none of us want to be here. I don't even need to be in Alaska; I just want to be far away from here.

I leave for college in two weeks, which is later than most schools but works for me. Two more weeks at the bookstore, two more weeks to figure out what to pack, two more weeks to figure out how I'm supposed to act like an adult. It feels weird to be going to college when things are continuing to get worse everywhere. It feels weird to ignore what's happening and act like this is the new normal. That this is *just how it is now.*

My school sent out an email last week about storm shelters and flood insurance, just to prove that everything was absolutely fine. Even if anything happened in Vermont, I'd be safe, and classes would continue, because that was obviously my biggest concern.

The anxious energy at the dinner table is palpable. Mom insisted on eating outside, "under the open sky." I think that it's just an invitation for bugs to bite me and take a swim in my water glass. Still, I know better than to complain. I'm not foolish enough to think that spoiling Mom's *special* dinner is a good idea.

Thea decided on hamburgers for her final meal, which I appreciate. They're one of my favorites, and Mom is able to make them well. No one says anything as we eat. The entire world is silent except for the clicking of silverware on our plates.

At first, I don't notice when it starts to drizzle. I hadn't even noticed that there were clouds in the sky in the first place. The darkness helps to hide them, and I never expect to see an abundance of stars in New Jersey. One day, maybe in Alaska, I'll go to the middle of nowhere, armed only with a feeble flashlight, and then turn it off. Then it will be only me and the stars. All of them, in all their glory. In Alaska, the world will all fade away into nothing.

Mom wants to ignore the drizzle, I can tell. She worked hard on this dinner, and she wants us to sit here and finish, even if that means soggy hamburger buns. No complaints.

We continue to eat, until I can't take the quiet anymore, swiftly standing from my place at the table and grabbing my empty water glass, the skin on my hand starting to itch slightly.

"Is anyone going to say anything?" I ask. "Or are we going to eat in silence, because I can do that inside."

"Liz . . . ," Dad warns, placing his knife back down on the tablecloth.

"Thea leaves tomorrow, and you and Mom hate each other so much that you can't even pretend that things are okay?"

Thea rolls her eyes. "Don't make your tirade about me, Liz."

"Or how about don't go on a tirade at all," Dad says. "This is supposed to be pleasant."

"That's easy to say when you're leaving us soon," I snap, something foreign possessing me. "Are you guys going to get a divorce?"

"Don't say that," Mom says. "Don't say things like that."

I've gone too far to turn back now. I might as well dig my grave. "Why don't I get a say in anything?" I ask. "Why don't *we* get a say in anything? You and Dad argue about everything and don't even include us in the conversation!" Mom opens her mouth to speak, but I keep going. "Dad, I want to go with you to Alaska. I don't want to go to college, and I don't want to stay here to rot." I somewhat enjoy the shocked look on Mom's face, but before she can say anything, I turn and stride toward the back door.

"I'll be inside if you care to include me in your next conversation." I make my way up the back stairs, my sneakers pounding against the wood. It takes a couple of tries to get the door open, but then I slip inside and shut it behind me, locking it.

I sit down at the kitchen table and revel in my glory. I can hear thunder rumbling above me, but I don't pay attention. If my rant didn't ruin dinner, the rain certainly will.

I set my empty water glass down on the table as the rain begins to pour down. It's torrential, the type of rain that's nice to get caught in when you've been overheating under the summer sun. I just shake my head as I play with my empty glass, pushing it back and forth on the wooden table. It's like a hockey puck, gliding precariously from one hand to another.

I stop only when I hear screaming.

It's not uncommon to witness a fight between my parents. They like to pretend that we can't hear them if they fight outside, but they forget that our house is old and the walls are thin. At this point, everyone in the neighborhood has heard one of their fights. I'll let them squabble on their own. I'm sure that Thea will join me eventually.

But the longer I listen, the more I realize that this doesn't sound like a normal fight. Neither voice stops to make room for the other. Instead, they shout together, the sound raw and rabid.

Something is wrong.

It's like there's something static in the air, the hairs on my neck standing on edge. I abandon my glass, moving toward the door. Something has to be wrong for them to be fighting like this.

When Thea's voice joins their shrieked chorus, I hesitate. Thea doesn't yell. Thea never yells. Something is terribly wrong.

As if summoned by my thoughts, Thea appears at the kitchen

door, her figure illuminated by a flash of lightning. My heart begins to pound as I stumble forward. What is happening?

As I get closer, I get a better look at Thea. Only it doesn't look like Thea at all.

Her face is bright red, blistering as the rain pours down. Her clothing barely clings to her figure. Her pale skin hangs off her body like it's been melted by a blowtorch, turning to liquid before my very eyes. Small threads of tissue graft larger pieces to the bloody meat that dwells underneath. At her shoulders and elbows, the places where there's no barrier built by fat and muscle, I can see glints of white bone, cartilage still gripping the joints. The skin on her forearm bunches around her wrist like excess fabric as the rain bites moth holes through her stained shirt. My heart drops as I stare, motionless, unsure if I'm looking at a human being or a ghost. This can't be real. This can't be real life. This is the type of monster that haunts my very worst nightmares.

All I can do is watch, my feet suddenly rooted in place, as Thea pounds on the glass with a bloody hand. She fumbles with the doorknob, her raw skin unable to grip the cold metal. I can hear her wails through the glass, even if I can't see the tears in her eyes. *The rain,* she gasps as she braces herself against the door. *Please, Liz. Help.*

But I don't move forward. I can't. I can't even breathe as my heart seizes up and my insides turn to stone. Instead, I stumble backward, my feet tripping over one another and sending me tumbling toward the ground. I fall with a thud, biting my lip so that the taste of blood fills my mouth. A crash echoes through the house.

I struggle to get back onto my feet, my limbs shaking too

hard to function. My hands clench and quiver as my nails dig into my skin. I'm paralyzed by fear, by confusion, by a million thoughts racing through my head, making it impossible to think. Nothing computes. Nothing makes sense.

But I shove myself back onto my feet and take a few staggering steps toward the door. I feel like I've never moved my body before, each muscle made solid by years of stagnation. My fingers reach out for the lock, the lock I turned when I returned inside.

Thea's screams echo on the other side of the glass as I try to twist the lock and open the door. But the metal doesn't move, no matter how hard I push, my fingers turning white from the amount of force they're applying. Again and again I use the heel of my palm to shove against the lock, praying for it to give. Maybe if I had a few more seconds, I could get it open. Maybe if there were just a few more moments, the lock would budge. But it doesn't.

All I can do is watch as Thea's knees buckle and she falls to the ground, the back door still shut. All I can do is watch as her chest stops rising and falling. All I can do is watch as she stops moving completely.

CHAPTER THIRTY-ONE

Tonight I dream of death. I can practically taste it on my tongue. I dream of darkness, and cold, and nothingness.

The dream is like an amalgamation of every doomsday movie I've ever seen, replayed in my mind, ricocheting off the sides of my skull. My dream disobeys the rules of physics, buildings warping, streets bending upward to meet the sky.

When I was little, like really little, I read a book about the end of the world. I think it was my first. I guess it was sort of a gateway drug, and then fiction gave way to real life, and here we are.

I checked the book out from the library, its cover worn and slightly stained. It was the last book in a companion series to an original series, which I loved. Even though my favorite characters were gone and the plot was starting to get questionable, I kept on reading.

The end was near for our intrepid heroes, and I read page after page after page in the way that only kids on summer vacation can. The characters raced against the clock, attempting to stop members of a rival family from becoming immortal as the sky turned yellow and all hell broke loose. Nine-year-old me vowed to notice if the world was ending, and to never ignore my gut instincts if the sky began to change color. Surely that was the telltale sign that everything was going to shit.

It makes sense, now, that the sky in my dream is yellow, even though the clouds rolling in over the actual horizon are a sickening gray. In my dream, the ground is covered in soot. Volcanic ash descends from the sky, piece by piece by piece, never lasting long enough that it sticks.

The dream continues to twist and turn, thunder rolling in the distance, and as the sky turns from yellow to red, I start to fall. Straight through the road and the abyss that lurks underneath it. Straight through the open sky. I fall, holding nothing and picking up speed, until I jolt awake, cold sweat on my brow.

Dim sunlight has just begun to trickle in, at least whatever sunlight can make its way through the foreboding clouds that cover half the sky. In the back of my mind I know we can't have more than twenty-four hours left, if we're lucky. I know I have to get up and get to work. As much as we can do before it comes.

I throw off my covers and pile them at the end of the mattress. Quickly, I tug on my socks before turning toward Maeve.

"C'mon, sleepyhead. Time to seize the day."

I expect a groan from her direction. I expect her to tell me to never call her sleepyhead again. I expect her to remind me that I'm normally the one who sleeps in late. But there's no reply.

I walk over toward her, the floorboards creaking underneath

me with each and every movement. Stooping down to nudge her awake, I realize that something's wrong.

She's gone, blankets piled up where she used to be, leaving an empty space in the shape of her sleeping bag. Just like in one of those corny '80s comedies my dad used to make me watch on the weekends.

And then I remember what I said last night. What I told her and the way her face looked as the words sank in. *Leave. When I wake up, I want you to be gone.* She did it. She really did it, and I told her to.

Fear knots in my stomach, and I start to sweat. I rush out of the bedroom, half expecting Maeve to be sitting in the well-worn armchair, laughing about how panicked I am, just another teen-movie cliché. But Maeve is nowhere to be found. All I find is my notebook sitting on the kitchen counter, a piece of paper and a pen draped carefully across the cover.

I take a step forward, willing my legs to move even though they don't want to. I reach out with a shaky hand and lift the paper, unfolding it. Anything would be better than this. Even my not-quite-a-nightmare of a dream would be better than this. At least I know that's not real.

Curving letters slope across the page, black ink slightly smudged in some places. It looks like it was written in a rush.

To Elizabeth Swann,
To Liz.

I'm sorry that I had to do this. I know that you told me to, but I'm still sorry.

It's my fault that the woods are off-limits. It's my fault that you're still here, because I didn't try hard enough to persuade you to come with me. I'm sorry.

But I'm not going to let myself die with you. No matter how much you like your books, and your tragic endings, I'm not willing to go out like that. This isn't one of those romances where one of us has to die for the plot to progress. My life is worth more than the fate of a building. Yours is too.

If you come to your senses, there are directions on the back of this paper.

I will remember you for the rest of my life. No matter how long it is. I can only hope that yours is just as long.

Don't forget me.

Love,
Maeve

As I fold the paper and stare out the window, I realize that once again, the cycle has repeated itself. Once again, I'm alone. Once again, I have no one else to blame but myself.

CHAPTER THIRTY-TWO

There's this thing someone with too much time on their hands made up called the butterfly effect. I don't know why they decided to call it the butterfly effect, because that seems like false advertising to me. The whole idea is that each moment affects every other one, and that the smallest occurrence, like a butterfly flapping its wings on the other side of the world, can set off a domino effect that could change everything. It's like when you miss the traffic light by milliseconds, making you miss your train. Maybe waiting on that train was your one true love, and maybe, now that you're stuck waiting on the platform for the next train, you end up meeting your archnemesis. The dominoes keep falling. When you're born everything is perfect, and you're headed down the path called destiny without a care in the world. And then, with every shitty occurrence, things just get a little bit worse.

Some look at the butterfly effect and marvel at how lucky they are to avoid a downward spiral of small tragedies. I have a philosophy of my own. Anything that can go wrong will go wrong. Some call it Murphy's Law; I call it being realistic. And my lifetime of adherence to Murphy's Law has led me to this point. No butterflies, just poor life decisions.

Maybe it all went wrong when I allowed Maeve to stay. Without her, I would have two functional arms. I wouldn't be hurting so much. I wouldn't have let my guard down and allowed everything to get so out of hand. There wouldn't be anyone marching toward me with knives and guns and who knows what else. There wouldn't have been anyone to leave me. No one there to lie to me. I'd just stay here, unbothered. It would be my choice alone.

But maybe my worst mistake was fighting so hard to survive. Outlasting everyone I knew or loved or cared about. Because maybe if I'd never tried, it wouldn't hurt so hard to fail. Because when you survive this long, you start to wonder if it will ever be worth it. I'm starting to think that it may never be.

I fold up Maeve's letter and place it on the kitchen counter, hoping that it might just burst into flames from the sheer anger radiating out of my eyeballs. It's my fault that I seem to attract the worst of the worst. It's my fault that I'm such a mess that nobody stays. Everyone leaves. *What can go wrong will go wrong.* I would get that tattooed somewhere on my body, but I'm sure that with my luck I'd probably get an infection and die.

When I was fifteen I gave myself a stick and poke with a slightly bent sewing needle and Sharpie ink, taking inspiration from a '90s punk-rock song about tongue piercings. If I was metal enough, it wouldn't hurt, right? Well, it hurt like a motherfucker, and I was doing it to myself, poking the probably hazardous Sharpie ink into my skin over and over until a poorly drawn infinity sign was permanently affixed to my upper arm. It was sloppy and I hated it, but I had done it to myself, so I couldn't complain. Soon enough it was faded and gone, all except for a few dots.

That's what I'm thinking as I head back down the stairs into the bookstore. I repeat it over and over in my head like a mantra. *You did this to yourself, Liz; you can't complain.*

And my brain is right, like it normally is, so I do the only thing I know how to do when the people I care about are gone. I do what I did after my parents and after Thea. After Eva. And now I'll do it after Maeve. Just keep moving on. Take one step and then another, wondering if it'll ever be worth it.

Before I can wallow in my mushy feelings for just one minute longer, I turn my attention to the front door. The front door that cannot and will not lock. The front door that seems to have something personal against me.

I decide to take my one-handed rage out on the door, like people used to do at those overpriced rage rooms comfortably nestled in dying malls. Just ten dollars to shatter five beer bottles with a baseball bat, like you couldn't do the same thing for free in your garage. I tuck the rejected wood planks under my good arm and collect the leftover nails in the palm of my sweaty hand. I tend to get sweaty when I'm nervous, but why would I be nervous right now? It's not like a group of bloodthirsty and grudge-holding individuals is headed my way.

Maeve said that the woods people would be here before The Storm. In and out before the rain comes. So we're going to go about this *Les Mis* style. If I keep them out long enough, they'll run out of time. They'll have to leave as The Storm inches closer.

I place a square of wood above the doorknob and use the dead weight of my nonfunctioning hand to hold it in place. The pressure sends a searing shock of pain up my arm, but I ignore it. I'm sure dying via woods gang or burning alive in acid rain would hurt quite a bit more. As they used to say, what doesn't kill you makes you stronger. Or what doesn't kill you right now helps ensure that you will not die a slow and painful death later on.

I shove a nail between my unmoving knuckles in a maneuver that would probably cause my high school carpentry teacher to die from shock. Then, with a few haphazard swings of a hammer, the nail is in place. Hopefully, it will hold better than the dysfunctional lock would have. It will hold. It has to.

• • •

The bookshelves were hard to move, but I did it. Sure, it wasn't an elegant or graceful process, but it's done, and two shelves now lie horizontally across the front windows along with two reading chairs, a cash register, and a fake woodburning stove I found in the basement. As ridiculous as it seems, I didn't want to use the books. Hell, maybe they'll all get destroyed anyway, but it seemed sacrilegious to use them as barricade material. I doubt they even stooped that low in *Les Mis.*

I walk over to the Science Fiction shelf and select a book. *A Canticle for Leibowitz.* Seems like the right time. As the sky continues to darken outside, I lean against the counter, flipping through the pages. It's not as bad as I expected, even though it's all about monks and takes place over thousands of years. They're trying to preserve parts of humanity, which is something I can get behind. It's not as bad as my dad told me it was, however many years ago that was, although I'm sure it felt scarier to him when the apocalypse was still something to prepare for. It all feels unreal, like my life before never really existed in the first place, like one of those oversaturated prologues in rom-com movies. The family is so smiley and happy that you know they're going to get into a car accident before they do. Except my family was never smiley and happy. They're just gone.

The wind howls outside and metal scrapes, a trash can being pulled down the road. My eyes shift to watch, and I place my book back down on the counter, dog-earing the page. As I look out the window, a hazy figure appears in the distance, emerging from behind the hardware store, details obscured in the semidarkness. The clouds barely let enough light in for me to see my surroundings inside the bookstore. There's nowhere near enough sunlight to discern what's going on outside.

As the figure inches closer, my stomach drops. I can feel my hands begin to sweat once again as I stare out the window, not daring to move. If I don't stand my ground, I'm weak. If I run and hide, maybe I deserve to die. My mantra just repeats itself in my head. *What can go wrong will go wrong.* But it can't. Not this time. This time it has to go right.

Eventually, I realize that it's not just one person I'm seeing; it's four. Of course it is. I'm sure that they think Maeve is still here, lurking somewhere inside the bookstore's walls. She stabbed someone for me. Surely they'd assume we would stick together after that, right?

But the woods people are wrong. It's just me in here, with one good arm and only a fraction of the strength required to fight off four adults. Maybe ten years down the road I'll think this whole thing is funny and be able to laugh, but right now it feels like a poorly timed joke. I adhere myself to the wall, allowing the shadows to swallow me entirely, until I'm certain I can't be seen from outside.

What can go wrong will go wrong, my brain reminds me.

The figures inch closer, maneuvering around the debris in the roads around the town square. The shortest can't be any taller than five two, with sleek black hair all tied up into a ponytail that sways as she walks with a slight limp. I recognize her immediately, a wave of guilt simmering in my stomach. Becca. My eyes zero in on her, blocking everything else out as the seconds pass. Becca. Here. Now. I don't have time to fathom how she's well enough to be here right now, after I saw her bleeding on the ground nearly a week ago. But I should know better than to think anyone is dead if I haven't seen their breathless body. It's the oldest trope in literature. Now she's back, and this time it's personal.

She crosses her arms and turns to the man next to her, who's almost as short as she is. A knotted beard makes its way down his neck, and he scratches a scruffy mustache with a stocky finger. Her friend from the woods, Tristan, I'm sure. The other man, or boy is probably more accurate, is thin and tall like a beanpole, a mess of unkempt hair making him look like he's halfway between human and Q-tip. He stands behind the other two, hands in pockets as he kicks at the debris in the road. Benji. The final member of their party, muscular and broad shouldered, steps out from behind the tall boy, her braids tossed behind her back.

As her blond hair comes into view, her bright red sweater becomes more vibrant in color. I retreat, backing away from the front door, away from her. As if out of impulse, my eyes flick over to the blade sheathed at her hip.

She looks away from her traveling companions and into the store as if she's peering into my soul. As if she can sense me looking at her.

And I say it even though there's no one here to hear me. It's more of a prayer than anything else.

"Eva."

CHAPTER THIRTY-THREE

AUGUST 29: AFTER THE FIRST STORM

The water made it all the way up to the top stair of the porch. I watched it rise through my bedroom window. People always said that this area was prone to flooding, but with these water levels, I wouldn't be surprised if it was practically the whole state, considering this town's elevation. I never used to believe them. I never thought something like this would happen to us.

When the water receded, it took my parents with it. I'd have to assume that it did. Either that, or the water turned them into nothing right in front of my eyes and I didn't notice it. I'm not sure which option is worse. Then came the cold, winter-like weather. It's been freezing for a week now, frost covering every surface that isn't burned already. I'm sure that it would be snowing if there were any water left in the sky.

When I look out my bedroom window today, all I can see is yellow grass and a mound of dirt underneath the tree house. Everything I see is dead. All of it. Maybe this is my punishment. Maybe staying alive is my punishment because I don't know where to go from here. Maybe my death will be ten thousand times more painful than theirs and I'll suck it up because I deserve it. I deserve it all.

I won't get any sleep tonight; I know that much. The gunfire has started in the streets. The last of us killing any other survivors for food, water, whatever they can get their hands on. Mom was wrong when she said that this sort of thing doesn't happen in New Jersey. Maybe this is just how we are. Doomed to destroy each other.

Everyone's probably scared and willing to do what it takes to keep themselves safe. I wonder how many people will be left by the time they stop shooting. I'm not sure if there will be anyone at all. And what about me?

I'm not sure if I deserve to live.

CHAPTER THIRTY-FOUR

I don't move at all until the first brick comes crashing through the front windows. It's like all my joints have been glued together, locking each kneecap and elbow into place so that I'm forced to stay statue still. It's a feeling I've felt before, a year ago, staring through a window not entirely unlike this one. It's a feeling that I was hoping I would never have to feel again.

⫛⎍⍀⊑⊬⦚ ⫽⍋⍙ ⊬⍜⎍ ⫯⌷⫯⍜⍑, our alien overlords remind me, which roughly translates to *You're fucked.*

In response I say: *Will you please just shut up? Now is absolutely not the time.*

My eyes flick toward the discarded hammer on the ground. I might feel stronger if I was holding it in my hand, feeling its weight and knowing that I would have something to defend myself with if it really did come down to it. Because in the darkest crevasses of my mind, in the gaps between the individual neurons that are currently firing a mile a minute, is the reminder that there is only one way that this ends. And as I stare at the four people creeping toward me down the road, I'm not sure that I totally like my odds.

I'm no killer; that much is clear. I will never be the hot, zombie-killing, hammer-swinging badass I wish I could pretend to be. I will never be the type of person that strikes first and thinks later. So I leave the hammer alone.

I watch the group's approach, inching closer and closer until I can make out every detail of their faces. Why is Eva here? Did she come willingly? Was this all her idea?

I can't quite decipher what lurks behind her eyes, but the feelings I had days ago, watching an old friend approach my front door, are gone. If Eva hadn't left months ago, none of this would be happening. We'd be here together, with no one on their way to destroy everything I care about. And I would have never let myself care about Maeve in the first place. There would have been no void in my life available to fill.

I can't help but jump when there's a thud on the door, a boot colliding with the wooden frame. The door bends, curving like a crescent moon, but it doesn't give. The portion I nailed shut does its job, keeping me safe enough for just a minute longer. Benji curses aloud, muttering something to the rest of the group that I can't hear over the howling wind. I'm just glad that my haphazard construction held.

Benji stalks back into the road and grabs another faded brick, testing its weight in his long fingers. He doesn't hesitate like I would, my mind racing through the plethora of ways that everything could go wrong. He squints and pulls back his arm, not even realizing that I am watching him from inside.

Benji hurls the brick through the window, the sound of splintering wood and shattering glass radiating through my bones. He's managed to hit the cross section of the wooden beams framing the windowpanes, completely destroying the top half of the window. Below the gaping hole, the remaining panes cling to their wooden frame, half-ready to go crashing toward the floor.

I gasp, backing up until my spine presses up against the Business section bookshelf. I look behind me, seeing rows of shelves and no exit. I'm trapped, left with nowhere to run. Breaching my door is an inevitability, and I spent so much time barricading myself inside that I didn't allow for an escape route. Another brick lands with a thud next to my feet, vibrating the wooden floorboards and sending a jolt through my nervous system. The impact is hard enough to leave a large, scraping dent in the hardwood floor, like claws across a chest. I wonder whether I should pick it up and throw it back at Benji. I'm not sure what good that would do.

But it's enough to force my body back into a semifunctioning state. If I have nowhere to run, that means that I have to hide. I have no other choice. And so, I beeline toward the kids' section, the pastel carpet practically glowing in the dim light like a beacon. I don't stop moving as voices echo from outside. I don't think about what they're saying to each other. I don't have time. I don't stop moving until I turn the corner into the depths of the Children's room and am safely out of view of the front door, suddenly eye level with a copy of *The Bad Beginning.* Sounds about right.

I peer through the crack between two sets of bookcases, pressing my chest against the shelving until my lungs are almost too compressed to breathe. I can feel my heartbeat in my teeth, each pulse radiating through my jaw. In a perfect universe (read: absolutely not this universe), I would have had oodles of time to come up with a concrete plan with no flaws whatsoever.

I would have boarded up the windows. I would have booby-trapped the place, Kevin McCallister–style. I would have had time to think about the decisions I was making, and how to prepare myself for not only The Storm but also The Scary People Headed My Way. But now, I'm doing both on the fly. What in god's name have I gotten myself into?

Becca, with deep circles under her eyes, takes the next swing at the window with her sleeved elbow, sending the glass crashing down toward the ground. As she admires her handiwork, I realize the flaw in my super-awesome barricade plan. I didn't build it high enough. A barricade does absolutely nothing if they can just climb over.

As she reaches a hand through the window, I search the shelves in front of me for something to use for protection. Sure, it might have been better to be hiding next to the Classics section, where books balloon past the five-hundred-page mark more often than not, but beggars can't be choosers. My eyes rest on a "pet rock" kit, still priced at $12.99, box unopened. Even though it doesn't quite pack the punch of *Anna Karenina,* it'll work. It has to.

As quietly as I can, I open the flaps of the rock's cardboard carrier and feel its heft. It can't weigh more than two or three pounds, but I'm hoping it'll hurt like it weighs ten when it comes time to throw it.

I can hear Eva's voice echoing through the open space, the flimsy shelving doing very little to dampen the sound. I can't make out each distinct syllable, but I know the sound well enough, know the way her voice sags when she's upset, to know that she isn't saying anything good. Someone else coughs, probably choking on the dust they've created with their destruction.

Either on that or the sawdust that I never quite got around to cleaning up. Glass crunches underneath someone's boots. I close my eyes and listen. One pair of shoes thudding to the ground. Then another. Then another. Then another.

They're inside now, all four of them. It's too dangerous to peer through the crack in the shelves, because with four sets of eyes, one of them is bound to see me or spot a shift in the shadows as I move back and forth. I don't like those odds. So I just press my body into the white wood shelving and wait. Wait until I have no choice but to spring into action. Wait for a miracle.

As if sensing my thoughts, the floorboards creak, and Eva's voice once again floats through the air.

"Liz?" She says my name like it's a question. Like I might not even be here at all. But we know each other too well, right? We both know that I'm the one who stays behind.

"Maeve?" Benji echoes. "Liz?"

I don't answer. I don't waste my breath, no matter how much I might want to. I just bite down on my bottom lip until I think that I might bleed. Any sound that I make can be used against me. Anything I do can be used to pinpoint my location. And sure, they'll find me eventually, but I'll take every spare second that I can get.

Eva continues anyway, as if she never expected a response from me in the first place. "Liz," she repeats. "We're not here to hurt you."

I remember what I saw in the woods. I remember the feeling of Benji's knife against my throat. I remember the way that Becca looked at me so intensely that I thought I'd burst into flames. I remember what Maeve did to protect me. She wouldn't have done that if she hadn't had to. She wouldn't have attacked Becca if she hadn't known that they were willing and capable of doing the same thing to me. Just like they are now.

"This can all end peacefully," Eva continues. "They'll forgive you guys for hurting Becca if you're willing to negotiate."

She's saying what her friends want to hear, not what she believes. Because Eva was the one who showed up here in a half-assed attempt to get me to leave. To persuade Maeve to drag me to safety. She knew it wouldn't bode well for me if I stayed. And this whole thing wouldn't have started with a brick through the window if any of them had any sort of intention of peace. Even if it would be easier to believe Eva and reveal myself, I know that I can't.

Eva's different than she used to be; Maeve was right. She's not the person who used to make book puns on slow workdays, or who used to slingshot rubber bands at me when I was working at the register. She's grown harder because being soft is no longer an option. She's almost unrecognizable, donning this new, stronger version of herself. I should have tried harder to stop her from leaving. I should have stopped her from changing at all.

I try to track the distance between my body and their voices. Maybe fifteen feet? I let out a shuddered breath as I press the back of my head against the shelf behind me. I try to remember what it felt like to be here a year and a half ago, when things were happy, and bright, and normal. If you had told me a year and a half ago that Eva would be leading a violent and likely murderous charge through the bookstore in an attempt to take control from me before an impending apocalyptic storm . . . I would have thought that sounded awesome, in theory. But I would have also called you crazy.

I hear them pause by the back door.

A familiar voice, Becca's, speaks to Eva. "Where does that go?" she asks.

"Upstairs."

"Upstairs?"

"Yeah," Eva says. "There's an apartment up there. I think it's where the two of them have been living."

"Would she be up there?" Becca replies. "You know her better than we do."

Eva pauses. "No," she finally decides after a few beats. "She wouldn't. She's somewhere down here, I'm sure. Both of them."

"Whatever you say," Becca grumbles, and the sound of footsteps returns, slow and methodical.

I'm screwed. They're headed this way. It's only a matter of time.

I wrap my fingers around the rock and bring my arm back, ready to throw, before pausing and looking at the freestanding picture-book shelf that forms part of the doorway into the Children's room. Eva and her friends wait on the other side. It's about three feet wide, extending almost fully to the ceiling, and double-sided. On the other side, it's filled with young adult graphic novels and nonfiction, with a "beach reads" display still out from last summer. It created a bit of privacy for the kids in the Children's room, which juts off from the main room like an L. It hides me from view now, too, as I tuck myself around the corner and out of sight.

I used to remove this shelf for author visits and events in order to "open up the space." Sure, it used to annoy me because it was heavy and nearly impossible to move, but now it's an opportunity.

I set down my rock and move forward, carefully placing

the sole of my sneaker on the carpet so that it doesn't make a sound. I don't hesitate. I don't have the time. I just push with all my might, as my biceps twinges and my palm burns. I push until the shelf gives way and begins to topple.

It doesn't fall quickly. Instead, it wavers back and forth, making me wonder whether it's even going to fall. But then it does. And it is beautiful. I can hear a low, rough voice curse loudly as a scuffle ensues. Rubber squeaking against the floor as all four intruders attempt to escape impending, bookshelf-shaped doom.

I grab the stone once again and quickly speed back around the corner and deeper into the Children's room, avoiding being seen by Eva as she stumbles into the wide opening I've created, the bookcase narrowly missing her right leg. I hear a howl of pain, which tells me that someone else wasn't as lucky. If I can hold them off for long enough, maybe they'll decide that this isn't worth it and they'll leave. Maybe, if I keep them here for long enough, Benji and Eva will remember why this place matters, and the person I used to be. Maybe they'll realize that I'm not their enemy.

I grip the stone, knowing that this time I'll have to use it. I've bought only a few seconds as Tristan struggles to wrench his foot free, and out of the corner of my eye I can see Becca turn erratically, searching for a clue to my location. Her lips are twisted into a grimace as she stares, ready to leap into action.

I see a hand enter my frame of vision and Becca takes it, squeezing Tristan's fingers as his knuckles turn white. As he leans closer, his face comes into view and my stomach flips. His eyes are filled with anger as he tries to stand. It's clear that he will not hesitate this time. He will not spare me like he did last time, not with his own survival on the line. All four of them are here, ready to finish what was started merely a week ago.

Becca leans over, wrapping her hands around the shelf and pulling upward as her friend begins to inch free. In this context, they look almost like they're siblings. Either that or they're dating. It's always hard to tell which. The pair turn to look at each other, and I watch as Tristan's Adam's apple rises and falls. He glances down at his foot and winces.

"Is it broken?" I hear Benji ask, his voice wavering.

"What do you think?" Tristan gruffly responds. I watch as Becca covers her face with her hands.

"Stay here," Becca mutters before turning to Eva. "Let's keep moving."

She doesn't wait for Eva to respond; she just turns the corner and enters the kids' room before I'm ready. Before I have the chance to move or retreat farther away from the main room. Before I have the chance to do anything at all. There's no warning. So I throw the rock in a last-ditch effort to stop Becca's approach.

As it makes contact with her forehead, her eyes flick up, registering my presence. She doesn't wince. She doesn't say a word. I start working on the Middle Readers' shelf. Sure, we've never moved it before, but that doesn't mean that it doesn't move.

I hear the wood groan as the shelf sways, my arm straining as the bookcase slowly leans away from the wall. This one doesn't move quickly. It doesn't catch anyone by surprise, and it doesn't have to. It just adds another barrier between me and Becca, broken shelving and ripped pages scattered on the ground.

She pauses for a second before resuming her pursuit, and my eyes scan her body, resting on the handle of a knife tucked into her boots. Blood seeps from a small cut on her forehead, the skin bruising already. She doesn't reach for the knife, not yet. She doesn't have to. As her eyebrows raise, a small smile on her face, I know that she realizes she has the upper hand. I can feel the presence of the wall behind me, even though I haven't reached it yet. I don't have to look to know it's there. I've run out of space, and I've run out of options, but how many options did I really have in the first place? I was never really meant to win, just to keep living for a few more minutes. Becca knows that too.

She begins to clamber over the pile of splintered wood and chapter books, the destruction covering most of the floor. It's more of a ragged scramble than anything else, her face contorted with effort. As she steps on a copy of *Under the Egg,* her foot slips into the pile and wedges itself beneath a fallen shelf.

I make the split-second decision to run. I'm not sure where I'm going, but staying put is not an option.

My legs churn, and I'm almost past Becca by the time she realizes what I'm doing. She reaches out an arm, her left boot still pinned, as I rush past. I sidestep, my body moving before my brain can even process it, my shoulder throbbing as it collides with a graphic-novel display. I ignore the feeling and struggle to turn, moving past Benji, who is stooped down, trying to stop the bleeding on Tristan's leg. He scrambles to his feet as I speed past.

I continue moving, heading toward the door and my flimsy barricade with no idea what I'll do when I reach it. Outside isn't an option. To get outside I'd have to climb over my barricade, wasting precious time that I don't have. If I do, Benji catches up, and it's game over. Like the energy that courses through my veins, this is not sustainable. None of this is.

Once I make it to the other side of the counter, I pause, my breath shallow as I look at the ragged group, still lingering at the back of the store. Becca has wrenched herself free, and she stands beside Eva, finally holding her knife in her hand. Her jaw is rigid, her stance tense. Becca's eyes burn, staring through me rather than at me. I am not a person to her; I am an obstacle in her path. Slowly, Benji rises, too, helping Tristan up from his place on the floor. Even though Tristan continues to bleed, he doesn't seem to notice as he slowly shifts his weight and reaches for the axe that is tied to his waistband.

Only Eva hesitates, no weapon in her hand, her blue eyes searching for something in mine. I'm not sure what she wants me to do.

It's Tristan who advances first, his motions staggered and uneven, leaving a trail of blood behind him. His face is pale, a sheen of sweat across his forehead, but his gait shows no sign of fatigue.

He pauses, turning around to look at Benji, who has reached the sealed apartment door.

"Benji," Tristan says, gesturing haphazardly as he sucks in a breath. "Search for the other one. Make sure she isn't hiding out somewhere."

Benji nods and skitters away, disappearing up the stairs and into the apartment above. Without him, the air is a little staler. Without him, I can feel ten tons of pressure rest upon my chest. Eva watches him go, biting down on her bottom lip as she fumbles for something in her back pocket.

I know that she knows Maeve isn't here. We both know Maeve, and we both know me. Under any other circumstances, it would be me hiding upstairs in the apartment, holding my breath and letting my organs burn inside me, while Maeve was brave downstairs. Eva knows that it would never be the other way around. But she says nothing.

Tristan doesn't hesitate. He strides toward me, as quickly as his leg will allow. There is nowhere for me to go.

As the distance closes, Becca just two feet behind him, I reach for the hammer on the floor. But before my fingers can make contact, a primal grunt erupts from Tristan's lips as he swings his axe, the blade mere centimeters from my head. I have to admit that I'm glad he missed. I've begun to get rather attached to my head. Instead, his axe collides with the previously repaired hole in the wall, breaking the patch in two and sending splintered wood scattering in all directions.

I scramble to recover, reaching back down to grip the handle of the hammer, my knuckles bleaching white, almost falling as my foot collides with my makeshift barricade. This is where I die. I look behind me at the rows of paperbacks. Edgar Allan Poe. Seems fitting.

"Eva, you don't want to do this, right?" I say, peering past Tristan, unsure why I'm even wasting my breath. "You know this is wrong. Please tell me that you know that this isn't right." I search her face for something. What, I don't know, but anything to make me believe that she isn't okay with this.

Eva opens her mouth to speak, but she's quieted by Tristan, an arm's length away from me. "That's not what this is about. Either you die, or we die, and I don't like your odds."

"I can take one of you out with me," I challenge, raising the hammer clenched in my fist. "I can do it." The words sound fake and hollow, but I try to pretend otherwise.

"I'm not sure that you'll last that long."

And with that, he moves forward and in one swift motion presses the blade of his axe against my throat, the back of my head slamming against a wooden chair, still stacked against the front door. He presses harder than Benji did that day in the woods. I can feel the axe slice through the layers of my skin, the warm blood slithering down my neck. I don't dare to move. I don't dare to speak. I don't dare to swallow down the copper taste in my mouth. One false move and the axe cuts through. One false move and I'm gone.

The gravity of the situation catches up to me now. After years of reading books about death and war and swords and pain, I'm finally experiencing all of it. And I'm afraid. I'm not cut out for the types of stories I like to devour.

I'm too scared to act when it really matters. Too scared to move as Thea banged on the back door. Too spineless to say anything as Eva walked out of this building and didn't turn back. Too chicken to tell Maeve how I felt, to do whatever it took to get her to stay. And now, the one time I've tried to fight, it crumbled so quickly.

The prospect of death is more terrifying than anything I've ever encountered. The idea of things being over. Fade to black and then nothing after. I won't remember the feeling of Maeve, of being held by her. I won't remember her sad birthday candle or slightly grating jokes. I won't remember any of this at all. I will simply be gone, nothing left but dead cells and dead flesh. And one day, those things will be gone too. And Eva will be gone, and Maeve, and Benji, and Peacoat Man, and there will be no one left to remember me at all.

It's a beautiful tragedy to think that this is my fate. The only way to make the pain and heartbreak and grief stop is for everything else to stop with it. Maybe this was always inevitable. Maybe it was always meant to end like this.

"You don't have to do this," Eva murmurs. "Just say you'll give up the store. Right, Liz?"

Tristan pauses, relieving a fraction of the pressure he's putting on his axe as he looks over to Eva. I don't even have the opportunity to decide if I'd want to surrender.

"That's not how this works," he replies. "There are rules."

Eva shakes her head, her voice slightly broken. "She didn't do anything! Liz is innocent. Maeve attacked Becca, but she was just there."

"Maeve isn't here," Tristan replies. "We get the retribution offered to us."

Eva's eyes widen as she turns to me. "In what world does that seem right?"

"This world!" Tristan fires back.

"Are you with us or not?" Becca interjects, sounding irritated. "Because it's starting to sound like you're not. She tried to kill me!"

But Tristan shakes his head. "You should do it," he says, glancing at Eva.

"What? No! I'm not doing that, Tristan."

Becca moves forward, pressing her much larger blade into Eva's hand. Her fingers hang limply around the weapon's hilt. "C'mon, Eva, get it done. We don't have all day."

I can feel warm tears slipping down my cheeks and dripping off my chin. Eva closes her eyes.

"Don't be a pussy," Tristan snarls. "You got us here—now finish it."

I watch as Becca shoves Eva forward, forcing her knife into

the proper position against my throat as Tristan retreats. She doesn't grip it the way she should. She barely touches it at all, and the look in her eyes says she's terrified. But only one of us will end up dead at the end of this. I'm the only one who has a right to be terrified.

I clench my jaw. It's almost ironic that this is how it ends. It's almost Shakespearean. My freshman-year English teacher could probably find discussion material for a whole class in this moment. But the irony doesn't matter.

"Hurry up, Eva," Becca murmurs.

"Give me a second!" Eva snaps, her voice fraying at the edges as she holds Becca's knife to my throat, not pressing it any harder. "Don't make me do this."

I look away as Eva's hands begin to shake, staring out the obscured front windows. I will not look into her eyes.

Outside, there is only gray, enveloping the world and the places I once knew. A shadow lurks in the square like a ghost. Maybe my ghost. I'm sure it's not totally implausible to start seeing things in the seconds before you die, right? Either way, now seems like the perfect time to go insane.

I watch as the shadow moves closer and closer until it pauses at the front door. Maybe it's death? Or the Grim Reaper or something like that, my mind playing tricks on me. It wouldn't be the first time I've hallucinated in the past few weeks.

The shadow hesitates, but then it climbs through the hole in the window, hiking boots scrambling down the bookshelves before they land with a thud on the hardwood floor.

This isn't the Grim Reaper. My brain isn't that creative nor is it daring enough to make such a bold deviation from the original source material. And as the non–Grim Reaper pulls off her hood and unsheathes her knife from her hip, I smile and let her name escape from my lips.

"Maeve."

She came back.

She came back for me.

I can feel my pulse quicken as my mind realizes what this means. That I am enough. That I am enough for her.

Eva pulls the knife away from my neck as soon as her name is out of my mouth and turns, eyes wide. As soon as the blade is gone, I can breathe again. I let the cool air flood into my lungs as I stumble forward, farther into the store. No one stops me. I'm heaving in gulps of air like I've never breathed before, because I thought that I never would again.

"What, am I late to the party?" Maeve says as she adjusts her grip on her knife.

Tristan curses, looking from Maeve to me, back to Maeve. Then he turns his attention to Eva, striding forward and snatching the knife from her hands. She seems more than happy to let go.

"You should have just killed her and gotten it over with," he mutters. "Now we have two of them to deal with."

But Maeve isn't waiting for them to finish their conversation. Instead, she vaults over the front counter, her left thigh scraping across the shellacked wood. We don't have time for a happy reunion. We both know that, no matter how much I might want to hold her tight and never let go.

Tristan moves to the front of the group, ready to take command. But this time, Maeve moves forward to meet him. Checkmate.

Maeve takes the first shot, pouncing forward toward Tristan

with her blade gripped tight in her hand. It's a smaller weapon than Tristan's, but she wields it with much more agility than he does his weapons. Tristan howls as Maeve's knife slashes across his torso, too slow to even notice what she was doing.

Becca takes the sound as a sign to spring into action and lunge at me. She swings a smaller blade now, what looks like a kitchen knife, in a manner that can be described only as helicopter-style. Sure, I have no reflexes, and I'm definitely not trained in any type of combat, but neither is Becca. All I have to do is outlast her, until Maeve is free enough to help. All I have to do is evade her knife.

"Eva, move your ass!" Tristan bellows, passing Eva the knife he took from her. With a grunt, she attacks, her blade slicing across Maeve's biceps, maroon trickling out in thin streaks. Maeve grits her teeth, her eyes narrowing, but she doesn't make a sound.

Becca decides to change her tactic, pulling her knife back as we slowly circle one another. Her eyes flick away from my face, down to my torso, and she moves forward, lips pursed and pulled taut. She's got too much energy fueled into this one movement. There's no time to backpedal anymore, and I sidestep, sending her flying past me as her blade barely scrapes my stomach. It doesn't hurt enough for me to care.

Suddenly, the back door shoots open, flung open so quickly that it thuds against the wall. I turn to watch Benji stroll into the room and out of the stairwell, looking far too calm, cool, and collected for the present circumstances.

"I couldn't find her," Benji says, his voice smooth. "Maeve, I mean."

Tristan growls and gestures to Maeve, who laughs in return. "No shit, Sherlock."

Benji scrambles for his own makeshift blade, his hand sloppily grasping the handle. It's nothing special, just a piece of sharpened metal wrapped in the type of tape you'd use on a hockey stick. It looks foolishly small in his hands, but he holds it tight, assuming an offensive position across from Becca. I'm starting to feel left out. Don't bring a hammer to a knife fight, or whatever.

"Back down, Benji," I murmur as the pair begins to circle, mimicking the dialogue I've read in countless cheesy adventure books. I feel like I'm going to vomit. "I know you too well for this."

Benji shakes his head, an uncomfortable smile worming its way onto his face. "You don't know anything about me, Liz."

"I know you well enough to know that you don't want to do this. You're not that sort of person."

I keep talking because as long as I'm talking I can't be afraid. Okay, well, I'm still afraid, but I'm not about to pee my pants. That's an improvement.

"Shut up," Benji replies.

"Do you think Thea would want you to do this?"

"Don't talk about Thea."

Thunder punctuates Benji's growl, and in the silence that follows, I can hear the raindrops that begin to fall, hissing as they collide with the ground outside. I turn and watch as the grass outside shrivels and dies in mere seconds, my bones suddenly made from lead.

It's here.

CHAPTER THIRTY-FIVE

Becca stops moving entirely, staring at the weather outside like she's never seen rain before, lips slightly parted as a breath escapes her lungs.

"Shit," she whispers. It's a few days earlier than expected, something that Eva and her crew hadn't bargained for by the looks on their faces. At the sound of Becca's voice, the rest of them turn, Maeve included. They all stare out the window, watching the droplets fall as if they've been hypnotized. But I haven't been.

I take advantage of the seconds that I have and move forward, quickly enough that Benji doesn't have the time to react. I decide to employ a move that I learned from a slightly bratty cousin at Thanksgiving dinner, hooking my right leg around Becca's and sweeping her feet out from under her. Her tailbone collides with the floor before she can even realize what I've done. Before Benji can either.

And then I run, wrapping my bad arm around one of Maeve's and dragging her with me while the woods people are still distracted. I can hear Maeve say something, probably questioning what the hell has gotten into me, but I don't stop. I don't stop as Tristan exclaims and lunges, his grip mere inches away from snagging Maeve's T-shirt as we disappear through the back door. I shove it shut and lock it, listening to the cacophony that erupts as Tristan and god knows who else pounds on the wood.

"What the hell are you doing?" Maeve whispers as I pull her up the stairs behind me. "I almost had him!"

"*I* didn't," I mutter in response. "Either I took the opportunity and ran, or I was dead, so I ran."

"And what's your genius plan now? Now that you've run away? Because last time I checked there's no other exit from this, unless you plan on jumping out the window. We're screwed."

"There are four of them and two of us. We were always screwed."

"So you don't have any idea what we should do next?" Maeve confirms. I say nothing in response because I have absolutely no idea what we should do next, but I'm not going to give her the satisfaction of being right. So she shrugs and picks up the armchair, sending it tumbling down the back stairs. Sure, it seems like an overreaction to my sudden silence, but I decide not to question it. We all have our vices; who am I to judge Maeve if hers is throwing furniture?

Maeve notices the look I give her and rolls her eyes. "When they inevitably make it through the door, it's probably better that they don't have a straight shot up the stairs, right?"

"Right." And just like that, the barricade is reborn. I can't say that I missed it.

The rain pours harder outside as Tristan and co. break down the back door, the axe cutting *The Shining*–style holes through the wood. Maeve ignores the sound, picking up the microwave and unplugging it before sending it tumbling down the stairs. It collides with the armchair with a sad thud.

"Could you stop destroying the furniture?" I ask. "How would you feel if I threw *you* down the stairs?"

Maeve scowls as she reaches for the coffee table. "Do you have a better idea?"

I begin to scan the room looking for a "better idea." Worst-case scenario, we make our final stand up here and take the minutes we've earned to lower our dangerously high heart rates. Or we could try to talk them out of it with the door between us. Maybe, if they physically can't try to kill us, they'll listen to reason. But I know that I'm being ridiculous. This has gone too far for them to call a truce, especially when they have the upper hand.

The bedroom door is ajar, blown open by The Storm, and I peer through as a cutting board goes flying past my face, the blue tarp slowly disintegrating as the rain grows heavier, turning from drizzle to downpour. The whole place is bathed in blue light, like the inside of some alien spaceship in a cheesy sci-fi flick with badly CGI-ed aliens. As I stare, something clicks in my brain, and I turn to Maeve, who's still struggling with the coffee table.

"Maeve, stop. I have a better idea."

She cocks an eyebrow, finally surrendering to the power of the coffee table. "Do you?"

"Yeah," I reply, before adding: "We're going to *Home Alone* this shit."

CHAPTER THIRTY-SIX

OCTOBER 6: AFTER THE FIRST STORM

I watch from the counter as Eva pores over travel guides, flipping past pictures of the Sagrada Familia and Park Güell. On the floor next to her is a pile of Spanish-English dictionaries and "100 first words!" books from the Children's section. It's pouring rain outside, something that still sends shock waves through my body. Neither of us is brave enough to go out in it, even though it seems perfectly harmless from inside. So we've both got cabin fever; that much is clear as I thumb through a copy of *Republic.* Some of us, however, have it worse than others.

I clear my throat, struggling to recall my high school Spanish skills. "¿Has estado en Barcelona antes? Es mucho más bonito de lo que parece en esas fotos." *Have you been to Barcelona before? It's much prettier than it looks in those pictures.*

Eva looks up at me from the stool she's sitting on, a dazed expression on her face. Her forehead wrinkles. "What?"

I laugh to myself. "I don't know what you're doing with those dictionaries if you aren't practicing the language. I'm simply trying to help you with your conversational skills."

Eva doesn't seem amused. "Respectfully, Liz, I'm not in the mood for your antics," she grumbles.

"It could be fun, though! A little project. I could help teach you! Remember that time when we memorized the first page of *Crime and Punishment* out of sheer boredom? And I made flash cards?"

Eva can't help but smile, although she tries to fight off the expression. "I didn't memorize any of that stuff. You did."

"Yeah, but you tried, right?"

"And failed." She pauses, closing the cover of the Barcelona travel guide. "Remember those super-slow Sundays, before all of this?"

"Let me guess, mid-July?"

Eva shrugs. "Probably. It was a ghost town in here with everyone on vacation, and we spent way too much time trying to guess the most streamed artists on Spotify."

I remember. Of course I remember. I remember everything, whether I want to or not. "We never did guess number six, did we?" I breathe out, letting the memory fill the space between us. Why can't it be like that again? The store is just as empty as it was that summer, even more so. And we're together, right? Even closer than we were before. What piece is missing from this equation? "Who do you think it is?"

Eva rolls her eyes in response. "It's not like we can check anything," she mumbles.

"Yeah, but it'll be fun. Humor me, Eva."

Eva shakes her head. "None of this is fun. We're stuck inside, and even if we weren't, there's nothing left outside the front door anyway." She swallows. "I'm beginning to think that I wasted the best years of my life in New Jersey."

"But you were stuck with *me* in New Jersey," I offer. "So it wasn't all that bad."

Eva sighs. "Don't you want to go on an adventure after all this rain stops? Don't you feel suffocated here?"

I don't. Excitement and adventure are things that seem cool when viewed from far away but are terrifying upon closer inspection. Dreams look so much more compelling when they're far enough away that they still look like dreams. When they come closer, they morph into reality. Reality doesn't bend to the whims of a teenager, and excitement never comes in the form you want it to. It comes in the form of storms, and rain, and all the horrible things that lurk in between.

"I think I'm all good." I flip the page in my copy of *Republic.*

Eva stares into the distance, watching the rain fall outside. "I just don't understand you, Liz. You're going to go insane one day if you're trapped here forever."

I fully intend to.

• • •

It's drizzling, dark clouds still filling the sky. Yet Eva still stands at the front of the store preparing to go out.

There's a bulging backpack at her feet, straps slightly ripped from overuse. She's so focused on wrapping plastic bags around her sneakers that she doesn't notice me as I walk through the back door. Or maybe she does notice me and pretends not to.

Mom had a bad habit of doing that sort of thing. We called it selective hearing. She had supersonic hearing whenever Thea was sneaking out, or whenever I was watching a super-gory foreign film that she absolutely couldn't know about. Yet as soon as I had to talk to her about missing family dinner for a band concert or needing to borrow fifty dollars to pay for a field trip, she went deaf. It was rather convenient for her and annoying as hell for everyone else.

"What are you doing?" I ask, walking toward her in my socks and pajamas. It's too cold and I'm too tired to put on socially acceptable clothing.

Eva's head snaps toward me as if she forgot that I even existed. She picks up her backpack and hugs it to her chest before responding. "I'm just going out for a bit."

"In this weather?"

Eva nods. "We need food."

I want to take her word for it, but I watch as her biceps clench, struggling to hold whatever's in her enigmatic backpack. She wouldn't need so much stuff with her to gather food. In fact, she'd need the empty room in her bag to carry food back. If I had bullshit detectors, they'd be going off right now.

"What's in the bag?"

Eva swallows, looking down at her feet before shaking her head. "It's not important, Liz. You don't need to keep tabs on me all the time."

"What?" I pause, biting my lip. "I'm sorry for being concerned and trying to make sure that you don't end up dead without anyone knowing where you are."

"I'm an adult," Eva says. "I'll be fine on my own."

She says it so matter-of-factly that it catches me off-guard. *On my own.* Her voice is heavy, like the statement is final.

"On your own?" I ask.

"It's a figure of speech. I'll be back."

But she doesn't say when she'll be back, and she doesn't even promise that she will be. She just lets her lie hang in the air lifelessly.

"Where are you going, Eva? For real."

Eva exhales, slinging her backpack over her shoulder and zipping up her coat. She looks at me, saying nothing, before finally deciding to bite the bullet.

"I'm leaving, Liz," she murmurs. "I'm sorry."

The statement catches me off guard. I don't know what I thought she was going to say. Maybe that she was going on some super-groovy vacation and would be back in two weeks, souvenir key chains in hand. But that would be ridiculous, and this is real life.

I feel a pang in my chest, right underneath my ribs, as my intestines twist and turn inside me. And I'm sure that's not anatomically correct, but feelings often aren't.

"What?"

It's a ridiculous question to ask because I most definitely heard her the first time, but maybe it's safer to double-check. Maybe now, once she's been questioned, she'll change her mind or reveal that this was all a horribly cruel prank.

Eva reaches for the doorknob instead. "I'm leaving."

A million questions burst into my head, but I'm beginning to think that I might not have time to ask them all. I always thought Eva would be here forever, the same way I assumed that Thea would be. I never thought that there would be an end to this.

"Forever?" I ask. The question sounds small and pathetic.

Eva huffs again. As I look at her, her hand still on the doorknob, I realize that she never meant to have this conversation in the first place. She probably hoped to disappear before I even woke up. That way, she'd be far, far away by the time I realized that she was gone. But she wasn't so lucky.

Am I really not even deserving of a conversation? Of a goodbye?

"I don't know, Liz," Eva replies, before slowly removing her hand from the door. That's a good sign. Maybe if I try hard enough, she'll change her mind. Maybe she'll stay for just a little bit longer. That's all I need. Just a little bit longer. We can take it one day at a time.

"I might come back," Eva continues. "When things are a little bit different. But I can't stay here with you forever. I'll go insane. We both know that. There has to be life outside of this bookstore. There could be communities, towns with electricity. We're shutting ourselves off to the world, staying here."

This is about me, isn't it? There are a thousand things that Eva doesn't say, but I understand them all. *You're driving me insane, Liz. I can't just stay here with you forever. I need something more. I need something better. I don't need you.*

"Were you just going to leave and say nothing?"

She doesn't respond.

"Were you, Eva?"

She takes a hesitant step toward me. "I thought that it might be easier that way. If I told you, then you might try to persuade me to stay. But I can't do that. I won't do that."

"So this is goodbye?" I don't hug her. I'm not sure that she'd want me to. I don't think I could handle it if she pushed me away and said no.

"I'm sorry. I can't do this anymore."

"You can't do this with *me* anymore, right?" I clarify. I

understand what she means without her even saying it. I understand all too well. "Got it."

So we don't hug. We don't smile. We don't wave. We don't wish each other good luck. Instead, Eva nods as she opens the door and walks outside.

I don't try to stop her. No matter what I do, she's not going to turn around. She's not willing to go insane with me.

CHAPTER THIRTY-SEVEN

We wait at the top of the stairs, listening breathlessly to the scuffle below us. They'll be through in a matter of seconds, but we bought ourselves enough time to come up with something that qualifies as a plan. And all that it cost us was an armchair, a microwave, a coffee table, and four plastic cutting boards. What a bargain!

I look toward Maeve, who stands at the edge of the staircase, blade in hand. As she brushes her hair behind her ear, I can't help but notice how strong she looks, how striking. I want to ask her why she came back. I want to ask her what made her change her mind. There's nothing I want more right now than to tell her the thousands of things swimming around inside my brain, but I know that now is not the time. Later, when my heart stops trying to jump out of my chest and my hand stops shaking, we'll talk.

I place the hammer down on the counter and select a chef's knife, its rubber handle sticky in my sweaty palm. I'm probably no good at wielding a knife, but it's better than being the only one without a proper weapon, no matter how cool it might have looked. I back up, assuming my assigned position once again as the back door is pulled from its hinges with an echoing crack.

Maeve's eyes shift from the cut on my neck to the knife I still hold in my hand, fingers pale and shaking. Then she exhales, her chest collapsing in on itself as she reaches out toward me. I let her hold the back of my head and press my forehead against hers.

"We don't have time," she whispers, her breath on my lips. "But I want you to know that I'm sorry."

"I'm sorry, too—" I start, but she interrupts me.

"We're going to make it out of this. We'll have time for apologies later."

And then she lets go, and we're apart again. The world is back in motion, Tristan's face visible at the bottom of the stairs.

I straighten my spine as Maeve looks back at me, a slim trace of a smile on her lips.

"We've got this, right?" I ask, wondering if I really want to know her answer.

Maeve shrugs. "Sure, we do. I'll get them into the bedroom. You just have to stall for a bit and keep the others away. Don't open the door, no matter what, and I'll be okay. We'll be okay." She pauses. "Easy peasy, right?"

It's not quite a vote of confidence, but it'll do.

Tristan is the first one to come through the busted doorframe. He pauses, staring at the living room furniture that blocks his way before cursing to himself and starting the climb. He'll be up here in thirty seconds. All I can do is wait, assuming my assigned position.

"Don't shoot until you see the whites of their eyes," I murmur to Maeve as Tristan shoves his way past our coffee table.

"What? I don't have a gun," Maeve says. I wish *I* did.

But I just shake my head. "It's a Revolutionary War joke."

Becca scrambles up the stairs behind Tristan, and Maeve stumbles backward, positioning herself between the doorframe and the kitchen counter. The dynamic duo will have no choice but to take their fighting into the bedroom, just as we planned. What happens after that is up to Maeve. It's go time.

As Becca reaches the final stair, Maeve pounces forward with a wide slashing motion, sending Becca and Tristan skittering backward into the bedroom. Maeve follows, crouched in an offensive stance, sending one last look at me over her shoulder. With a wink, she disappears inside.

It's just me, Benji, and Eva in the empty living room. I lower myself slightly, my knees bent at odd angles, the chef's knife out in front of me. Benji quickly does the same before turning to Eva, who slowly lowers herself into position.

"So, Eva," I start as we begin to circle one another. Benji swipes at my leg, and I carefully sidestep. He's not subtle, and I can see his moves coming from a mile away. "Long time no see, huh?"

That sounded cooler in my head.

"I don't like this any more than you do," Eva replies, narrowing her eyes.

"I don't like this either," Benji chimes in, but I send him a death glare.

"I wasn't talking to you, Benji." I turn my attention back to Eva, who adjusts her grip on her blade. "I thought I knew you better than this."

Benji seems eager to say something about how he *also* once held a blade to my neck, but Eva jumps in before he can.

"If I had any other option, I wouldn't be here."

"So you were forced to come . . . is that it?" Maybe then this would all make sense. Maybe then I'd be able to understand what changed.

"I do what I have to in order to survive," she murmurs.

"And what about my survival?"

I watch as Eva's cheeks burn red. "I tried to get you to leave!"

"But you betrayed me! You were supposed to be my friend!" And that statement seems so small, but that doesn't make it any less true.

Before she can respond, Maeve appears in the doorway, her silhouette looming large. Blood stains the back of her sweatshirt, trickling down the back of her leg. I want to know what they've done to her, but I know I can't do anything about it. Not yet. Tristan and Becca stand in the center of the room, quickly advancing as Maeve reaches above her. She waits until they're in position. She waits until they're right underneath the tarp before she pulls it away, revealing the stormy sky.

I watch Tristan's face as he feels the first drops hit his skin. Eyes wide. His mouth hangs open before he lets out a scream, tongue catching the droplets like a kid on a snow day. I feel the hairs prick on the back of my neck, my skin crawling and cold as he wails and the rain floods in. And it doesn't stop. It spares no one. I know that all too well. I'm transported back to my kitchen at home, ears brimming with the sound of Thea's wails as she tried to find shelter. The way I just stood there, doing nothing, unable to save her.

I'm frozen now—we all are—my legs refusing to budge as Maeve escapes through the bedroom door, slamming it shut behind her and holding the knob closed. It's as if we've forgotten why we're here. Instead, we stand paralyzed, listening to the echoing sound of death. And even though it wasn't me who pulled the tarp off the ceiling, and it wasn't me who shut the door, I still share responsibility for the aftermath.

Maeve doesn't turn to face me, still staring at the sealed door. I hope that she knows that I understand what's going on inside her. That I feel her pain, and I share her burden.

We do what we have to in order to survive.

Benji is the first to speak, striding toward Maeve with his knife held out in front of him.

"What the hell have you done?" he howls, his shouts no match for Tristan's, but he tries anyway.

Maeve slowly pivots, her jaw clenched as she meets Benji's glare.

"I did what you would have done to me. I did what those two were *planning* on doing to me." It's a ragged defense, but Benji doesn't respond.

The shouts have quieted, the only sound left in the room being the raindrops as they pound on the roof. Do we keep fighting?

But the bedroom door slams open, propelled forward by a gust of wind, and shock radiates up my spine, rippling across my eardrums. All four of us turn to look, and Maeve adjusts her grip on her knife, taking a step back to prepare herself for what waits inside. I don't think I want to see a dead body. Another one. But it's like fate wants us to see. Like it wants us to understand what we've done.

Standing in the open doorway, however, isn't a dead body. It's Becca, limping but alive. Blisters cover the left side of her head like something out of *The Phantom of the Opera,* and when she reaches a shaking finger out toward Maeve, the skin is raw and bloody.

I blink, wondering if I'm seeing things. Maybe this is a manifestation of the guilt simmering inside me. Was there a way she could have survived the rain? But then I remember the bathroom, nestled in the corner of the bedroom, closed off and shielded from whatever came in through the roof. Becca was close enough to run, but behind her is a dark shadow. Tristan wasn't so lucky.

Becca strides toward Maeve, her finger pointed straight at her chest. Maeve stumbles backward until she hits the wall. Until she can't retreat any farther.

"You killed him," Becca growls, pausing a few feet away from Maeve. Then Becca turns to me, a crazed grimace forming. "You *killed* him."

Maeve sways slightly, like every ounce of life within her has been sucked out. Her lip trembles as she searches for the right response. I don't think there is one in this situation.

I watch as Becca grips her weapon, pulling it back as she prepares to go in for the kill. Maeve stumbles, reaching toward the wall behind her for support, her fingers tense. She makes no move to save herself.

As Becca moves forward, I do the same. I know what I have to do, and I know that I have to stop the cycle that seems to follow me wherever I go. I can't just stand by anymore as the people I love die. I can't just watch as everyone I care about leaves me behind.

Maeve's eyes go wide as she looks at me. As I move forward, ready to position myself between Becca's blade and Maeve.

I've almost made it when I feel a strong hand on my

shoulder, dragging me out of the way. Seconds pass like molasses as Eva lunges in front of me and Becca recognizes what's happening. But she's already in motion. She's too close. And the blade plunges in, maroon welling from the wound. Becca wanted to go for the kill, and she did.

Eva falls to the ground, a knife wedged into her stomach.

The four of us—Maeve, Becca, Benji, and I—stand motionless. And then it hits me like a wave. I rush to Eva's side as my knees buckle, slamming against the hardwood floor as the blood continues to pour from her torso. Too much. Too fast. And I don't know what to do. To my surprise, no one stops me. No one, not even Becca, makes a move.

My hands start to shake as I look at Eva's face. I watch as it goes from pale to gray, her skin fading into monochrome as she grimaces from the pain. I pull off my sweatshirt, wildly thrashing to get my bad arm out as the worn fabric clings to my skin. I bunch it up into a wad and press it onto her torso, wrapping it around my knuckles as hard as I can even though I'm not sure if I'm doing the right thing. But this is what I've seen in the movies, when people yell: *Put pressure on it!* So I do it because it's better than doing nothing. I do it because there is nothing else that I can do. Eva grimaces when I press the fabric against her skin, doing everything she can to avoid showing that she's in pain. But her eyes look like they're on fire.

Eva finally exhales, a gust of air escaping from her lips. "Liz, please."

I'm not sure what she's begging for. Salvation or release?

I try to keep my voice level as I respond. "You're going to be okay."

Eva laughs. Not her usual warm laugh, but she laughs because she has to. "Am I?"

I meet her eyes until I can't look any longer, swimming in them. Drowning in them. So I stare at my hands, and my fingers, now painted with red. I stare at my knuckles, turning white from the pressure. And I thank my lucky stars that my sweatshirt is red, because that lets me imagine that I'm anywhere else but here. I just stare at my hands and listen.

"I'm sorry," Eva whispers, her voice cracking on the last syllable. "I want you to know that I'm sorry."

"Please, Eva. Not right now."

She groans, and I hear the floorboards creak as Becca paces across the room. She runs her fingers through her dark hair.

"I'm sorry that this is what it had to come to," Eva murmurs, her face hollow. "I'm sorry that I turned you into this. That I didn't protect you."

"It wasn't your job to protect me." I feel like I've swallowed sawdust.

"You didn't deserve this. You didn't deserve any of this."

"No, no, I do. When you left, the first time, I didn't understand. I couldn't see that you were in pain too. I'm sorry. I'm so sorry." The apologies tumble out of my mouth like dominoes. I can feel the blood pooling around my fingers. It's still warm. "I understand why you left. I'm sorry I couldn't let you go."

Eva shakes her head, biting down on her chapped lips. "I only wanted a life bigger than all of this."

I stare into Eva's blue eyes as her lip trembles. I don't know what to say to make things better. I don't know if there's anything that I can say at all. I can only watch as the light fades completely from her eyes. Until I realize that my hands aren't moving up and down anymore as I hold them to Eva's torso.

She's gone.

No. Not now. Not right now. Not on top of all of this. *No.*

I lift my hands, finally realizing whose blood they're covered in. The person who I thought would always exist, even if she existed far, far away from me. These are not my hands. They are someone else's. They shake as I inspect them, looking for some small familiarities in these now-foreign objects. My limbs are not my own. This is not real.

I rub my knuckles against my thighs, scraping off the red with pure friction. I wipe them once, then again, then again, as the skin stings from the rawness. I rake my hands against my thighs until I no longer feel anything at all. Until there is no pain left for me to feel.

And then the tears start, sliding down my cheeks one after another and falling toward the ground. Toward Eva. I let my chest heave like it's about to burst apart. I let the wail escape from my lungs because holding it back would make me fall apart completely. This wasn't supposed to happen. Not like this. It was all supposed to stop before it came to this.

She didn't deserve this.

I run my bloody fingers through my hair, allowing my fingernails to scrape their way across my skin. I want to hurt like Eva did. I want to feel her pain. I want to bleed like she did, in a way that matters.

I rub my hands against my legs once again, over and over until the raw skin turns so pink that I can see my blood well up beneath the surface. I want to feel her pain. I need to feel her pain.

"Liz, stop."

Maeve's hand appears on my shoulder, and I reach for it, clinging to her fingers like they're all I have left. Maybe they are. I stare at Eva as the blood continues to leak from her wound, even though her heart has stopped beating. I watch as it stains the floor.

When I was little and would scrape my knees on the concrete sidewalk by the playground, Dad would lift me up into his arms. With his strong fingers, he'd brush the bits of stone that were still stuck in my skin and carry me over to the water fountain. As he let the water flow over my minuscule wounds, he'd murmur that he wished he had scraped his knee instead of me. I never understood why he'd want to take my pain away, because then he'd have to feel it instead.

But now, as Eva's blond hair is splayed across the floor, I feel what he felt. I know what he meant. As if in a trance, like I've lost control of my limbs, I reach for the knife that juts from Eva's torso. It's a chef's knife. A chef's knife like the one I brandished moments ago, now abandoned on the floor. That's all it took. With my hand wrapped around the handle, I pull it out.

As I rise from the floor slowly, like Lazarus from the dead, Becca stops pacing and looks at me. Everyone that's left looks at me, and my bloody hands, and the knife that they grip.

The question rises inside me, spewing from my lips like volcanic ash as I stalk toward Becca. It's an eruption.

"What the hell are we doing?" I bellow, my voice as coarse as sandpaper.

Becca stumbles backward, turning to avoid the open bedroom door. "This isn't on me," she retorts, reaching for a small steak knife sitting on the kitchen counter. "You killed Tristan. Don't you think you deserve to die?"

"Did Eva deserve to die?"

"She jumped in the way! How is that my fault? She did it for you! This is *your fault.*"

Benji scampers around the perimeter of the room, eager to join the last remaining person who's still on his side.

Becca looks down at the body on the floor before turning toward Maeve. "I didn't mean to kill her. I didn't want this to happen." She pauses. "I meant to kill you."

Maeve moves closer to me, reaching for my hand with hers. It's warm. It's safe. For an instant—just an instant—I forget Eva. Then, no sooner than it came, the feeling is gone.

"So do we just keep going?" I ask, my voice shredding. "Do you want to keep killing each other?"

Benji looks down at the body on the floor, and Becca follows, standing motionless. Thunder growls outside, shaking the windowpanes.

Before I can answer my own question, I feel something hot on my shoulder, small and spreading like flame. Maybe this is the pain I deserve, finally arriving, a few minutes too late. But as I look up at the ceiling, my breath catches in my throat. When I see the crack forming and growing by the second, paint chipping and falling as the roof caves, I grab Maeve's hand, lacing my fingers through hers. The entire room creaks from the force of the raging Storm. Acid rain has started dripping down from the ceiling, splashing violently onto the worn floors. We need to get out of here.

Now.

Without saying a word, I rush down the stairs, pulling Maeve behind me, my nails gripping her forearm and creating half-moons in her skin. She doesn't fight it, following blindly as her feet trip over each other. But Benji doesn't follow, Becca still at his side, rooted to the ground. He hesitates, seeming to wonder whether to abandon his last remaining ally.

I think of Becca, who seems still filled with anger and about to detonate, a thousand thoughts whizzing through her brain. It would be easier to say nothing and solve one of my problems without doing anything at all, but too many people have died today. We don't need more bodies.

"Get out of there now," I bellow up at Benji, praying he can hear me over the sound of thunder that looms outside. I don't have to tell him twice.

He reaches for Becca, hair flying as he pivots and makes his way through the door. Although she tries to resist, her husk of a body is no match for Benji's survival instinct, her knees bending and following as if on autopilot. He drags her down the stairs after us, feet thudding against each step, just barely out of the apartment as the ceiling buckles and the rain rushes in.

CHAPTER THIRTY-EIGHT

Benji doesn't hesitate to slam the door shut behind him, the sound ricocheting through the small stairway.

"What the hell is going on?"

He isn't talking to anyone in particular, his question broadcasted to all three of us. As we stumble out into the bookstore, he looks around, first at Becca and then to me, his mouth wide.

Benji's pale skin is flushed, the shimmer of sweat visible on his brow. "Does that mean that we're not even safe inside? What do we do?" No one answers.

The wind picks up, and I hear a rustle of metal in the parking lot, a grating noise, like nails down a chalkboard. Maeve turns slowly, staring out the back window as I try to come up with a coherent answer to Benji's question.

"We weren't able to finish the repairs in time. We were never ready to ride out another Storm."

Benji runs his fingers through his hair, his hand shaking. He looks to Becca for reassurance, but she's not present. Sure, her body is here, having been dragged down the stairs, but her mind is somewhere else far away. Half of her face is covered with blisters, an eye turned glassy white, the space around the iris filled with crimson from burst blood vessels.

I think about Eva's body, still up there, not even cold and slowly being destroyed. What did she do to deserve this? And why not me? Why was she more of a worthy sacrifice than I am? And now she's gone, and I'm here, and there's nothing that I can do about it.

"What about the generator?" Benji is asking, as the wind howls outside.

I don't care about the generator. I don't care at all. It can dissolve into nothing for all I care. I hope that it disappears completely.

The grating noise in the parking lot returns, louder than it was before, as Maeve gazes out the window, eyes darting back and forth. I try not to pay attention. I try to not acknowledge the hairs on the back of my neck that stand on end. But Maeve stays alert, and I can hear her suck in a jagged breath as glass shatters in the Children's room, a serrated car door crashing across the floor, thrown by the ferocious winds. Rain pours in through the broken windows.

Fear leaps into my throat as Maeve turns to me. "We have to get out of here."

But I don't hear her. All I do is watch as the rain makes its way inside and singes the bright blue carpet. All I do is watch as page after page of my books are destroyed. The car door busted through the last semidecent part of the wall, and now the western side of the building is exposed to the elements. If we stay here, either the wind or the rain will kill us.

"We should move into the basement," Maeve murmurs.

"There's a basement?" Benji parrots, his hand reaching for Becca's, her fingers limp in his.

"It floods sometimes," I respond eventually. "It's not safe. It's filled with overstock and books we never had time to return." As well as copious copies of *The Giver,* but I decide not to mention that.

But Maeve's eyes dart from the hole in the front windows to the destruction in the back.

"But it's safer than this, right?"

I don't know if it's safer than this, but the decision is made for me when the wind picks up again, causing the fractured pieces of our wooden patchwork to splinter.

I swallow. "It's safer than this."

I look for a way to lead them downstairs into the slightly murky and most-definitely-haunted basement. It won't be easy getting there. The entrance to the basement is on the other side of the room, which will require us to run under a leaking ceiling, past an exposed wall, the whole while praying we aren't trapped by the rain or falling debris. Kind of like a very real, very terrifying game of "the floor is lava," but the sky is lava and one wrong step means certain death.

But Becca makes no move to follow me toward the basement. She's staring blankly ahead, as if she's been hypnotized. It isn't until Benji places a tentative hand on her shoulder that she snaps back to reality.

"I'm not doing this," she spits, her jaw clenched, the syllables harsh and gritty. "I'm not going anywhere with you two."

Benji retracts his hand, turning to Maeve for whatever help

she can offer. But Maeve doesn't seem interested in persuading Becca to survive.

Benji leans in closer, whispering something into Becca's ear. Her face softens, but the look quickly dissipates, her face turning stony as soon as she glances back out the window. "I'll take my chances up here, alone if I have to."

"That's a suicide mission," Benji pleads. He pauses, biting his lip, before adding, "What would your brother say?"

In an instant, Becca's cheeks flush red, embers burning inside her, her gaze flashing back to Benji. "Who are you to talk about my brother? You don't know him at all."

Maeve shakes her head. "I'm going. Stay up here and die for all I care."

Maeve takes a step toward the basement like she expects me to follow. But I don't. Instead, I turn to Benji, who nods and follows Maeve across the room. Every step they take is preceded by a drop in my stomach. It's agony, watching Maeve carefully step around the room, fearful that one mistake could mean the end of the family I've only just found.

I take a deep breath before following in their footsteps. It's now or never. I step over a stack of Percy Jackson books, narrowly dodging a steady stream of water falling from the sagging roof. The wind pushes me back against the wall and sends droplets spraying across my legs. A low moan of pain escapes my lips as I bend down to grip the bubbling skin. Maeve and Benji are almost at the door to the basement now. Maeve hesitates, looking back at me.

I glance behind me and realize Becca isn't there.

She stands in exactly the same spot, looking out at the blue carpet on the floor, which is slowly dissolving in front of her. Harsh winds whistle through the store and send her dark hair flying around her face like one of those balloon men in front of a car dealership.

"Come on!" I shout over the roar of The Storm. "It's not safe."

"I know," Becca replies, her lips pursed into a thin line.

"You'll die."

Becca doesn't respond. The car door skids across the room as more bookshelves tumble, wood splintering against the rain-soaked floor. The glass of the only remaining window shatters, and I'm all too aware that *our* window to make it to safety is closing.

"Fine!" I yell. "If you want to die so badly, you've got it."

I'm scared, and I'm tired, and I know that if I don't move soon, I'll meet the same fate as Tristan, as Eva, as all the people who went before me. Like Thea. Have I really survived for so long just to give up now? Is this really how it's meant to end?

My feet pound across the floor, taking one step and then another. It's all I can do. I barely have time to think, barely have time to stop as I dodge books and falling bits of rain.

I stop only when I hear the screams, my head twisting out of pure instinct.

Becca is splayed on the ground, writhing in agony. A bookshelf lies on top of her legs, pinning her to the floor as water floods in. Her fingers are contorted, gripping the carpet fibers with what's left of her fingernails, clawing against the shelf by her feet. This does not look like someone who is ready to die.

I run forward and grab Becca, wrapping my fingers around her blistering and bleeding upper arm. The pain in my own arm, the one still mending after being eaten by the generator, is searing as drops fall down. I try to pull her up, but Becca doesn't have the force within her to move her legs.

I watch as her face morphs into Thea's, her dark hair turning lighter with each second, my imagination taking over and warping my reality. I watch as her dark eyes glow blue and her screams become all too familiar.

Maeve's boots squeak against the floor as she rushes forward to help.

"I need you to move her legs," I tell her as the wind swells, muffling my words. I will be brave. For Thea.

I brace myself and pull again, the edge of the white painted wood digging into the skin on my fingers. My Converse slide against the rough carpet as the shelf shifts, lifting from Becca's feet, only half an inch, but it's enough. Maeve reaches forward, dragging her legs out of the way and motioning for me to let go of the shelf.

I let it clatter to the ground as the sound of the screaming wind echoes in my ears, numbing the rest of my senses. I slide my good arm underneath Becca's torso as Maeve reaches for her feet, a safe distance away from the open window. I bite my tongue, the taste of blood flooding into my mouth, as I bend over and lift up, drops of rain finding their way onto my skin. I will not scream. I will not make a noise.

Becca is small, weighing no more than a minifridge, but it feels like so much more. My calves tense and my spine compresses as Maeve and I shuffle across the floor, my feet slipping and tripping over one another.

Rain lacerates my back. Books are flying around the room

like a tornado. I'm losing strength. Maeve and I are struggling to drag Becca to the safety of the basement. We're not going to make it.

I'm not going to make it.

I sink to the floor, clutching my mangled arm. I can't summon the strength I need to keep moving as Becca slips from my grasp. And suddenly, I feel a wave of something cool wash over me. A haze fills my senses, and it's like I'm a million miles from here. This doesn't exist. This isn't real. I've been so afraid for so long. So hesitant. So unsure. But I'm not now. If this is how I go, so be it.

The pain fades away as I think of Thea. My parents. Eva.

Maeve.

Maeve.

I look at her as she hands off Becca to Benji. She moves toward me, and I remember whom I keep going for. Taking one breath and then another. I feel her holding me, pulling me toward the basement. Out of the corner of my eye I see Benji sliding Becca's body across the floor behind me, his calves straining. And I crumple. There is nothing that I can do except let myself fall.

Brian Henderson

28 Years Old

Columbus, Ohio

I know this is probably slightly weird to say—and please, bear with me—but I really think that my life started when everything ended. I lived this life of constant work, constant studying, constant solitude. I was making my way through my residency, taking no prisoners or whatever. And when it happened, I was lucky to survive. Truly. I was under the overhang of the hospital waiting for my ride to pull up when the rain started, so I just went inside. I didn't run. I didn't panic. I just walked inside and helped whom I could. I did what I could to save those who were left. Protected them, too, from the flooding and violence that came after. But when the streets cleared and we were able to leave, we left together, because I was needed. And I was no longer alone.

CHAPTER THIRTY-NINE

We all sit in the basement trying to avoid thinking of the bodies that remain upstairs. The Storm still rages outside, and whether Benji and Becca like it or not, they're stuck here until it passes through. We're reminded of that every time we hear the wind howl above us and listen to the sound of shattered glass.

Maeve and I sit next to a shelf of overstock, our backs pressed against a pile of picture books. She holds my hand even though there's no one trying to kill us anymore, a blanket draped around my blistered shoulders. Even though Maeve is never afraid. She still holds my hand, her fingers laced through mine, squeezing tight with every sound that echoes from above. We sit on top of a filing cabinet as the water begins to seep in, acid slowly but surely covering the floor. It's too dark to tell the rain's depth, but we can hear it in the quiet of the basement, ebbing and flowing.

Benji and Becca remain by the basement door, perched atop a discarded desk, Becca lying on her back as Benji watches over her. Even though I'm too far away to make out the expression on Becca's face, I can see the way her shoulders shake as she silently sobs. Benji looks on from a few inches away, his hands pressed against his knees. He doesn't say a word. He doesn't even move. I'm sure that he has no idea what to say to Becca.

I want to say something to her, even though I know that I shouldn't. I want to tell Becca that I understand how she feels. I know what it's like to watch your sibling die and know that you can do nothing to save them. I remember the way you feel like you're underwater, the world eating you alive. You can't remember how to breathe anymore now that they're gone. Maybe she wishes that she was gone too. I did.

It hurts to know that I helped cause this pain. To know that I am responsible for the way Becca feels right now. But I had to do it, right? We had to do it. And unlike in the children's books pressing against my spine, there's no easy answer. There's no apocalyptic equivalent of *Aesop's Fables,* although it might be worthwhile to spend time creating one for all the postapocalyptic children who come after me. There's no right or wrong, just ten million in-betweens.

I don't know what will happen when the rain stops and the ground is finally dry. I don't know what Becca and Benji will do. Will they come after us once again, or will they remember Eva? Will they tell their people about her, and how she stepped in front of Becca's knife? Will Becca remember who carried her to safety? Will the peace we have right now last a little bit longer? A small part of me reminds myself that there might be nothing left to fight for when we emerge.

"I'm sorry, Liz."

I'm snapped away from my thoughts as Maeve squeezes my

hand. I can feel the heat rising to my cheeks at the reminder of her presence. Am I allowed to feel a sliver of happiness in a moment like this? I'm not sure whether I should feel guilty.

"Sorry about what?"

"Eva. Leaving. All of this."

"Eva wasn't your fault," I reply, squeezing her hand gently. "She made that choice on her own." I pause, listening to the building creak in the wind. "I would have done the same."

"Don't say that," Maeve murmurs.

"It's the truth."

"Fine." Maeve rotates herself until she's facing me before carefully taking my other hand. She holds both my hands in hers. "Then I'm sorry for leaving."

"You came back, right? You're here now. That's what matters."

"But it was my fault that these people even came in the first place. They wouldn't have even known about the generator, or about you, if you hadn't been with me."

I shake my head. "I'm the one who told them. And if I hadn't told Benji, then I would have told someone else. Either way they would have ended up at our door at one time or another. Maybe this was inevitable."

Maeve cocks an eyebrow, the faintest hint of laughter hidden under her voice. "I didn't take you to be a believer in the grand plan of the universe."

"I'm full of surprises."

Thunder rumbles outside, shaking the remaining glass in the building's windowpanes.

Maeve pauses, running her finger through the dust that coats the cabinet's surface. "Still, I'm sorry." A hardcover of *Parable of the Sower* slowly dissolves in the swirling water beneath us. It has to stop rising at some point. It has to.

"Stop with the apologies, Maeve."

"I'm serious. I should have stayed. Maybe things would have been different if I stayed." She looks down at my bleeding hand, wrapped tight in an old tote bag we found lying on the stairs. I pull it underneath the blanket I'm enveloped in, hiding it from her view. None of that matters now.

"Maybe things would have been different if I had left with you."

I have an urge to tell her about the butterfly effect, and how any one of the million decisions we've made throughout our lives could have been the one to lead us here. It could have been her choice of breakfast cereal at age nine that sent her spiraling down this strand of time. It could have been any combination of things, and none of those things are her fault.

"Whatever sins you think that you have to atone for have already been forgiven," I murmur.

Maeve laughs, for real this time, the sound cutting through the stale weight in the air. Benji looks over at us, eyebrows raised. "Are you suddenly getting biblical on me, Liz?"

"I read the whole thing a few months ago. I will go to some pretty wild lengths to cure my own boredom. Would you like a selection of fun facts about female Russian sniper Lyudmila Pavlichenko?"

"Are you sure that those facts are fun?" Maeve asks. It's not a no, so I decide to continue.

"Not-so-fun fact number one: she claimed to have killed three hundred and nine people, making her the—"

"Please, spare me the gory details," Maeve groans as she reaches for something behind me.

"What are you doing?"

She searches the shelf for something, peeling off a piece of plastic wrap and discarding it, watching it dissolve in front of our very eyes. Becca says something to Benji, who scowls, placing his hand on her knee. She pushes it off.

Maeve holds a leather-bound notebook. It's not my leather-bound notebook—the cover is still fresh and untarnished—but it's close enough. As she inches closer to me, she places it on my lap, its brown cover almost invisible in the too-dark room.

"What's this about?" I ask as she opens the book's cover.

"Remember how, when we'd just met, you asked for my story?"

"You said you weren't ready."

Maeve flips through the pages before landing on one. "I think I'm ready now, if you are."

I smile. "What, is this your big happy ending?"

"No, but it can be our beginning, right?"

I nod.

• • •

We write together, using the lone pencil that was left in the drawers below us, and I whisper my words into her ear. She inks them onto the page in her perfect handwriting, my writing made better by the fact it was done by her hand.

I write about my sister and my earliest memories with her. Dancing in the rain when we were five, not caring that we were soaking wet, not running from the thunder that rumbled overhead. Singing together in an elementary school talent show, dressed up in ridiculous costumes that didn't quite make sense. She refused to use a backing track, even though without it we sounded horrible. There were no computer-generated trumpets to mask our off-key notes. I write about staying up together late at night, whispering about god knows what. Telling each other secrets, the ones that we couldn't possibly imagine telling anyone else. They were secrets just for sisters. Secrets that would drive me wild if I didn't tell someone, so I told her. Doing dishes and singing show tunes together, even though she always sounded better than me. She'd be Maureen and I'd be Joanne, even though they were dating each other and we were siblings. Even though the notes were too high for me and my voice would inevitably crack. I didn't care when she laughed at me. I just cared that we were together.

Maeve writes about New York City and the way each block smelled like food or garbage, you just never knew which. She writes about the Jefferson Market Garden and how she had to do a project on it when she was in second grade. Apparently, there used to be a detention center there before it was turned into a library. She writes about the gate in front of her basement apartment that separated the descending stairs from the sidewalk. She used to set up lemonade stands there, right on Ninth Street on summer days. She writes about the little chocolate shop over on Bleecker Street that she used to go to with her dad before it moved when the rent got too steep. She writes about chocolate bunnies and candy raspberries. She writes so vividly that I can imagine the taste.

I write about Maeve, and her love for Fiona Apple. I write about her cart that she pulls around everywhere and the creaking sounds that it makes. I write about the way she smells and how she talks in her sleep.

And Maeve writes about me, and the generator. She writes about my well-worn Converse and how stubborn I can be sometimes. She writes about how much I snore and swats away my hand when I attempt to cross it out.

We write about us. We write it all down. We write until everything else disappears, just in case we do too.

EPILOGUE

The world has begun to come back to life, the smallest flowers peeking out from the ground as we slowly edge into April. The air smells sweet. It smells good. It smells like home. And sure, it smells the way the air smelled before everything went to shit, but I try to forget about that. I try to focus on the good.

Becca and Benji left after the sky cleared and Becca was well enough to travel. They didn't say a word to us as they left, but Becca looked into my eyes and nodded, and I understood. A truce, for now. Until things change, or we make up our minds about North Carolina. I try to focus on the good.

Maeve is lying beside me as I roll over in bed, the spring sun streaming in through the open window. The repairs to the bedroom took a long time, but we did it, and this time I was able to pitch in, my arm mostly healed. We measured and cut the wood, using an old carpentry manual I found in the DIY section downstairs. We even patched the roof and did it right this time. After all of that, we went back to my home and took the things we needed. And maybe even some things that we didn't. One by one, trip after trip.

The old rocking chair that used to be hiding up in the guest room now sits in the corner, a stack of books atop its well-worn upholstery. We almost collapsed trying to carry it the ten blocks from my house to the store, but we managed. And then we lay on the floor, swimming in our sweat and refusing to get up until we got too hungry.

The bookstore is no longer my glorified bachelor pad. Maeve has turned it into a home. Unfortunately, her definition of home includes an embarrassing selection of baby photos stolen from my old living room. Maybe one day we'll make it back to New York City and I'll be able to return the favor. Until then, I'll have to find other ways to embarrass her back.

I nudge Maeve awake as I crawl out of bed, the window-panes magnifying the sun's heat.

"What time is it?" she grumbles, pushing my grandma's old quilt onto the floor. It used to be draped across the end of my bed, used only when it got cold enough. Now it smells like Maeve.

I pull a T-shirt over my ratty tank top and walk through the bedroom door. Maeve follows suit, rubbing the sleep out of her eyes as we make our way down to the store.

A to-do list sits on the front counter, each letter written in perfect cursive. Repairs are coming along faster now that the generator is fixed—something that I had absolutely no hand in—but there's still work to be done. I read the entries, scanning each loop and line as I smile. Maeve plans on repainting the mural that used to adorn the walls of the children's room, which means I'm being sent to the hardware store down the road for more blue paint. Still, I fumble with the battery-powered stereo sitting on the Science Fiction shelf and wait for the dulcet tones of Pinegrove to waft through the air.

As Maeve walks past me toward the front door, she pauses, looking at the small knife that sits on the shelf above the counter. It's Becca's weapon, the handle worn, the blade since cleaned. Neither of us knew what to do with it, so it stayed here, like some shrine. We both remember.

I just nod in acknowledgment as Maeve continues forward, unhooking the metal sign that hangs on the front door. The windows still need to be fixed, but we have time. No matter what comes next, I'm certain that we will make it through to the *after*. We have time.

"Do you think there's a reason that we made it?" Maeve asks, turning to me like she senses my thoughts.

I smile, my teeth pushing against one another. "The cockroaches are always the ones who survive the crunch." Laughter invades the end of my sentence, and Maeve beams back at me. "You and me? We're just too stubborn to die."

"I'm glad you were stubborn." For a second, I don't really understand what she's saying. But then, I do.

"Me too," I say. "I'm glad you were stubborn too."

Through the remains of the front window, I can see Peacoat Man stumble down the road, Sawyer by his side. When he sees my shadow in the window, he smiles. I smile back.

ACKNOWLEDGMENTS

First, major thanks to Lily Dolin at UTA, who believed in this story from the get-go and championed it tirelessly. And to the rest of the agent-ing team—Viola Hayden, Ciara Finan, Atlanta Hatch, and Roxane Edouard—thank you! To my wonderful editor, Hannah Hill, and the rest of the team at Delacorte Press, thank you for embracing this story and embracing Liz and Maeve so enthusiastically. My thanks, also, to Carmen McCullough at Penguin UK for your insight and dedication all the way across the pond.

I cannot overstate my immense love and gratitude for the whole Watchung Booksellers gang—Margot, Maddie, Marni, Kathryn, Nicole, Aubrey, Katie, Emma, Felisa, Asia, Caroline, Evelyn (the Divas!). Thank you for the amazing space you've created and for welcoming me into it so wholeheartedly. This book would not exist without you.

Thank you to my parents, Peter (who *has* read *A Canticle for Leibowitz*) and Tim (who has a vast collection of vintage tablecloths), who have supported me and my writing since I was six and scribbling half-finished stories about magical subway cars.

I cannot put into words how much you mean to me. I love you always.

And thank you to Bea, who endured the many nights of me babbling on and on about the apocalypse at the dinner table. And thank you for rescuing me from prom. I'm sorry that I pushed you into the radiator all those years ago.

My gratitude, also, to the wonderful people in my life who taught me to work hard and chase my goals: Aunt Betsy, Kathleen, Anne, Maggie, Kat, Daniela, and Grandpa. Special thanks to Uncle Joel, Aunt Karen, Phoebe, and Uncle Nick, who all read drafts of *TLBOE* in various stages of completion and kept reading anyway.

Thank you to the incredible teachers who encouraged me and my work—especially Mr. Hernandez, Ms. Duerson, Ms. Dorian, and Ms. Schulz.

Finally, thank you to the people who unknowingly created my writing soundtrack: Julien Baker, Alanis Morissette, and Harvey Danger. You have absolutely no idea who I am, but you might be the only reason that I sat down and finished writing this book.

ABOUT THE AUTHOR

Lily Braun-Arnold is an undergraduate at Smith College studying English. When she isn't writing, she can be found working at her local independent bookstore, Watchung Booksellers, or daydreaming about living in outer space.